The Ashburn Family

Geneva Durand

Contents

A note of explanation: Of course I took inspiration from my family, but mixed in a good dose of imagination, so the Ashburn family is not my family and many incidents in this book have no similarity to anything from my childhood.

Also, in the fear that someone might suppose that Jen Ashburn is meant to be me, I have made a point of making her significantly different. And now I am afraid you will think Jen is me anyways.

My characters name themselves, and I mostly can't help it. But I would never let a character who was meant to be me take a name so similar to my own. Jen is not meant to be me at all.

To everyone who commented on this book before publication: thank you. It would not have been the same without you!

To my parents
who kept their priorities straight
when the world's were crooked

Chapter 1—Cleaning Day

Jen   Hannah & Essy   Madeline

Kyle   Roy   James   Joe   Mich   Fred

The Ashburns were the family everyone in the neighborhood told stories about. Generally, your average American only recognizes the kid whose ball falls in his doggie yard every Friday, the old man across the street who waves from behind his trash can, and the hardcore jogger whose neon green jacket is unmistakable. But the whole subdivision knew the Ashburns.

There were reasons.

First of all, succeeding grades of young Ashburns had practiced their letters in chalk on the driveway—mostly, but sometimes they overflowed to the street—and, of course, they wrote their names. Madeline thought Ashburn was much easier to spell than Madeline, so one year Ashburn was scrawled in sloppy pink letters all up and down Middleton Lane.

Also, knights was a favorite game. Bloodcurdling warcries, such as, "An Ashburn, an Ashburn! Meet an Ashburn, meet death!" frequently rang through the neighborhood. Since bicycles were the Ashburn children's trusty steeds, the shouts were not at all confined to their own back yard.

Most days the neighborhood calmly smiled behind frilled curtains and later laughed at the dinner table. But there was one day they had learned to dread.

Cleaning day.

To do the Ashburns justice, cleaning day did not happen very often. Mrs. Ashburn saved the biggest cleaning for May 30th, the day before her and Gerald's anniversary; but other cleanings happened throughout the year, about once every other month, timed to fall right before the arrival of—as the children put it—people that don't like us. Mrs. Ashburn once told them that everything had to be clean for Aunt Clarissa, because she didn't like a mess. This had been misinterpreted.

Once upon a certain Friday the Thirteenth Aunt Clarissa was expected at four in the afternoon. Thursday the Twelfth had disappeared, between one thing and another, and Mrs. Ashburn decided that with an early start, the cleaning could be done in plenty of time for her brother and sister-in-law's arrival.

It was Mrs. Ashburn's philosophy that cleaning day ought to be a day of joy. She called it "house blessing day"—in front of the children—and started it off by playing a recording of Handel's Messiah. In theory, as soon as they heard the first notes, the children sped off to their places to clean—that is, to bless—the house. In practice, Mrs. Ashburn usually had to shout, "The music's on!"

Since you can learn a lot about a person's personality by the way they clean—or don't clean—this seems like the perfect opportunity to introduce the nine Ashburn children.

Kyle, fourteen, was the oldest. Kyle had grown five inches in the last year and considered himself quite a young man. He ruffled his blond hair and put on sunglasses every time he stepped out the door, and then pulled the glasses down and looked over them when he wanted to make an impression.

Kyle ruled over the kitchen during cleaning days with a rod of iron, and smashed dishes in the same style. But he delighted in scrubbing dirt and grime, and even took apart the sink drain and stuck his fingers in it to clean it out, which none of his siblings would have dreamed of doing. Mrs. Ashburn decided that a few plates and glasses was a cheap price to pay for a shining kitchen. Kyle unplugged the oven to sweep behind it and took the toaster apart to get all the crumbs out. Once, in an excess of zeal, he had even tried to take the back off the fridge so he could clean the inside.

Jennifer—always called Jen, to distinguish her from Mrs. Ashburn—took Joseph, Micheal, and Madeline to the back yard, "to keep them out of hair's way," she said, conflating a couple of her mother's frequent sayings. The quartet trooped out of the house singing and shouting, "Comfort ye, comfort ye, my people!" Mrs. Wimpole, rocking on her porch across the street with a hot chocolate, fled to her living room thinking the words were especially inappropriate.

These four were the reason the neighbors dreaded cleaning day. Joe was five, Mich and Mad were three, and twelve-year-old Jennifer could make as much noise as the toddlers. Besides, she banged the trees harder and with a bigger stick.

As for Jen herself, she was a bookworm, and loosely speaking a tomboy, whose favorite thing to do was wrap her wet hair around a thick headband and see it come out in long curls the next morning (not for looks—it didn't in fact look any good—but because she liked to bounce the curls on her hand), and whose darkest secret was the fact that she talked to herself, in the bathroom, about anything and everything.

Ashburn number three, Roy, was a thin, shy, glasses-wearing boy, who still could be surprisingly mischievous at times. He was neat by nature and by reaction, for neither Kyle nor Jen were particularly organized. He took care of the living room and school room, and Mrs. Ashburn was confident that the Queen of England herself would not have been able to find anything out of place there once he was done.

James cleaned the laundry room—also known as the mud room, because it was the way in and out the back door—and garage. Though only eight, he was already a start-from-scratcher. Everything got thrown on the floor in the middle of the room before he felt ready to begin. And then he began by sitting in a chair and slowly sipping a glass of water, pretending it was coffee, which seemed to him a very grown up thing to do. After that, he got busy and worked hard until things were back in their places. James was a reserved boy who kept his own counsel—or maybe he was a boring sap who didn't have many ideas; none of his siblings were quite sure.

Hannah and Esther were the last two in the cleaning line-up. They were twins; but though they looked identical, their personalities were so different that no one ever called them "the twins;" that name belonged only to Mich and Mad. Hannah was sweet, calm, imaginative, and afraid of her own shadow. Essy was fun-loving, lively, practical, and fearless. It was Essy's great grief that she and Hannah could not pretend to be each other without giving themselves away in seconds. Hannah was not so sorry.

Mrs. Ashburn's theory was that you had to be seven before you could help bless the house; but Hannah did not do well with sticks and stones, and Essy did too well. So though they were only six, the two girls cleaned the children's rooms—one large girls' room to Hannah, and one large boys' room to Essy. Hannah vacuumed the floor and wiped down the windows she could reach. No bribe would have convinced her to even look under the beds. Essy wouldn't clean under the boys' beds either, but that was because they were so cluttered.

There was a tenth Ashburn also, who had not yet arrived on the scene, but was due any day now. He was a sleeping partner in Mrs. Ashburn's share of the chores; the bathrooms and dining room.

Around three o'clock Mr. Ashburn came home from work—early, so as to be in time for Aunt Clarissa's visit. The cleaning party was still going, so he went and locked himself in the basement, the only safe haven for junk, dust, and early husbands.

Jen and the children were singing Old MacDonald as loudly as they could, and the right hand neighbor had turned on his stereo system to try to drown out the noise. Kyle had broken three plates and one glass so far. Roy, with a pair of earphones, was on his hands and knees "swabbing" the dining room floor. He had a butter knife between his teeth and growled "Arrr!" at anyone who got in his way.

Essy was lying on the couch reading something by Ballantyne. At the beginning of every chapter she resolved to go outside at the end of it and help Jen, but she always found a good excuse to keep reading. Hannah, with a mop, was shadowing Mrs. Ashburn as she scrubbed the tubs.

"Hannah," said Mrs. Ashburn, suddenly sitting on the floor, "is your father home?"

"Ye-s—he's in the basement."

"Tell him I need him quick," said Mrs. Ashburn.

Hannah rushed off and knocked on the basement door—not loudly.

"Oh boy," said Mrs. Ashburn. "Jerry! Jerry!"

"Oh, Essy, come help," Hannah panted, knocking again.

"Hannah's calling you, Essy," Kyle shouted, "and someone's knocking on the door."

"I'm reading," said Essy, without having heard what Kyle actually said.

"Kyle!" Mrs. Ashburn screamed, "get your dad! The baby's coming!"

Kyle dropped the casserole dish he was scrubbing and flew to the basement door in excitement. Roy flourished his knife after him and growled over the two distinct footprints he left on the ceramic.

Kyle knocked with vigor, just as he did everything else, and was about to run at the door with his shoulder when it opened and Mr. Ashburn, armed with a notebook and a highlighter, stuck his head out.

"My dear, I think someone's here," he said. "I heard knocking."

"The baby's here!" Kyle said—not very accurately, because the baby was still coming.

"Oh!" said Mr. Ashburn, confused. "Did *it* knock? Oh! That baby! Already?!"

"No not yet," Mrs. Ashburn gasped. "Hurry!"

"Coming dear, coming!" Jerry fumbled in his pocket for the keys and grabbed a baseball cap hanging on the wall. He rushed into the hall and sat abruptly on the floor to pull on his shoes. "I'm ready—I'm ready!"

Hannah tugged at Kyle's sleeve. "Aunt Clarissa is here," she said in an awed whisper. "I heard the doorbell."

"Oh boy!" said Kyle, and he remembered his broken casserole dish and ran off to sweep it up, shouting as he went. "Esther, tell Jen to stop that noise! Roy take off those 'phones. The baby's here and so's Aunt Clarissa!"

"What'd you say?" asked Essy, putting her book down reluctantly.

"'Do your duty 'til the stars fall!'" Kyle repeated, heavily paraphrasing his previous remarks. "Nelson at the battle of Trafalgar," he winked to Roy.

"Nelson said, 'England expects every man to do his duty,' Ky."

"Oh well, it's about the same thing," Kyle retorted, with a fine disregard for details. "Essy, tell Jen that Aunt Clarissa is here."

"She is?!" Essy exclaimed, bouncing up and straightening her skirt.

Kyle dropped the whole dustpan into the trashcan and went to open the door. "Where are my sunglasses?" he muttered. "I might need them if they want me to help take the suitcases out of the car."

His dad caught him in the entryway and said in one breath, "Jennifer and I are leaving Kyle and you're in charge and be nice to your Aunt Clarissa and don't let Mich make Uncle Bob swing him for too long and pray that the baby gets born nicely. Bye!" He whisked out by the garage door and the car flew into the street. Aunt Clarissa, standing on the doorstep and preparing to ring the bell a third time, raised her eyebrows suspiciously at the disappearing vehicle.

"Well, the van's still parked, so they can't have *all* run away," she said aloud. "Besides, although it sounds like pigs and cows in the back yard, it's probably the children."

"It's Old MacDonald, sweetie," said Uncle Bob.

"Old Who? Oh, Kyle! Good afternoon."

"Greetings, Aunt Clarissa," said Kyle politely. "Hi Uncle! Do you want me to help with the suitcases? Because then I'll have to go get my..."

"Oh no, we can do that later, Kyle," Bob said. "Come inside."

"Yeah, come inside," Kyle repeated graciously. "Essy will tell Jen and the rest of the little ones to stop," he added, with a pointed glare in her direction as he brought the guests into the living room.

"Please sit down. Excuse me, I have to get back to the kitchen. The fridge is unplugged because I'm scrubbing behind it so I have to finish or the ice cream will melt."

Essy delayed long enough for a high five with Uncle Bob before she bolted out the back door and, watching her opportunity, jumped on top of Jen between drum beats. "They're here!" she shouted.

Jen got up. "Silence!" she roared.

Old MacDonald stopped instantly.

"They," Jen said impressively, "are here. Joe, sneak in by the back door and change your dirty shirt. Essy, please take Mad and wash her face. Mich, put the snake down and clean your hands. Let's go say hi."

Mich rubbed his hands on his pants.

"How can you touch a snake? It's dead. You don't know what it might have died for," Essy said. "It's not hy... hygen... how do you call that, Jen?"

"It's not hygiene," said Jen.

"Anyhow you might get sick," Essy finished.

"I wubbed the sick on my pants," Mich explained.

"Rub it on the grass silly, not your pants," said Jen, and Mich obediently laid down and rolled over three times.

"That's enough, let's go. I wish the neighbor didn't make so much noise with his music! It's awful," Jen grumbled.

"Hurry up!" Kyle shouted out the kitchen window. "There's no one to entertain the relations except Hannah."

"Coming, coming," said Jen, pulling Mich through the back door and pointing Essy and Mad in the direction of the bathroom. "Where're mom and dad?"

"The baby's being born," said Kyle.

"What?!"

"So they left."

"Oh!"

"Roy is almost done swabbing and I'll finish blessing the fridge in just a minute. Take some donuts and water and go be polite. Here Mich, you carry the napkins."

Back in the living room, Uncle Bob was enjoying himself hugely. Hannah was talking.

"What time is it?" she began by asking.

"3:30," said Aunt Clarissa.

"I knew it must be early," said Hannah.

"It's 3:30 in the afternoon," Uncle Bob explained.

"Yes, it's earlier than four. How did you get here so fast? Was it the fairy pigs?"

Aunt Clarissa's eyes opened wide and Uncle Bob almost choked. "There wasn't as much traffic as I expected," he said, "but maybe that was because the—uh—the fairy pigs helped things along."

"Fairy pigs like things to be a mess," Hannah explained. "They like to mess up my hair especially and they live under people's beds. So I guessed they brought you here early so we couldn't finish cleaning. Did you know mommy..."

But just then Jen and Mich came into the room. "Hello!" Jen called out merrily, as if there had been a crowd of fifty.

"Good afternoon, Jennifer and—is that Joseph or Micheal?" asked Aunt Clarissa.

"It's Mich," said Uncle Bob, offering the toddler a knee. Madeline and Essy appearing in the doorway at that moment, Mad took the other.

"Where did your parents go?" Aunt Clarissa asked Jen, as she accepted a glass of water.

"Unk Bob, was you ever found a dead snake?" Mich demanded.

James came into the room suddenly. "I need another cup of coffee," he announced. "Daddy took all my neat pile and shoved it out of the way of the car so I need to start over again. I can't start without a cup of coffee first."

"That seven-year-old drinks coffee!" gasped Aunt Clarissa.

"James is eight," said Essy.

"Not real life coffee," Hannah added quickly. "It's water coffee and only looks black if you shut your eyes hard."

James stared at Aunt Clarissa. "Oh!" he said. "Hi. Where did mommy go anyways?"

"Mommy and daddy went..." began Jen, but Hannah interrupted.

"Will you stay long enough to see the baby?" she asked Uncle Bob.

"The baby!" cried Aunt Clarissa. "Has it been born too?!"

"All but," said Kyle joyfully, coming in and plopping down on the sofa.

"Did they go to the hospital?" asked James.

"No!" Mad exclaimed, shocked. "Hospilals are bad places. People who go there die. Right, Unk Bob?"

"I think you have cause and effect messed up," Uncle Bob suggested.

"I love messes!" Mich shouted. "Where is it?"

"Have a donut?" Jen asked, coming to Uncle Bob's rescue.

Roy, standing mostly out of sight behind a bookshelf, mumbled something. Kyle caught the word long and replied, "I guess it could be a couple hours. They should be at the hospital by now. I don't know."

But the baby was in too much of a hurry to wait for any hospital. Halfway there, Mr. Ashburn pulled off to the side of the road and called 911.

"This is what comes of being in denial, and trying to clean—I mean bless—the house. I never did believe in cleaning—I mean blessing—day—" he said, sweating.

Mrs. Ashburn groaned. "Oh, call it cleaning, it doesn't matter! oh! it's coming!"

"Fred—Fred, his name is Fred. F-r-e-d. I can't remember anything else! What do I do?!"

"Oh boy!"

Fred Ashburn was born somehow, and the firemen got there in just enough time to hear his first cry. So the next day the fire department brought Mrs. Ashburn flowers and took a picture together. It showed up in the paper, and Aunt Clarissa was shocked.

Chapter 2—Scyllis

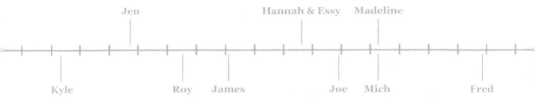

The Ashburn children were homeschooled. But once Grandpa Ashburn said that they were backyardschooled, and he had a point.

The Ashburns' back yard had trees on three sides—not so many trees that the right and left hand houses weren't easy to see, but enough to cast shade at almost any hour of the day except high noon. There was a maple—a fine tree for climbing, and for hanging targets on, and for driving nails into with a forlorn hope of maple syrup—and a dogwood which Jen loved to photograph, and an oak tree with a tree fort—actually more like a tree platform—and a tire swing. Also there was a tree of some prickly variety that the children all hated, and a pear tree that bore the hardest pears you ever did see. Soaked in water overnight and then well cooked, the pears made decent pies.

Over the years the backyard grass saw a jungle gym, a trampoline, a badminton court, and an above ground pool. It struggled with the gym, flourished under the trampoline, hung on through the badminton court, but after the pool, the grass was no more for a long while.

There were also a few blueberry bushes which did double duty as goal posts. Mrs. Ashburn sighed; but she and Uncle Bob had played one-on-one "basketball" with potted plants on the driveway in their childhood, so she said nothing. Still she couldn't bear to watch the soccer games.

Behind the lawn grew trees and weeds and brambly bushes, and piles of sticks and stones and other things Mr. Ashburn didn't want in the yard. The ground sloped down to a little creek—a very little creek which had water only when it rained. Half a dozen yards behind that was a wall. Behind the wall was a highway. Not just any highway—The Highway.

The Highway was the Ashburn children's Seven Seas, their Wild West, and their Last Frontier. On the other side of that wall were bandits and pirates, evil knights and captive princesses, trolls and shadowy villains. On this side, they built teepees and forts and other snug hideaways where they could safely discuss their plans.

One day Essy, Joe, Mich, and Mad were plotting a voyage of discovery. They were under a tent, which looked surprisingly like three towels hanging on the branches of a tree.

"We need a compass," said Essy.

"What's a com—com—" asked Mich.

"It has a needle," began Essy. She stopped, doubtful how to explain a compass.

"I'll get one," Joe volunteered, and came back a minute later with a handful of pine needles.

"Well, I suppose we can pretend," Essy decided, putting them in her pocket. "Here's a fishing pole," she added, flourishing a stick. "Otherwise we'd have to use our fingers and we'd catch nothing but seaweed. You can't imagine what that tastes like." ("Grass, I bet," put in Joe.) "What else?"

"A famper for us dirty fings," said Mad decisively.

"Oh! We won't be gone *that* long."

"Let's bring an Adult along," suggested Joe.

"What for?" Mich asked.

"To cook the lunches, of course."

Mich nodded appreciatively.

"Which adult?" asked Essy.

"Not a real Adult, silly. A pretend one. I'll get it." Joe took off his coat, wrapped it around a stick, and held it up.

"But how can a pretend Adult cook our lunches?" asked Essy doubtfully.

"They're pretend lunches, silly!" Joe sniffed.

"All right. We have pretend compasses to tell us where to go. We have a pretend Adult to cook our pretend lunches. I think we need a pretend…"

"Will you stop saying pretend!" Joe exploded. "You can't really truly pretend if you say so all the time!"

"Well then, where's the pret—I mean boat!"

"It has to be a wocket," said Mich. "We tant get over the wall in a boat."

"It's not a wall today, it's a shining sea," said Joe.

Mich wrinkled up his face and stared at the wall. "I tant shut my eyes so hard," he announced.

"Look the other way then," said Esther. "*I* don't see why you can't pretend with your eyes open as well as with them shut. It's all pretend anywa—"

Joe growled threateningly.

14

"Where are we going which I was about to say if you'd let me," Essy retorted.

"We're just seeking adventure," said Joe.

"All right. Oh bother, here comes Hannah and Fred." Essy's face fell, for when Hannah arrived on the scene there were no more compasses and fishing poles. Instead there were sea monsters and mermaids. If Essy were in charge they would have shipwrecked on a desert island and built a canoe to escape; Hannah's barque reached fairyland and there was a tribe of pixies ready to escort them to a golden palace where they could live happily ever after.

"Shucks!" said Essy, who got her vocabulary out of books like *Old Yeller*. "Now we can't have anything real."

"Hurray," said Mich.

"If you ask me," said Joe, "fairy feasts are a lot better than eating bark."

"Fairy feasts are all air," said Essy. "Bark is real good if you chew hard and think about bacon."

"What are you children doing?" asked Hannah loftily, seating herself next to Essy and arranging Fred in her lap.

"We're planning an expedition across the shining sea," said Essy.

"Oh goodie!" Hannah exclaimed. "I love sea expeditions, there are so many creatures to run from."

"Let's have a new one this time," said Joe. "I'm tired of mermaids and sirens."

"We'll have Scyllis," Hannah announced.

"To cook food in?" asked Essy, surprised.

"Not a skillet, a scyllis."

"What's a scyllis?" asked Mad.

"It's a rock monster," said Hannah, "at least I think so. There was another one too, but I forgot his name. We have to sail by very softly, or we'll wake him up." She stood up, handed Fred—now about eight months old—to Essy, and arranged the other children in a line. Then Hannah took the lead and walked slowly forward, rocking back and forth to simulate ocean waves.

Fred giggled.

"Shh! Scyllis will hear you."

But Fred only giggled louder, and Mad giggled too. Essy was tickling them with her bunch of pine needles.

"Shh, children!" cried Hannah, turning. "Essy..."

But Mad lunged at Hannah, and tickled her too, and soon the six children were rolling and crawling in a complicated tangle, making enough noise to wake up a dozen rock monsters.

Suddenly a terrifying roar stopped them in their tracks. Another roar, a little smaller but equally terrifying, sent them scurrying into the tent.

"It's Scyllis," panted Hannah.

"No such thing," gasped Essy, looking terrified nonetheless.

"It got Joe," said Mad soberly.

"Shucks!" said Essy, brightening suddenly, "it *is* Joe, I bet!"

"I don't think shu—that word is very ladylike," remarked Hannah. Nevertheless she edged closer to Essy.

Ten seconds later Joe tumbled into the tent, followed by another ear splitting roar and a shower of loose stones and dirt.

"It tant be Joe," said Mich.

"No, it isn't me," Joe agreed, trying hard to look scared and not laugh.

"It's real!" gasped Hannah, clutching Essy by the shoulder.

"All right," said Essy. "Let's fight it. Where's my fishing pole? I need it for a sword."

Here came a roar that sounded like at least three monsters.

Essy paused. "M—maybe we should send the pretend adult out to be a scout," she suggested. "I should stay to defend Hannah and the others. —Joe, what're you laughing about?"

Joe giggled. "Aren't you gonna go fight it yourself?"

"I would but this stick is rotten," Essy explained.

The monsters outside started to laugh. Crestfallen, Essy spotted Kyle, Jen, and Roy.

"All right," said Kyle, "it's dinner time, kids. Scared you, Essy!"

"Shucks! —Don't look like that, Hannah. You give me a better word!"

"What were you children doing?" Mrs. Ashburn asked when they trooped inside.

"Oh," said Kyle, "a little natural history, some biology, a bit of physical education, but mostly anthropology."

"I see," said Mrs. Ashburn. "Well, take some soap and try to learn some chemistry before you sit down at the table."

Chapter 3—The Inner Works

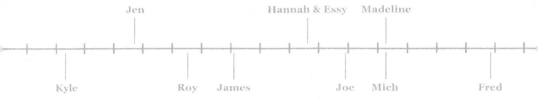

Back when Hannah and Essy were two Mrs. Ashburn fell heir to her parents' home on Middleton Lane. The family sold their small old house and used the money for remodeling. They added a large dining room onto the back, turned the old dining room into the second half of the living room, and knocked out walls upstairs until it was just two large children's bedrooms. Besides that, downstairs had a guest room, the parents' bedroom, a small office for Mr. Ashburn, and a school room. Lastly, a new garage had been built and the old garage closed off and made into a music room for the banishment of all instruments. Mrs. Ashburn was committed to her children's musical education but hated having to remind herself of that whenever she "couldn't hear herself think."

Outside, the house had a simple layout with a lot of roof, pale blue siding, white accents, and an overhang in front of the door supported by two pillars. "Technically," Roy once said to Kyle, "the pillars make that roof a portico."

"And the blue siding makes the house an ice palace," Kyle retorted.

The name stuck, and the house was known as the Ice Palace from then on. Even Mr. Ashburn accidentally invited his workout buddy to the Ice Palace one evening.

Mrs. Ashburn started married life with the philosophy that children should learn to love to help out. She reasoned that as they grew, the children would see her picking up toys, setting the table, washing the dishes, cooking, and so forth, and would naturally desire to imitate her. This youthful enthusiasm, she resolved, would not be spoiled by assigned tasks. Instead, each child would organically grow to take responsibility for some particular thing, joyfully shouldering a part of the burden and becoming a productive member of the household.

It was a lovely theory, Gerald said. He stroked his chin as he said it, a sure sign of inward doubts. But he saw Jennifer square her jaw, and said no more.

Mrs. Ashburn might have stood a chance with someone else's children somewhere. She just possibly might even have stood a chance with her own children, had they been in a very different order. But Kyle and Jen got through the chore imitating phase with only the vaguest notions of how to do the chores at all. Worse, they were both perfectly happy watching their overworked mother do everything by herself while they played. Jen enjoyed mothering Roy—for no longer than fifteen minutes at a time—but for tables and dishes and food prep she cared not at all. Kyle thought leaving messes behind was good fun. "It's just a phase," said exhausted Mrs. Ashburn, and bit her tongue three times a day when she felt like saying, "Clean up!" But she had almost no time to teach her little savages.

Mr. Ashburn, to his credit be it said, made a valiant effort to retrieve the situation. He took a day off from work and spent the whole time, from seven in the morning until eight at night, "sightseeing" with Kyle and Jen, and talking to them very seriously about how mother needed help. Jen took care of Roy for a whole hour the next day and Kyle set the table for breakfast.

On the strength of that one day of rest Mrs. Ashburn made it through the next four months. But when James came along Mr.

Ashburn said firmly, "Dear, you're running on fumes. Those children need to take some responsibility for the messes they help make. I don't care if it does spoil their attitude for work; you can't keep doing everything around here, Jennifer. I want you to promise me that Kyle and Jen will have chores assigned to them before I come home tonight."

"Jerry," said Mrs. Ashburn weakly, "don't you think this is just a phase? Pretty soon they'll..."

"It's been a phase long enough," Gerald said resolutely.

Mrs. Ashburn was secretly relieved.

So then Kyle took over setting the table and Jen put the clean dishes away. Those two jobs being the simplest, they got handed down from child to child.

When they neared their teens the children learned how to cook. Jen was a good cook, Essy even better, and James had a genius for it. Hannah was hit or miss; sometimes her dishes were delicious, but other times she forgot to put flour in her bread. Which was of course the fairy pigs' fault.

Roy hated cooking. Mrs. Ashburn made him learn a few basic dishes ("so he can give his wife a break once in a while"), and then looked around for another job for him. In the meantime she told him to go take care of the flowerbeds—which was the same as saying, tear everything out and start over.

Roy took that job seriously, and the Ashburn yard began to bloom. He worked intensively in season, and Mrs. Ashburn frequently said so to grumbling cooks in wintertime.

Kyle mowed the grass and James took out the trash.

Dishes were Jen's care five days out of the seven. She wiped them clean and filled the dishwasher as tightly as possible.

"Will anyone do dishes in heaven?" Hannah once asked.

"Of course not!" said Jen. Then she added thoughtfully, "Well, maybe, but it sure won't be me."

"I thought you liked it," said Hannah.

"Good night, no," said Jen. "All this half-chewed food?"

"Lots of times you do it on my day," Hannah explained.

"That's by accident, 'cause I forget. Wait, is today Tuesday? Snap! Again?! You can finish," she growled.

Besides chores, there was school.

School in the Ashburn house was not all play—though a lot of it was, and play is surprisingly good school, if it is active, creative play. But there were things to be learned whether or no; and depending on the child's inclination, a given lesson could be very hard work indeed.

At first math was a good joke to Kyle. He made the stupidest mistakes. Then Jen caught up to him, and he got a little frantic. He put forth his best effort to beat her grades. Jen said, "Well, if I spent as much time studying as Kyle..." and did not mind her A-.

Jen thought school was good fun. She got things the first time, for one thing, and she was a bookworm anyways, for another. Mrs. Ashburn arranged things so that 80% of Jen's work was reading, and Jen counted all that as "free time" without a clue that it went on her report card. All Mrs. Ashburn had to do was leave the right book on the coffee table. The few minutes a day Jen had to spend in front of a textbook and a notebook filling out the answers to math questions made her feel grown up and important.

Roy was studious and went far into the hard sciences. But it did happen sometimes that everyone thought he was reading chemistry and it turned out to be a pirate story.

James did as little school as possible, but that little he did well. Besides, he spent his free time tearing broken household appliances apart and reading books like *The Way Things Work,* so Mrs. Ashburn wrote Applied Mathematics on his report card and gave him an S for satisfactory.

Hannah and Essy learned to sew and crochet and cross-stitch. Besides that, Hannah wrote birthday cards and Essy drew them—a valuable pair of complementary skills that made them much admired in their circle of acquaintances close enough to be on the birthday card list.

When Fred was born, Joe was just learning to read. In after years Kyle said about all the younger children, "I did twice as much work as these whippersnappers"—with an air of "and behold how much smarter I turned out." But they certainly all learned to read and write somehow, and that they picked up a bit of math somewhere became evident the day Mad beat Kyle in an impromptu multiplication quiz.

Besides the standard subjects, the Ashburn children memorized Bible chapters. Mr. and Mrs. Ashburn's college friends the Martins thought they were prodigies. But Jen said, "In the middle ages Pastors in the Alps would memorize the whole New Testament"—and the Martins mentally added, "historical prodigies, too!"

Mrs. Ashburn decided not to mention that her children also memorized all one hundred and seven answers to the Westminster Shorter Catechism questions.

There were two other non-negotiables of Ashburn schooling: music as aforementioned ("it develops brain cells," Mr. Ashburn said to an uninterested James), and spelling.

At first, spelling lessons came out of a green book with red binding that was called The Blue Backed Speller. Kyle had no trouble convincing all his siblings that it was the same book great-grandmother had used in her one-room schoolhouse. The preface said things like "this little book is so constructed as to condense into the smallest compass a complete SYSTEM of ELEMENTS for teaching the language," and "the modifications in this revision are not of a character to embarrass those teachers who use the previous editions in the same class."

Mrs. Ashburn struggled through words like vend and glib. But then she came to lesson 32, which included engross, carouse, and purloin. That was pretty rough, and at 44—gusset, lamprey, mercer—Mrs. Ashburn snapped the book shut. Kyle looked it over, curious to see why the lessons were stopping, and said innocently, "Oh mother, isn't it important for me to learn to spell circum-fluent and suc-ce-dan-eous?"

From then on Mrs. Ashburn made lists of words her children misspelled in their other work and used those instead.

A little after the failure of Mrs. Ashburn's theory, Mr. Ashburn pasted these house rules on the wall of the stair landing, right next to his wedding picture:

1. Make your bed.
2. Do your kitchen duty.
3. Say good morning.
4. Do your school work.
5. Then you may play.

Such were the inner workings of the Ice Palace.

Chapter 4—Caleb Calhoun

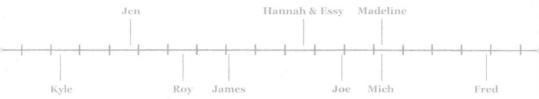

The left hand house had been vacant for several years. It was weedy and seedy and the Ashburn children called it Bleak House. That was Jen's idea.

Then one day a backhoe and bulldozer and some other machines with the word "caterpillar" on them showed up.

"They must turn into awf'ly big butterflies," said Joe at the dinner table.

"It's just the company name," Essy snorted. "Butterflies!"

"I knew that!" stormed Joe. "You haven't got any imagination!"

"Are they going to tear Bleak House down?" James asked.

"Probably," said Mrs. Ashburn.

"It's a big contracting company," Mr. Ashburn added. "They'll build a little mansion over there instead and you'll have to find a fancier name for it."

"The real Bleak House was actually pretty big and nice," said Jen.

"I thought the name came from a story," said James.

"The real Bleak House in the story, I meant."

"I wonder who will live in it," Kyle said. "If it's lots of people we can't call it Bleak House anymore."

"I hope they'll be nice people with no family ghosts," said Hannah tremulously. "Please would you pass the salt, Mich?"

"I'm not scared of a family ghost," Essy boasted. "I don't believe there's any such thing anyways. You prolly made it all up about Mrs. Wimpole."

"You spoil everything, Essy," Joe complained. "I'll be scared of the ghost for you, Hannah."

"Oh goodie!" said Hannah gratefully, resolving to people the new Bleak House with dozens of ghosts and forgetting that she hadn't wanted any.

"Me butter!!" wailed Fred. He'd been banging with his knife for several minutes now and was tired of being ignored.

"How do you ask, Fred?" said Mrs. Ashburn.

Fred said please by curling his hand. This was an accepted hand signal, not to be mistaken for a defiant fist.

"Well anyway I hope it'll not be old people. And not stupid kids either who play video games all day," Essy said.

"You probably won't ever even meet them," said Hannah.

"I will too!" Essy fired. "I'll be good friends with them before you've come out from behind the curtain, Hannah Ashburn!"

It was several months before the new Bleak House was finished, and then a For Sale sign stood sentinel over the yard.

One day three weeks after the sign went on guard duty Essy sat down to weave a dandelion crown under the maple tree. The other kids were chiseling steps into the wall with flat rocks so they could climb over and get to The Highway. Essy had bruised two knuckles and cut a third and thought it was a stupid idea.

The noise of a couple cars turning into the Bleak House driveway made her look up. This had happened several times already, and so far nothing had come of it. Essy recognized the real estate agent's Toyota but looked more closely at the potential buyer's SUV. Out stepped a businessman, greying a little at the temples, his wife, who would have been pretty if she hadn't looked so tired, and last but not by any means least to Essy, a boy about her own height slid out of the car seat and looked little and forlorn by the big house.

Afterwards Essy said she knew right away that they were going to be the neighbors. But she said it so long afterwards that she may have been mistaken.

There was a retaining wall on the edge of the property, from which she could see most of the driveway and the back door, and Essy, not wanting to miss anything, took her flowers and sat down on the wall, dangling her legs over and whistling innocently. Three quarters of an hour went by, and Essy was just thinking of harvesting more dandelions for a second crown, when the mother and son came out the back door.

"Looks like a nice yard," Essy heard her say. "You can play if you like Caleb. Don't get your shoes dirty."

"Yes'm," said Caleb, and he went and sat down on the grass.

This was not a promising beginning, for Essy did not favor little boys who couldn't get their shoes dirty and liked to sit calmly on the grass. But she called out, "Hullo!"

"Hi!" said Caleb, a little startled.

"Come on over," Essy suggested, not being sure in her mind about the rights of going onto the neighbors' property uninvited.

Caleb came obediently.

"What's your name?"

"Caleb."

"I heard that one. What's the other one?"

"Alex, or Calhoun?" he asked.

"Are you Caleb Alex Calhoun or Caleb Calh—"

"Alex is my middle name. What's your name?"

"Oh! You're Caleb Calhoun! That's awesome. I wish my parents had named me Ashley. Then I'd be Ashley Ashburn. I could be a famous actress."

Caleb stared at her.

"I'm actually Essy. Good afternoon," she said primly, bending over and stretching out her hand.

He shook it.

"Now that we're introduced you can sit up here and talk to me. Are you going to live here? How old are you? What's your favorite color? Is this all of you?" Essy arranged the dandelion crown firmly on her head.

"All of me? I'm growing as fast as I can!"

"Silly! I meant did you have brothers, or sisters, or things like that."

"I have a cousin," Caleb said doubtfully.

"That doesn't count unless they live with you."

"She doesn't. She lives in England. She's old—she goes to a university there."

"Oh! Well, you can answer the other questions now."

"I don't remember them all," he said. "But I'm eight."

"Jolly! I'm eight too."

"What's jolly?"

"I mean 'I like it.' People in old books say it that way. When's your birthday?"

"August 17th."

"Oh larks! —That's ark—arkaic too," Essy explained. "What I mean is that I'm happy because I'm older than you. My birthday is August 3rd."

"You're not very much older. I don't see why it matters," shrugged Caleb.

"Of course it matters. Hannah is only 39 seconds older than me and she gets to tell me all what to do and I can't ever contradikt her," Essy retorted.

"Well I'm not going to never contradict *you*," Caleb said darkly.

"Yes you are."

"Am not!"

"You have to, because I'm older. But let's not argue yet. We can do that tomorrow. I mean whenever you move in. When are you moving in?"

"I don't know. Maybe we're not going to live here."

"Oh!" exclaimed Essy. "That would be awf'l!"

Caleb was surprised, but also flattered. No one had ever cared where he lived.

"You haven't asked me anything," Essy pointed out.

"Oh," said Caleb, who was not used to sustaining a conversation. "Um—who's Hannah?"

"She's my twin sister. Do you have a twin—oh, I forgot, you haven't got anyone."

"Do you just have Hannah?"

"Oh no, I got lots more. Of course only Hannah is my twin. But there's Kyle and Jen and Roy and James and Hannah and me and Joe and Mich and Mad and the baby."

"Oh!"

"Come on, do you want to meet us?" asked Essy, getting off on her side of the wall and offering Caleb a hand.

He took it and stood up, but hesitated. "I don't know—I don't think..." he looked back at Bleak House.

"Oh, do you have to ask your mom?"

Caleb fired up at "have to." "I don't—" he began, but fortunately Essy interrupted.

"I'll go with you! I want to meet her. I mean, I'll go if you invite me. I don't wanna be rude."

"Oh," said Caleb blankly.

"Well'm I invited?"

"Uh, I guess so."

Mrs. Calhoun appeared at the back door just as the children approached. "Caleb—"

"Greetings, Mrs. Calhoun," said Essy. "I'm Esther Ashburn. I'm your new neighbor. I mean I'm one of your new neighbors."

"Hello, Esther," said Mrs. Calhoun, with an odd sound to her voice. "Caleb, we're just leaving."

"But you're coming back right?" asked Essy anxiously.

"Um... we're not sure yet," said Mrs. Calhoun, coming across gruffly because she had no idea how to talk to this little girl. "—Caleb."

"Bye," Caleb mumbled, disappearing.

Essy ran back to the wall and waited until the family pulled out. Then she waved violently. "Goodbye Mrs. Calhoun! Goodbye Mr. Calhoun! Goodbye Caleb Calhoun!" she shouted. Then "Goodbye real estate man!" as an afterthought.

The Calhouns moved in a week later. Essy came over with Joe and a plate of cookies.

"I don't want to be a nu—a nu—a bother. So I'll just leave the cookies," she explained to Mrs. Calhoun. "But I hope you unpack fast. Caleb can bring the plate back tomorrow."

"Does your mother—does she know about this?" asked Mrs. Calhoun.

"Yes, she was so glad that such a nice family took the house. I told her all about Caleb."

"I mean, does she know about the cookies."

"Oh, yes. She ate one."

"What I meant was, does she know you brought me cookies?"

This was a sore point with Essy, who had purposefully asked her mother could she take cookies to the neighbor, with just enough ambiguity that Mrs. Ashburn was likely to guess it was Mrs. Wimpole, with whom Essy was on the best of terms (in hopes of one day seeing the Wimpole ghost, if truth be told).

"Ye-es. No. I asked her, but she maybe didn't understand," said Essy truthfully.

Mrs. Calhoun was not sure if she really wanted to meet Mrs. Ashburn or if she really didn't want to meet her. However, this acquaintance with the neighbor girl without knowing anything about her family was too awkward. "I'll take the plate over myself tomorrow and say hi," Mrs. Calhoun said, trying to sound friendly but actually sounding frigid.

Essy quaked a little, wondering what her mother would say about the plate of cookies. But she smiled nervously and said, "Come on Joe. See—you—tomorrow. And oh, please don't worry about it if you forget to come!"

Mrs. Calhoun started to wonder if they should have scouted out the neighbors before buying the property.

Caleb's mother showed up at eleven o'clock the next morning. Essy had made a clean breast of the cookies over the dinner table, so she had nothing to fear.

"Oh boy," Mrs. Ashburn said, "what will they think of us! Letting you and Joe go over there with a plate of cookies." She laughed. "Essy, next time you make it clear what you're asking permission for. I'm happy to have a friendly daughter but sometimes the friendly daughter should go with the friendly mother. Okay?"

"Yes'm," said Essy, relieved.

"Yes'm and she won't do it again until next time, mum," laughed Kyle.

"You're awf'l mean, Ky! I've never taken cookies to the neighbor without permission before."

"Took 'em to the neighbor's dog," Kyle began.

"But that was—"

"Children," said Mrs. Ashburn.

"Peace," said Kyle grandly.

Essy crinkled her nose. "*I* wasn't the one arguing. You peace if you like. Mommy may I please be excused?"

"Me too," the other children shouted.

"You may all be excused, children," said Mrs. Ashburn, and with that permission granted the table was solitary in seconds.

So that was how Mrs. Ashburn was ready for the doorbell at eleven the next day.

"Mrs. Calhoun? —I recognize the plate! Please come in. I've a too friendly daughter, but in this case I'll have to thank her for the pleasure of your acquaintance," Mrs. Ashburn laughed.

Mrs. Calhoun relaxed into a smile. "I've a lot of unpacking to do," she said, "but I'd be glad to sit down in an orderly living room for a minute."

"Whew," Jen whispered to Roy, "hers must look awfully bad right now."

"This is my youngest, Fred," Mrs. Ashburn was saying. "Jen, Roy—and Essy you already know. The others are outside or upstairs."

Mrs. Calhoun sat down. "It seems like a quiet neighborhood," she began. (Jen elbowed Roy and he coughed.) "Nathan and I lived in the city for most of our lives. This suburban peace is new to us."

"I hope you keep enjoying it," said Mrs. Ashburn.

"We moved mostly for Caleb's sake," Mrs. Calhoun explained. "The schools here are better. Where do your children go?"

"Oh, we homeschool."

"Oh. Well." Mrs. Calhoun's eyes darted around the room and rested on a globe. After a second of awkward silence she said, "Well. I'd better…"

But Mrs. Ashburn thought this was no footing to end the interview on. She was guilty of interrupting for once, and asked about city life, and about Mrs. Calhoun's job, and Mr. Calhoun's, and Caleb's school, and their family, and their church, and the only subject she avoided was politics. The conclusion Mrs. Ashburn reached was that Caleb was not likely to do her children harm and they were likely to do him good.

Then Mrs. Ashburn noticed that Mrs. Calhoun was trying to weigh the same question, though with less success. This pleased her as being the mark of a careful mother—at least that is why she thought it pleased her, although there is something to be said for imitation being the highest type of flattery and that sort of thing. Anyways, she invited the Calhouns to dinner on the spot.

"It'll be a deal more comfortable than a half-unpacked dining room," Mrs. Ashburn said, "though I warn you our dinner table may dispel your notions about peaceful suburbia."

Mrs. Calhoun laughed. "Well, thank you very much for the invitation. I guess we can take our chance of that. And now I'd really better get back to unpacking. It's been good talking, Mrs. Ashburn."

"The mother is all right," she said to her husband later. "I suppose the kids are too, though there are so many of them. I counted thirteen coming in and out of the room during the conversation. I guess I might have counted the same one twice. But there have to be at least eight."

Meanwhile Mrs. Ashburn looked in the kitchen and said, "Oh boy, I really should remember the pantry before I invite guests."

And thenceforth Caleb of Bleak House and the Ashburns were friends.

Chapter 5—Her Own True Knight

Jen

Hannah & Essy   Madeline

Kyle   Roy   James   Joe   Mich   Fred

One afternoon Caleb looked out the window when he was halfway done with his homework and saw the Ashburn children—minus two-year-old Fred—and their bikes rolling out into the street. "Can I go outside mom?" he shouted. "Thanks!"

"He's going to play with those Ashburn kids," thought Mrs. Calhoun, and sighed. "I'll have to do an extra load of laundry. I should really tell Nathan to buy some Tide stock."

"What are you guys doing?" asked Caleb, arriving breathless after dragging his bike the length of his driveway.

"We're playing knights again," Jen explained.

"Yes, but different this time, because Hannah doesn't want to be a knight anymore, she wants to be a lady," said Kyle. "So we're doing knights and ladies, and right now the knights are picking their ladies."

"You pick a lady," Roy explained, "and then you're her true knight and have to defend her and make sure she gets everything she wants."

"Actually you just have to joust on the bicycles and claim that your lady is the prettiest," said Kyle, because all the boys were looking a little alarmed.

"I'll be Essy's knight," Caleb offered.

"No you won't, you're a wimp," Essy said decidedly. "Joe is my knight."

"I don't wanna be your knight!" Joe snorted.

"That doesn't matter, sweetie," said Essy graciously.

"James is my knight," said Hannah timidly, rightly interpreting Caleb's glance. "None of the other girls want James," she whispered in his ear.

"I'm Mad's knight," boasted Mich.

"I don't want a lady," said Roy. "I'm the Knight of the Forlorn Hope and my lady died many years ago."

"But I want a lady," protested Caleb.

"I guess you could be the herald," said Kyle doubtfully.

There was a general outcry.

"Caleb can't yell loud enough." "He doesn't know the game." "You have to be herald, Ky. You always are."

"But I'm Jen's knight already, and Caleb doesn't have anything to do," said Kyle.

"I'll be Jen's knight," offered Caleb eagerly, "and then you can just be herald all the time."

Jen frowned.

"Well..." said Kyle.

"I'd rather pretend to be a knight myself," said Jen. "I'm only a lady because there are so few. Oh, I guess you can be my knight," she finished ruefully.

36

"All right, I'm Jen's knight," Caleb announced proudly. "An Ashburn, an Ashburn," he shouted. "Meet an Ashburn, meet death!"

"You're not an Ashburn," said James.

"A Calhoun, a Calhoun! Meet a Calhoun, meet—"

"You can't have our same motto," exclaimed Essy.

Caleb huffed.

"How about, 'By the sword of Calhoun!'" suggested Jen.

"But that doesn't say anything about dying," Caleb objected.

"'Death by the sword of Calhoun,' then," said Kyle. "Let's get started. Who wants to challenge first?"

Roy swung a leg over his bike and threw down an old winter glove. "I, Knight of the Forlorn Hope, hereby proclaim before all men the greater fairness and beauty of the Lady—"

"You'll have to name her," said Jen, giggling, "—call her Merika."

"Lady Merika," Roy went on.

Kyle shouted with laughter. "Nope, nothing," he choked. "Just a—funny looking cloud in the sky. Go on."

"I hereby proclaim the greater fairness and beauty of the Lady Merika and will defend that saying with my body, without fear or attaint as to the truth of the same!"

"He's an awf'ly funny knight with those glasses on," Essy tittered. "Come on Joe, aren't you gonna say about how I'm more beautiful?"

Joe picked up the glove. "I, Sir Joe Ashburn—what do I say?"

"Do maintain the greater fairness and beauty of the Lady Esther and will defend that saying with my body, without fear or attaint as to the truth of the same," said Roy, who knew all the formulas.

Joe repeated it—mostly, and then Kyle took over as master of ceremonies.

"All right," he said. "The course is about twenty yards, so back up, both of you. Spectators to the sides, please! Joe's turn first, since Roy challenged. Here's the lance for Joe. Jen, give Roy the shield."

The shield was a badly battered cardboard box, with a sharpie drawing of an eagle on one side and a hole in the bottom, stuck on the end of a three foot stick. One rider held the shield, the other armed himself with a lance—in other words, a stick—and tried to knock the box off while both cycled past each other. The rule was that the shield bearer couldn't pull the shield toward his body, only wave it up and down. Also, there was a chalk line down the middle of the road which divided one rider's course from the other. These safety measures were all owing to Kyle.

Once the riders were in their places, Kyle took up position as herald. "Oyez, oyez!" he cried. "Sir Roy of the Forlorn Hope challenges Sir Joe of Ashburn to mortal combat—is it single combat or mortal combat, Roy?"

"Single combat," said Roy.

"To single combat," Kyle resumed, "in defense of which lady is prettiest."

"That's not..." began Roy.

"No, but it's too long the right way," said Kyle. "Ready?" He took a deep breath and raised his hand impressively. "Let them go!" he shouted.

Roy, who was an excellent bike rider, gave his tire a little jerk and made it squeal as he started. Then he flashed down the course, shouting the Ashburn war cry. He held the box steady to give Joe a chance, since he was only six. Joe tipped the box, but failed to knock it off the stick.

The boys switched weapons and ran the course again. Roy took the box off in one clean stroke.

"Hurray," shouted Mich, and the other children clapped.

"Lady Merika is fairer than you are," said Joe to Essy as he dismounted.

"Well, she's dead anyways," said Essy.

James stepped forward for the glove. "I'll do it next," he said.

Essy said, "You have to say the part about Hannah being the most..."

"That's silly," said James. "I won't."

Kyle shuffled his feet before crying out his formula. It fell a little flat.

James beat Roy and then Mich. Kyle went and handed the glove to Caleb.

Caleb took it with a deep breath and rattled off, "I, Caleb Calhoun, Knight of Bleak House, hereby proclaim before all men the greater beauty and fairness of the Lady Jen and will defend that saying with my body, without fear or—or—anything of the same!" It sounded a little like he'd been rehearsing it—which he had.

"Oyez, oyez," Kyle shouted. "I, Kyle Ashburn, herald of the Ashburn family, do claim the helm of Sir Caleb Calhoun of Bleak

House by this reason, that he hath never yet entered joust or tourney."

Caleb looked confused.

"That means," Roy explained, "that you have to pay the herald, because you've never done this before. Everyone has to pay the herald the first time."

"But we played knights last week," said Caleb.

"Yes, but I forgot this part then," said Kyle. "What do you have?"

"I have forty-seven cents," said Caleb doubtfully, putting a hand in his pocket and dragging it out full of coins.

"The quarter will do," said Kyle. He handed it to Jen. "She'll give it back when the game is over," he explained.

"Go take your place," urged Roy.

"Go beat 'im!" said Jen, curious to see how Caleb, who'd only jousted the littlest children last week, would do against James.

"Oyez! Oyez! Oyez! Sir James of Ashburn challenges Sir Caleb of Calhoun of Bleak House to single combat in defense of which lady is prettiest! Ready? Let—them—go!"

"Death by the sword of Calhoun!" Caleb shouted.

"Meet an Ashburn, meet death!" James retorted, and they met in the middle.

Caleb caught the box on the tip of his stick and sent it flying all the way to the curb.

"I went easy," James complained. "I didn't think he was that good."

"That's your fault," said Jen smugly.

James switched for the lance. At the words, "Let them go!" he swooped down and Caleb saw his life flashing before his eyes. Scared stiff, he dropped the shield just as he arrived at the middle of the course. So James completely missed.

Kyle grinned. "That's a new technique."

"It's not fair!" said James.

"We'd better outlaw it now," Kyle agreed. "But it wasn't in the rules before. You're beat."

Caleb put his chin up and grinned, and Jen slapped him on the back. "Not bad!" she said. "James is hard to beat."

"Clever, clever," added Kyle, who'd been beaten by James himself a time or two.

"He just dropped it 'cause he was scared," Essy snorted.

"If you were a knight and not a lady," said Caleb with an unexpected display of spirit, "I'd fight you!"

"Okay, time for round two! —Where're you going, Caleb?" Kyle asked.

"That stick had sap on it. I'm gonna wash my hands," he said.

He left a very blank silence behind him.

"Oh boy!" Kyle finally said. "Sorry, Jen."

Later that evening Jen growled at her reflection. "Really gotta do something about this," she reflected. "Essy isn't ever taking him for her knight now. I'm stuck." Jen leaned against the door and stroked her chin. "I'll just have to make a man out of him," she decided.

Chapter 6—Stiffany

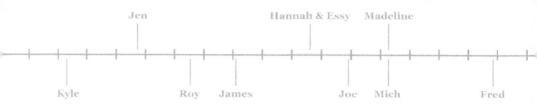

Jen | Hannah & Essy | Madeline

Kyle | Roy | James | Joe | Mich | Fred

The Ashburn family was noted for its hospitality. That was what Kyle said one day when Fred, waking from a nap, asked why there was so many peoples. At any rate, enough friends had cracked the joke about revolving doors that it was becoming stale.

On a pleasant afternoon in June the Martins were due for a three day stay. These were the same Martins who made the remark about young prodigies mentioned earlier. Mr. Paul Martin had been Gerald Ashburn's closest friend in college, and Amy and Jennifer used to do their homework together. After college the couples moved far apart, but they kept in touch and managed to visit each other at least once a decade.

Mr. and Mrs. Ashburn prepared by reminiscing about the old days. "I wonder if Paul still eats Doritos with his cupcakes," Jennifer speculated.

"Last time he visited he was on a diet," Gerald remarked.

"Yes, but he might be done with it by now. Wasn't that seven years ago?"

"At least. I don't think the twins were born yet," said Mr. Ashburn.

"I was pregnant with Joe, I'm sure. Almost eight years, then. Caroline must be near graduating now!"

"There's another one, isn't there?"

"David," Mrs. Ashburn recalled. "He was five then. And there was a baby. Landon, I think."

She paused and caught the sounds of their own children laughing and shouting.

"I do hope they'll get along," she said.

Jen was making dinner for the guests with a book in one hand and a spatula in the other. The book was receiving most of her attention.

Essy came up and planted herself next to Jen. "What're the people like?" she demanded.

"What people?" asked Jen absently.

"Aren't you making dinner?"

"Mmm."

"Stop reading, Jen. You can't cook good and read. Last time you burnt the boiled potatoes."

"'Cause I sat down. I'm not sitting down this time."

"Well put it down anyway. I wanna talk."

Jen sighed. "What?"

"What're the people like?"

"The Martins? Oh, I dunno, it was a long time ago. Caroline was a snob," she added.

"Was she the cool kind of snob, or the annoying kind?" asked James, coming in for a glass of coffee-water.

"Oh well... she might be better now. That little baby was spoiled rotten," Jen replied.

"Should I hide my toys?" wondered Joe.

"Not a bad idea," Jen agreed.

So when Mrs. Ashburn came to see how the preparations were going she found her children hastily stuffing their most treasured possessions under their beds.

"Children, you don't have to..." she began—but she thought better of it. After all, bones of contention were better buried.

The Martins had driven seven hours that morning and when they arrived some of them looked a little jaded. But not Landon.

"Ugly house," he said, climbing out of the car and swinging a pair of toy nunchucks around. "Blue is for the sky, not for siding. Uncle Harvey said so."

Jen heard and said sweetly to Mrs. Martin, "Oh my, is that the baby! Oh how he *has* grown. I remember when he was just this big!" she simpered, measuring off about a foot with her hands.

"This is little Jennifer, isn't it?" smiled Mrs. Martin—punishing her very effectively, though unintentionally. "Here's Caroline— she's so grown you probably don't even recognize her!"

Jen stewed and Kyle snickered.

Had Jen but known it, Caroline's face as she grumbled "Hi" only reflected her own frown. But Jen did not know it, and immediately stamped on her mental tablets, "Snob. Confirmed."

"Ho, ho," Kyle whispered to Roy, "it'll be open warfare soon. Go it, lil' sis!"

Mr. and Mrs. Martin sat down with Mr. and Mrs. Ashburn in a corner of the living room. Mrs. Ashburn nodded to Kyle. "Why don't you go show the children around? Enjoy yourselves!" she said.

So the children trooped off to the school room, and when in the pauses of their conversation the parents heard voices they thought, as parents like to think, that the young people were getting along beautifully.

Jen began the war by being killingly polite.

"Would you like a glass of water, Miss Martin?" she asked.

"Thank you, Miss Ashburn," Caroline replied loftily. "I... only drink lemonade."

"Oh! So... sour," said Jen, and Kyle discreetly put his hand over his mouth.

Hannah and Essy were sitting on a desk, since there were not enough chairs in the room, and David who had brought up the rear, stood by the doorway looking awkward. So Hannah patted the empty spot next to her and David, sitting down, began to swing his legs.

It was a case of curiosity overcoming shyness, for Hannah had a question for him. "Is it true that your sister's a snob?" she whispered, her eyes round as saucers.

"Of course not!" exclaimed David. "I mean... not very often," he whispered back. "Why?"

"Jen said so."

"Then Jen's a snob," David huffed.

"Is not!" cried Hannah, unconsciously speaking aloud.

"Must be," David growled.

Then he and Hannah suddenly realized everyone was looking at them.

"What on earth are you arguing about, Davy?" Caroline asked.

"Nothing," he mumbled, and went back to swinging his legs.

"David's a little shy," Caroline explained.

"I'm not shy," said Landon. "Which one of you is Kyle?"

"Me."

"You got a C on your history test," he chortled. "I *always* get As."

"I used to think it was a shame geniuses die young," said Jen reflectively.

Caroline smiled involuntarily and then looked carefully at her bracelet.

Meanwhile Hannah and David were whispering again. "What's a snob, anyway?" asked Hannah.

"It's a... a... it's someone who's always got their nose in the air," said David.

"Oh!" said Hannah, and stared at Caroline closely. "I guess your sister isn't a snob then," she concluded. Caroline had the snubbiest of snub noses.

"I meant," began David, "well, I meant... a... never mind."

Hannah was looking at him carefully, meditating something. He fidgeted, but she evidently reached a favorable conclusion, for she asked, "Do you wanna see my dolly?"

David's eyes widened. "Uh... uh... sure..."

Hannah jumped from her seat, dragging David after her.

"Where're you going Hannah?" asked Essy. "Aren't you gonna play?"

The others were arranging a game of twos and sixes.

"When we get back," said Hannah, and she and David disappeared.

Caroline and Landon stared after their brother. "Gosh!" said Landon.

Dead silence fell on the group and Caroline shot an angry glance in Landon's direction. It fell harmlessly from his armor of oblivion. "Is this *your* notebook?" he asked, pointing at Jen. "Stupid drawings. Look like a dead poodle dog."

"Rude..." began Jen reflexively. "It's rude to point," she added, after a momentary pause.

"It's a goody-goody!" Landon squealed. "Two shoes! Sheesh!"

"All ri—ight," Kyle interposed, "let's start the game!"

"Landon Martin," Caroline said sharply at the same time.

Jen tilted her head to one side, looking at Landon, and stroked her chin. Mich and Mad saw it and caught their breath apprehensively. But nothing happened right away, and they forgot about the look.

"Whenever anyone rolls a six," Kyle explained, "that person takes the pen and starts writing. When we roll a two you have to pass your paper to the left. First person to a hundred wins!"

About halfway through the game Caroline had the pen and was writing numbers furiously when Essy rolled a two and passed her a new paper. Caroline stared at it. "What in the..."

"Jen writes in Roman numerals sometimes," said Essy.

"XLVIII? Uh... mmmf... What does the L mean?" asked Caroline.

Jen laughed in a superior way.

"Two!" cried Kyle, and the unreadable paper moved farther down the line.

David and Hannah got back just as the round ended.

"What were you two doing?" asked Landon.

"Showed David my doll," said Hannah.

Caroline looked at David in disbelief, and even Jen grinned a little.

"David liked her, didn't you?" Hannah said defensively.

"Mmm guess so," mumbled David.

Landon snickered.

"What's your doll's name?" said Caroline, asking the first question that came into her head, to relieve David.

"Stiffany," Hannah replied.

Landon laughed annoyingly. "Stiffany! Stiffany! You're so fff-funny!" he mocked.

Jen, in the background, stroked her chin thoughtfully and called Essy over.

They played another round and then Jen suggested cupcakes. Coincidentally, Essy appeared just then with a plate full. Yellow cupcakes they were, and the center one had a generous swirl of frosting and sprinkles.

Landon squealed and dove for the frosted one. Jen caught Roy's eye and winked.

Caroline saw the wink and looked slowly towards Landon.

He crammed the whole cake into his mouth. Then he coughed and sputtered. "Eww! Ishtissherrble! What *is* this?" Landon wailed.

"It's poetical justice," said Roy.

"Also known as mustard," Kyle grinned.

Caroline laughed heartily.

"Nasty!" screamed Landon, spitting cupcake bits all over the table. "Who made that?"

Back in the living room Mrs. Martin gushed, "Oh they're having *such* a good time to—geth—er!"

After dinner the children all went upstairs to play sandwich.

"If Caroline can handle this," said Jen magnanimously to Kyle, "I'll change my mind."

Sandwich was a game Kyle and Jen had invented with the help of two old memory foam mattresses. The goal was to sandwich someone between the mattresses and eat them. The challenge was to avoid being wrapped up from behind and sat on while you were eating the person under you.

Caroline looked at the mattresses on the floor and opened her eyes wide. "We're supposed to do what?" she asked.

"We all try to..." began Kyle.

"Your 'splanations are boring," said Essy, pushing David over. In another instant James had wrapped him up neatly and he and Essy, sitting on top of him, began to eat calmly.

"Yum!" cried Jen, dropping the corner of the second mattress over the eaters and throwing herself on top, where she was promptly joined by Landon and Roy.

Kyle winked at Caroline. "Let's roll 'em up," he said, and the two of them each grabbed a corner. Jen wriggled away, but Roy and Landon were being eaten in no time.

"This one tastes like mustard," Caroline laughed as Landon screamed.

"Hurrah," David shouted, finally managing to crawl out of his sandwich.

When at last the game stopped everyone was hot and panting.

"Whew," said Caroline, "I need a glass of water!"

"I thought you only drank lemonade," Jen grinned.

Caroline burst into laughter. "That was a joke, Miss Ashburn," she retorted. "Sour! You were awful snobby."

"Your mom called me little Jennifer," Jen explained, laughing.

"Oh yeah, was that it? Now I know how to get under your skin. When it comes to that," she added, "don't ever call me Lina."

"Won't," Jen promised. "Lemonade?"

"We had a wonderful time!" said Mrs. Martin when they left three days later.

"Yes, we had *such* a wonderful time," said Landon, making faces. "Stif-fan-ny," he mouthed distinctly.

"Nasty boy," Essy muttered to Hannah. Then she remembered the mustard frosting she made for his cupcake, and giggled.

Chapter 7—What Children Think of the Zoo

"What've you been up to, flutterbudget?" Mr. Ashburn asked one evening, scooping Hannah up and putting her on his shoulder.

"We've been playing zoo, Pa," said Hannah. She always called Mr. Ashburn Pa when he called her flutterbudget.

"Playing zoo? So this is why there is a layer of leaves in the trash."

"The panda was eating them," Hannah explained.

"Who was the panda?"

"James. He didn't acksually eat the leaves. He tried to but he said he couldn't shut his eyes hard enough."

"What else did you have in your zoo?"

"Well, there were kangorillas and zoophelants," Hannah said. "But Essy got tired of jumping everywhere and Joe didn't like having to drink through his nose, though I told him all the zoophelants do that. Mich and Mad kept 'scaping so finally we let them be monkeys and we played they had 'scaped out of a circus train and when we caught them we would get lots of money so we could buy a .22."

"What do you know about .22s?" asked Mr. Ashburn, chuckling.

"They're in fishing magazines," Hannah replied promptly. "Essy said so. Oh daddy, what does a rihornotamus really look like? I said it had a horn but Essy said it didn't and James said there wasn't any such an'mal."

Later that night Mr. Ashburn said to Mrs. Ashburn, "These children really need to visit the zoo."

So it was arranged for the next Saturday. Hannah was tremendously excited, and therefore so was Joe—which meant that Fred and the twins were also excited.

Caleb came with them, and this was how.

"Oh mommy, can Caleb come with us?" asked Essy on Friday morning.

"Why—I suppose we could invite the Calhouns. I'll think about it," said Mrs. Ashburn distractedly. "I smell something burning. Is Jen in the kitchen?"

Essy decided that her mother's "we" gave her carte blanche. Less than an hour later, Mrs. Calhoun heard the doorbell. Opening the door, she beheld this spectacle:

Miss Esther Ashburn, dressed in her very best Sunday outfit, with three dandelions in her hair, holding a crookedly folded sheet of notebook paper with a daub of playdough stuck to the outside.

"Greetings and salutes, Mrs. Calhoun," said Essy, who had gotten her lines from Kyle (in response to "What's the right way to say hi to someone when you really want them to do what you ask?"). "This is to inform you that on the—that on the—I forget what, but it ended with please accept this invitation for your per—perusal. Please say yes, oh please!"

Mrs. Calhoun took the paper, removed the playdough seal, and read aloud, "Jennifer Faith Waring and Gerald Fredrick Ashburn invite you to share in their joy at the zoo, on May the Thirty-First in the year of our Lord 1983. Reception immediately following. RSVP. P.S. You are looking very well today and Mrs. Calhoun please come to the zoo with us and bring Caleb."

"I copied the first part from mommy's wedding invitation," said Essy truthfully. "It's in a frame halfway up the stairs next to their picture. I changed where it said wedding to zoo, of course. Won't you come?"

"It's October," said Mrs. Calhoun thoughtfully.

"Yes but it's beautiful weather for October!" said Essy, afraid that the month was an objection.

"I meant, May 31st is far away. When *are* you going to the zoo?"

"Tomorrow. And we're all going and we're all going to see if there are rhinotums, or something, and whether they have horns or not. And Caleb wants very much to see the horns."

"Well, I'm working, but Caleb and his dad can probably go."

"Oh," said Essy, "that's splendid! I mean not about you. I mean, I wish you could come too. I mean I'm happy Caleb can come. I'll go tell mommy!"

"Um—yes. Goodbye to you too, Esther. I will *never* understand that child," sighed Mrs. Calhoun.

The Ashburns' house was a buzz of excitement the next morning—or most of it was. Jen lounged on the couch with a book (it was *The Life and Times of Jesus the Messiah* by Edersheim, in one 1,000 page volume—as previously mentioned, Jen would read anything) and Kyle sat down to clean his sunglasses. They had both been to the zoo before and agreed that it was "not so whippy."

"But," said Jen, "let's give it a fair chance with the others. It's always seemed to me that the best thing you can do with a zoo is tolerate it in order to not disappoint your parents, but maybe most kids love 'em."

"I guess that's possible," said Kyle doubtfully. "I'll look as cheerful as I can then, but I can't jump up and down for joy about walking all day and hunting for animals in their own cages with my eyes, so there's no use trying."

"No," Jen agreed, and went back to her book.

It was Mich and Mad who were jumping up and down for joy, and also for the pleasure of hearing their boots make a racket on the floor. "We goin' zoo, we goin' zoo," they chanted. "Raaar! Fffft! Bzzzz!"

"Don't remember there being bees," said Kyle.

"I'd like to see a monkey," said Roy. "And a parrot. I think if I were a pirate I'd rather not have one, but anyhow I should know about them."

"I wanna see the tigers," said James.

"Caleb and his dad are coming," said Essy, to anyone who cared to listen. "They're going to follow us in their car. Daddy you won't drive crazy will you?

"Eh what?" asked Mr. Ashburn. "I didn't know the Calhouns were coming. Drive crazy! What're you talking about, tiddlywinks?"

"Me 'oo!" wailed Fred. "'Oo urt!"

"Got 'em on the wrong feet," said Jen, picking Fred up to fix his shoes.

"All right, hop to, in you go," exclaimed Mrs. Ashburn, holding the van door open. "One—two. Three, four—five and six. Jen, Fred, Joe—where is James? Last one in is a rotten ninja!"

Snap, snap, snap, went ten seat buckles, and Mr. Ashburn was decidedly the last one in and buckled.

Mich talked nonstop on the way. "We're gonna crash," he said. "I can tell we're gonna crash. Gonna crash, gonna crash... we crashed! Oh bother, now we have to walk the rest of the way. Look! We dropped a wheel over there..."

If it had been up to James they wouldn't have gotten into the zoo at all. He stood outside admiring the signage and wondered audibly why anyone would pay to go past it. "Bet these animals are cuter than the ones inside anyway," he said.

"Wanna walk," said Fred, and Jen let him out of the stroller. "Wanna push," he said. Jen was about to get in herself, but Mrs. Ashburn exclaimed.

"Jen! You'll break it."

So Fred rolled his empty stroller down the sidewalk. Not very straight, because he couldn't see a thing.

"Yeah, I've been to the zoo before," said Caleb, in answer to a question from Essy.

"How'd you like it?" asked Essy.

Caleb shrugged. "It's just an'mals," he said. "Guess it'll be fun with you guys though."

"Ah, the zoo," Mrs. Ashburn was saying to Mr. Calhoun at that moment. "So much better than an amusement park, don't you think so?"

"Much more educational," Mr. Calhoun nodded, "and kids like it just as well."

"Cheaper too," said Mr. Ashburn cheerfully. Then he ran away before Mrs. Ashburn could wither him with her glance.

"Well, flutterbudget," he asked Hannah, "shall we go see the mammals first, or the reptiles?"

"I wanna see the kangorillas first," Hannah declared. "Which way are those, Pa?"

"Hmm... mmm... the kangaroos are to the left, and—so are the gorillas, so let's go that way."

"Me tired!" Fred announced.

"Get back in the stroller, then," said Jen.

"No 'toller. 'Tary," he said.

Kyle put him on his shoulders.

"Are those kangorrillas?" asked Hannah presently.

"Kangaroos, yes," said Mr. Ashburn.

"Thought they'd be cleaner," Hannah explained. "The zoophelants too. Don't they get any rivers to take baths in in this zoo?"

"Um... don't think so, dear," said Mr. Ashburn.

The gorilla's cage was under maintenance. But the monkeys pleased Roy. "Milk!" they screamed at him. And, "Milk!" he screamed back.

They got to the tiger cage and James stared moodily at the great cat. "Why doesn't he do something?" he asked.

"It's hot," Mrs. Ashburn explained.

"Lazy bum!" James shouted. "Yaaah! Get up and roar!"

"Tigers don't roar anyway," Caleb said. "They purr."

"Lazy bum! Get up and purr!"

But the tiger only flicked its tail.

Hannah wouldn't go into the reptile house. Jen spent so much time in it that Kyle said she was going in for herpetology.

"What's herpetology?" Essy asked Jen when she came out.

"Study of... something. Why?"

"Kyle said you were doing it."

"Must be reptiles then," Jen grinned. "No, but there's air conditioning in there," she said.

"Oh look!" Hannah squealed suddenly. Momentarily, Mr. Ashburn thought she had finally found an animal to be excited about. She had—a squirrel.

"I ti—ired," Mich yawned.

"Me too," said Mad.

"See if you can both fit in the stroller," Mr. Ashburn suggested. Fred was asleep on Kyle's back.

"Might be time to head home, honey," Mrs. Ashburn said.

"Probably," Mr. Ashburn said cheerfully. "Been a wonderful day, hasn't it kids? So much better than an amusement park."

"What's a—a 'musement park?" asked Essy.

"A place where..." Mr. Ashburn began.

"Never mind, Jerry," said Mrs. Ashburn hastily. "Caleb, do you know where your dad went?"

"Here I am," said Mr. Calhoun in his grave voice. He opened a bag and displayed a dozen cool popsicles.

"Yay!" Joe shouted. "Thank you!"

And so with tired eyes and sticky faces the Ashburn children made it home.

"So how was the zoo, Hannah?" Mr. Ashburn asked as he put her to bed.

"Well, there were lots of an'mals," she answered. "But I think it's more fun to play kangorillas and zoophelants than to see them."

Chapter 8—Family Ghosts

One evening at dinner Caleb asked his dad, "What's a knight?"

"It's when things get dark," Mr. Calhoun said absently.

"I think he means with a K, dear," said Mrs. Calhoun.

"Oh. It's a person who—who wears armor and—"

"I know," said Caleb. "I meant, what does a knight do?"

"Well he—he fights to defend his country or his family or his lady or—"

"So if you are someone's knight, you have to fight for them?"

"Well—or, you know, help them when they're in trouble. Chivalricaly speaking," Mr. Calhoun said, forgetting who he was talking to, "a knight was supposed to be willing to do anything for his lady, even participate in adventures meaningless in themselves but thought to bring honor or pleasure to her. Of course, in actual medieval practice—" he stopped and looked at Caleb. "Why are you asking about knights, anyway?"

"Oh—uh—just—because—" Caleb mumbled. "Mom, can I be excused?"

"Yes—but go clean your room before you play."

Caleb went to his room and picked up a notebook. He tore out a blank page and wrote, "a knight fights." He laid it on his night table and sighed.

"It was awful good of Jen to let me be her knight," he reflected. Then he added determinedly, "So I'll be a good knight."

These reflections sprang from a game of knights the children had played together that afternoon. Caleb had been Jen's knight again, and disgraced himself by dropping the shield twice—which was now against the rules of the game, and resulted in disqualification. Then when Jen ran the course with him a couple times for practice, Essy stuck out her tongue and said that it was pretty funny for a lady to be coaching her knight.

"You should challenge Joe for that," Jen said.

"I'm tired of this dirty stick," Caleb complained.

"Coward!" shouted Joe gleefully.

"He's not a coward exactly," Jen explained calmly, "just a— well, never mind. I'll do it myself. Sir Joe, prepare for battle!" she finished cheerfully, for Jen loved to joust.

So for the rest of the game Caleb clapped for Jen and enjoyed himself—nevertheless with a sense that he had not done the proper thing in the eyes of the Ashburns. Especially he felt this when Essy stuck her tongue out at him again.

From the window of his room Caleb had a good view of the Ashburns' maple tree. Essy, with James' help, had rigged a pink bandana to a high branch with a loop of string. When the bandana rested at the bottom of the loop, the Ashburns were busy; but when Essy pulled it to the top, Caleb was welcome to come.

Right now the flag was flying high and Caleb rushed to put his room to rights.

Essy was sitting on a branch of the tree, her heart sore within her. Hannah and Joe were plotting ghost stories and had told her plainly they didn't want her.

"You need to help me," she said when Caleb came. "Get me—let's see—a white towel."

Caleb resented the tone. "Why?"

"Because!"

"Because why? Don't be so bossy."

"Bossy?! You're my neighbor, Caleb Calhoun. I own you."

"You're *my* neighbor," Caleb retorted. "So I own *you*."

Essy thought for a while. "But you were my neighbor first."

"Do you mean because you're older?"

"Exactly," said Essy, who had been thinking no such thing.

"Bummer!"

"I'm not a bummer!" Essy retorted, firing up. "I'm just older than you, Caleb Calhoun!"

"Silly girl," he sniffed. "You don't know what bummer means."

"Well I think it's mean to call people names they don't know."

"I didn't call you no names. You're a real silly girl," Caleb retorted.

"Well fine!" Essy stormed. "I don't want your help anyways! I'll go see James!"

She was gone before Caleb gathered his wits. So he wandered into the house and found Joe and Hannah sitting on the school room floor and shivering with scared delight.

"What's wrong with Essy?" he asked.

"She's too brave," said Hannah.

"She ruins everything," said Joe. "Do you wanna hear our ghost stories?"

"Sure," Caleb said, joining the circle.

Meanwhile Essy found James in the garage, taking apart a broken sewing machine.

"James, I want your help," she said.

"With what?"

"Hannah and Joe are busy thinking of ghosts for Bleak House."

"Well?" asked James.

"They kicked me out, but I heard about a few of them," Essy explained. "One used to be a pirate, and he buried treasure under the dining room floor. He died and now his ghost tries to find it. But two other people found the treasure and unburied it, and then they fought and murdered each other because they couldn't agree what to spend it on. They haunt the living room, because that was where they killed each other. Then came the last ghost—she wasn't a ghost then of course—and took the treasure and bought herself lots of rich clothes and married a prince for his title and lived a miserable life. Now she haunts the place too because she stole the treasure."

"Well?" repeated James.

"Joe made up the part about the pirate and the treasure and Hannah did the rest."

"Well?"

"Well, don't you see?" said Essy. "It isn't healthy to believe in ghosts—I heard Aunt Clarissa say so once. We have to cure them."

"How are we supposed to do that?" asked James.

"I don't know. I was thinking about—a white towel," Essy said doubtfully.

"Nah, that's not scary at all. Where's Roy? I bet he could dress like a pirate ghost pretty good. You could be the lady." James got excited and threw down his screwdriver. "I bet we could scare them pretty bad," he grinned. "Let's see…"

The next week Mr. and Mrs. Calhoun went on a date and Caleb spent the whole afternoon with the Ashburns.

Caleb found Essy insufferable that day. So did Jen.

"What's with you?" she asked, when they went outside to play after dinner.

Essy smiled and stuck her chin in the air.

"Spill it already," Jen said. "You'll explode with conceit."

"You look real silly with your hair curled," Essy told her.

Caleb growled. "You look silly when you put dandelions in your hair," he snapped.

Jen laughed. "Let it go, Caleb, I know my hair looks silly. If Essy wants to enjoy her secret in solitary bliss, it's her business. Let's go swing."

"I think your hair looks nice enough anyway," he said, running toward the tree.

Essy watched them go with a superior air, and then went to find James.

"It'll be dark at seven," James was saying to Roy. "I heard Caleb say that his parents wouldn't be back until ten. Where's that notebook with the ghost lady's journal?"

"I got it," Roy said. "I wrote all sorts of stuff about parties and what not. I bet even an antiquarian would think it was real until he analyzed the ink."

"Are we ready to go?" asked Essy, bouncing around.

"Just about. Where are the blue glow sticks?" James asked.

"Here," exclaimed Essy, holding up a backpack. "And my costume, too."

"I've got mine," said Roy. "Let's go."

James slung a backpack over his shoulders and stuck an old knife in his belt. "Where's everyone else, Essy?" he asked.

"Jen and Caleb are at the swing. The others are in the fort, except Kyle who's studying like he always does."

"We'll go out the front door and make a run for it," said James. "It's not too light right now anyway, and they won't be looking. Ready?"

Dashing across the yards in the growing twilight was an adventure in itself, and Essy thoroughly enjoyed the guilty run. The trio slipped inside the Calhouns' back door and dropped their loads.

"Hello, Frankie," Essy said, petting the dog.

"Just be patient a second," James added, "and we'll have a job for you. —Okay, kids. First thing is to move all the furniture just a little bit. They say that when you move furniture over a few inches people lose their bearings and run into it. You go walk around upstairs with a few blue glow sticks in the meantime, Essy. Maybe we can scare them a bit ahead of time. Be sure to close the curtains so they can't see you."

Essy went upstairs and drew all the curtains. Then she snapped on a handful of glow sticks and walked with a ghostly tread back and forth behind Caleb's window.

Presently she heard her mother's voice across the lawn and saw Jen take Mich, Mad, and Fred inside. Essy rushed toward the stairway.

"The little kids are going in," she called down. "It's almost time!"

"All right, hurry up and change," James replied. "You too, Roy. Wait, hand me the book first." James rolled it up and tossed it to the dog. "Fetch, Frankie! Good boy. Here, again. Fetch! All right. Now listen up Frankie. Fetch—to Caleb. No, the book! Fetch! Good boy," said James, opening the back door and letting Frankie run across the lawn.

James chuckled. "That should bring them here. Now... where's the electric box? No sense letting them come turn all the lights on... Are you two done changing yet? I'm gonna cut the 'lectricity!"

Essy came down, dragging a mile of white cloth behind her. "Is this good?" she whispered to James. For some reason, they all started whispering as soon as the lights went out.

"Perfect," James said. "Well, a little long. Try not to trip over it—lady ghosts usually don't even walk, let alone trip. Let me help you fit it all in the closet—here, I'll take the glow sticks. Roy, you start stomping up and down the dining room floor as soon as I've locked the kids inside. I'll run around and creak doors and wave glow sticks, until the time comes for me to tumble down in a murdered heap in front of them. Oh! Look, they're coming, they're coming! Hurry, Essy!"

"Wh—wait, what do I say, what do I say?"

"Anything—anything but boo!" Roy hissed, rushing off to his post and running into the cabinets on the way.

"Wait when do I come out!" Essy asked in an agonized whisper through the crack of the closet door.

"At the psychological moment!" James exclaimed. "Now shh!"

Essy, waiting in her stuffy, dark closet, thought it was almost an hour before her timorous siblings arrived at the back door. It was certainly a long time, for they had caught sight of the blue light crossing and recrossing Caleb's window earlier, and were very nervous.

"We *have* to take the dog back," said Caleb.

"And if there are ghosts don't you want to see them, Hannah?" asked Joe.

"No!" said Hannah, wide-eyed. "You don't need me, anyway."

"All right," said Joe.

But Hannah found staying alone in the dark yard worse than the ghost hunt, so she was with the others when they finally made it to the door.

"Anyway I've lived here for more than a year, and I've never seen a ghost," said Caleb. "And people write journals when they're alive, not when they're ghosts, so a journal doesn't prove anything."

"But the blue light..." suggested Joe.

Caleb was silent.

"Let's hurry and put the dog inside," Hannah whispered.

Frankie barked.

Caleb opened the door and stepped in boldly, fishing for the light switch.

"We should have brought a flashlight," Joe said thoughtfully, stepping inside.

"Hurry, put the dog down and let's go," said Hannah.

"Wait, here's the light—" All three distinctly heard the click, click of the switch as Caleb flipped it back and forth. "It's—not—working," he said breathlessly.

Hannah gasped and grabbed tightly onto Joe.

Just then the back door slammed shut.

Caleb jumped at it and twisted the door handle. "It's locked," he gasped.

From the dining room the sounds of trampling feet were heard. Somewhere in the house Frankie barked.

"I'm not afraid!" Joe screamed.

Slam! This was James coming in the front door—and locking it.

Caleb ran, crashing into furniture and falling over strategically placed cushions on the floor. He caught a sudden glimpse of Roy the pirate, illuminated by a blue glow stick in each hand, and shrieked. He slammed into the front door, fumbled for the lock, found it, and fled into the night, leaving the door wide open behind him.

Meanwhile Joe, whose imagination was not only capable of summoning ghosts to fight, but also capable of arming him with weapons to fight them, flourished his fists and screamed defiance.

"Shh, shh!" hissed Hannah. "Let's just go! Oh!" she gasped, hearing an unearthly groan and the swish of cloth. Essy, tired of waiting, swept out of her hiding place and burst upon her siblings' terrified eyes, a whirlwind of white bedding.

Joe crouched against the back door, fumbling with the locks while Hannah prayed in a whisper, "Dear father, please let us escape and don't let the ghosts get Mr. and Mrs. Calhoun when they come home. Amen."

As he ran down his driveway Caleb heard familiar shouts from the Ashburns' yard—"James, Hannah, Essy, Joe! Where a—re yo—u! Cale—eb! Roy!"

The next minute he had flown across the lawn and was hanging onto Jen for dear life, shaking and gasping and all but sobbing.

"Good night! Caleb! What's wrong?"

"There's a g-ghost," he shivered, "a pirate!"

"Oh! Is that all?" asked Jen.

"Fiddlesticks!" said Kyle, who was helping Jen look for the children. "Ghosts aren't real."

"There's one at my house," Caleb said, "and it scared me and Joe and Hannah."

"It scared you all right," Kyle retorted. "Where are Joe and Hannah?"

"They're still there, I guess," said Caleb. "It locked the door and I ran away."

"What? How..." Kyle began, but Jen interrupted.

"Some knight you were!"

"But I'm not Hannah's knight," Caleb said, surprised. "I'm your knight."

Kyle laughed. "Once a knight always a knight! You can't be brave for your lady and no one else."

"Oh," said Caleb, feeling that there was a little too much to this knight thing.

"Come on," Kyle added. "Let's go see what's up over there."

"It's just that if you're not brave for anyone else," Jen explained as they walked, "you're not very likely to be brave for your own lady. See?"

"I guess so," said Caleb.

Kyle and Jen walked up the drive while Caleb trailed a little behind. "I say, Jen," Kyle whispered suddenly. "That's broken glass. There's something going on, anyway."

"Well, so much for a locked door," Jen said, pointing to the open front door.

Kyle walked in, glancing sharply from side to side.

"Yo-heave-ho, and a bottle of—" came from the dining room in a sing-song voice.

"That's Roy," Kyle whispered. "I've heard him practicing the whole last week. What's going on here?"

Jen tripped over something in the entryway and for a second lay there, terrified. It was a body, soaked in—blood?

"Ky!"

Kyle dropped and the next instant had James in a chokehold.

"Ow! Ky!" James shouted.

"Oh, it's you. I should have known. What on earth is going on here, James?"

"I'm the ghost of a murdered man," James explained. "It's tomato sauce, Jen, with a little black paint."

"I hope it won't stain the floor," Jen said drily. "Why is this light not working?"

"I turned 'em all off," said James. He pulled a flashlight out of his pocket and switched it on. "Just give me a second."

With the lights on, the Calhouns' usually elegant home looked like a war zone.

"Were you all the ghosts?" Joe asked, coming in from the back room and looking proud of his own bravery.

"Yep," said Essy gleefully, spinning around in her makeshift dress and promptly tumbling to the ground.

Roy looked around at the mess, and looked rather ashamed of himself.

Jen glanced at her watch. "Well, they said they'd be home at eight. You kids have about three minutes and... twenty-four seconds to clean it all up. Let's get going!"

"Eight!" James exclaimed. "I thought it was ten."

"Well, you thought wrong," said Kyle. "Now listen up. Jen and I'll help clean, but only if you three are going to confess handsomely. We have literally nothing to do with this and you'd better not expect us to shoulder any blame."

"All right," said James ruefully. "But it wouldn't have been near such a jolly mess if Caleb hadn't torn through like there was a whole zoo chasing him. He broke the front door glass and I'm not much looking forward to explaining that."

"You'll have to do it, anyways," Kyle said, picking up a broom. "It's your fault for scaring him."

"Hmm!" grunted James, scrubbing the floor with the tail end of Essy's dress.

Caleb tugged on Jen's shirt. "You—you won't tell Essy how scared I was, will you?" he whispered.

"No-o," said Jen. "I guess not. But you need to toughen up, little boy, or..."

"I'll try," said Caleb. He hugged Jen gratefully and then went to help clean up with a lighter heart.

Later Hannah said to Joe, "I don't think we should make up ghost stories any more."

"Why not?" asked Joe.

"It puts too much temptation in Essy's way," she said sadly. "You oughtn't tempt your brothers and sisters more than you can help."

Chapter 9—Why Fred Learned to Write

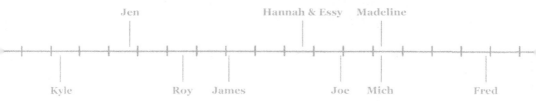

Jen   Hannah & Essy   Madeline

Kyle   Roy   James   Joe   Mich   Fred

About this time the twins had a sudden mania for going to the bathroom after bedtime. Mrs. Ashburn might have wondered more about this, if it weren't for an even more sudden mania on the part of her youngest son.

Fred wanted to learn how to write. Day in and day out, he followed her around, scratching lines in a notebook and demanding, "What letter's dis, mommy?"

This sudden swing toward studiousness puzzled Mrs. Ashburn greatly. But clearly it must be taken advantage of. Fred was soon to turn four, and Roy had been spelling his name at that age.

So Mrs. Ashburn taught Fred to recognize F, R, E, and D, and he spent long hours practicing them with his chubby fist curled around a crayon.

"How wong," he asked one night at dinner, "do it take to wite?"

"Oh..." said Mrs. Ashburn, "you could probably learn in six months or so, if you try hard."

"Like in Januwerry?"

"Mm—maybe *next* January. Or February, or..."

"Wanna wite in Januwerry," Fred insisted, "not in a different werry."

"Well, try very hard then," Jen suggested.

"Why does he want to write?" asked Mr. Ashburn.

"What kind of a disease is consumption?" Mad asked suddenly.

"It's when you eat too much," Essy explained, looking critically at Mad's full plate.

"That's not what it means!" said Kyle. "If you die of consumption that means something consumed you. So it's like being eaten by a dinosaur," he winked.

"Consumption," said Mr. Ashburn, "is the old name for tuberculosis."

"It means you cough a lot," said Mrs. Ashburn.

"It's actually a bacterial disease caused by the growth of—er—tubercles—in your lungs," said Jen.

"But why *does* Fred want to write?" Mr. Ashburn asked.

"If you were going to the moon, which one of your siblings would you take?" Roy asked Essy at the same time.

"Take me!" Mich shouted.

Essy frowned.

"I'd take you," Mad said. "Except I wouldn't go with you."

"You mean you'd send him off by himself?" Jen laughed.

Mr. Ashburn tried again. "Fred, why do you..."

"Daddy," said Mich, "why is the sky blue in the daytime?"

"Well," said Mr. Ashburn, "it has to do with the way the sunlight..."

"Can you tell me in a poem?" Mich asked.

Mr. Ashburn opened his mouth, but nothing came out, and Mrs. Ashburn rescued him by saying, "Shall we read our chapter now?" —referring to the Bible chapter they always read together right after supper. "It's almost time for Winkin', Blinkin', and Nod to go to bed," she added.

"But we're not tired!" Mich and Mad exclaimed. Fred hadn't learned to recognize himself under the nickname Nod yet.

"It's not about how tired you are, it's about how tired you make everyone else," Mr. Ashburn said, reaching for his Bible.

About two hours later he realized no one had explained why Fred wanted to learn to write.

After she had been in bed for three minutes Mad whispered to nobody in particular, "I need to go to the bathroom," and went. Arrived, the first thing she did was pick up a corner of the mat.

Underneath was a square of toilet paper, with these words written in pencil in a very bad hand. "Mad, sky is black. Mich."

She took another square of paper and a pencil from the drawer, and bent over it laboriously. "Mich," she wrote. "Dangerus. Be Ware. Mad. P.S. Goodbye."

When she came again in ten minutes there was another message. "Mad, what dangerus? P.S. You made the pencil wet. Mich."

"Mich, dangerus, is bad things. Because of Fred—" here Mad found it necessary to flip the square of paper. Trying to write on both sides tore it beyond repair, so she started again, on a longer strip this time. "Mich, Fred is dangerus. Because he nos, and now he wants to rite. Be Ware. Mad."

Mich wrote back, "Mad, he prommised to be seceret. Honor of a Ashburn. No fear. Mich."

"Madeline, what are you doing?" Jen asked, catching her slipping through the hallway.

"I'm going to the bathroom," Mad gulped.

"Well hurry up," Jen said. "You're supposed to be in bed."

This time Mad wrote, "Mich, good. Jen told me to hury up, so no mor tonite. Mad. P.S. Goodbye."

So now you know why Fred wanted to learn how to write.

In the end it was Madeline, not Fred, who ruined the scheme. For one night she fell asleep on the bathroom floor and Jen found her there with the tell-tale pencil in her hand and a half-written note crinkled in the other.

The twins shrugged and said they were getting tired of the game anyway. But Mrs. Ashburn found Fred sobbing in his bed.

"What is it, honey?" she asked.

"I just learned to rite my name!" he wailed.

Chapter 10—James the Hero

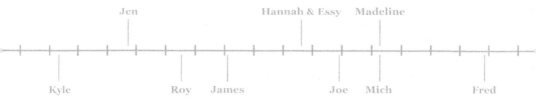

The Ashburn children could get a lot of fun out of a cardboard box. Roy had invented the shield, and Kyle gave the youngest ones box rides, but James invented the traffic light game.

This game featured a box with three colors of construction paper glued to three different sides. Of course the paper was red, yellow, and green. One child held the box and stood in front of the Ashburns' driveway. The others had to respect the signals as they bicycled past. It sounds dreadfully simple, until you begin to speculate on how fast a child can turn a box around from red to green and then through yellow to red again, before you have a chance to get through the intersection. Then the policeman swoops down on you and fines you—if he can catch you—anywhere from three to fifteen slaps on your right hand.

Sometimes the police chases became dramatic. This usually happened when Kyle was the policeman. He slapped hard.

One day Jen came out of the old garage turned music room singing, "Oh I'm sick and tired of the violin, never wanna see one in my life again!"

Kyle, who was studying for the ACT, threw his books down and said, "Let's go outside and do something! Get the kids together, Jen. I'll start losing brain cells if I prep another minute."

"What should we do first?" Jen asked, once they were all outside, with bikes, skateboards, a few cones, and three cardboard boxes piled around them.

"Let's play leapfrog!" said Mich.

"I want to play knights," Joe announced.

"How about we go get the chalk," Hannah began, "and draw..."

"And draw holes in the middle of the road," Essy finished.

"It's awful cold," said Roy. "We'd better play something exciting, like capture the flag."

"Exciting?" Jen repeated sarcastically.

"Can we play duck duck goose?" Fred asked.

Roy rolled his eyes.

"Let's just play *something,*" said Mad.

"But what?" Kyle asked. "We seem to be faced by insurmountable opportunities."

"How about the traffic light game?" James suggested.

"I'll be the traffic light," Jen said.

"And I want to be the policeman this time," James added.

"You just wanna get me back," Kyle said. "We'll see about that!"

The game went smoothly until James caught Kyle running a red. Kyle ran the red and kept right on going, flying around the corner of the road despite James' loud siren calls. James took off in hot pursuit and the other children appointed Essy to represent the police force.

Kyle was already out of sight by the time James took the turn. That wasn't a problem, since there was only one way to go, but at the first intersection he had to stop and guess.

"Little rascal," James muttered. "I guess I'm not likely to catch him now, even if I go the right way. Oh!" he exclaimed suddenly, catching sight of a cloud of smoke rising from a house on the right. Through the windows on the south side he could see an orange glow.

For a few seconds James was paralyzed by astonishment—and excitement too. Then he dropped his bike on the curb and ran to the door of the house. He started to pound, shouting, "Fire! Fire!"

Someone driving down the road jumped out of his car. "How long has this been going on?" he asked, running up. "Have you called the fire department?"

"No," James said, "I don't have a phone. Who lives here?"

"Don't know," said the man. "I'll call."

"It's an older couple," said a neighbor, appearing on the scene. "Maybe they're not at home."

James put his ear to the door and listened hard. All he could hear was crackling noises. He grabbed a flower pot from the porch and threw it at the nearest window.

"Hello!" he called, bending cautiously inside to unlatch the window. "Anyone home? Fire!"

"Help!" cried a voice, and James turned excitedly.

"Did you hear that?" he exclaimed.

"Hear what?" asked the neighbor.

James dove headfirst into the house.

"Hello!" he shouted again. Here inside he could feel the heat of the fire on his right. He ran toward it. "Say something!" he shouted. "So I can find you!"

"Here, here!" a voice called.

James flew around a corner and stopped abruptly, facing a wall of heat. Three sofas, in flames, lined the walls. Smoke made it impossible to distinguish any of the details.

Suddenly he felt something touch his leg—a hand. He bent over and saw an elderly woman, lying on the floor, trying to crawl away from the couch that had almost been her deathbed.

"I can't walk," she said in a cracked voice. "You're a brave boy, but you'd better save yourself."

James grabbed both her arms and dragged her out of the room. Her slippers were on fire, and he tore them off as soon as they were out of the smoke. Then he threw her over his shoulders, fireman style, and paused, unsure which direction the door was in.

"That way," she said in his ear, pointing to the left. "Past the kitchen."

It was hot in the kitchen, and the hiss and crackle of melting paint and snapping structural joints blended with the roar of flames in James' ears. Chunks had fallen from the ceiling and several appliances were melting.

"The back door," she gasped, pointing ahead, past the central countertop.

James kicked the door with his leg and it opened outwards. Stooping, he ran through the doorway into a utility room. Smoke filled his eyes and he stumbled blindly through, crashing into the next door, which flew out, door frame and all, much more easily than it should have.

James jumped to the ground, tripping and falling face first on the grass, gasping as the load he was carrying knocked the breath out of him. Behind him the flaming walls collapsed. He scrambled desperately forward, but the roof, sliding off the walls, pinned his legs to the ground.

"Someone!" James shouted. "Back here!" Then the pain got to him and he lost consciousness.

One of the firemen walked to the Ashburn house after the fire was mostly out with a neighbor who had recognized James. Jen was still outside picking up balls and pieces of chalk.

"Hi Mr. Thomas," Jen said.

"Hello," said Mr. Thomas. "Where's your mom—or your dad?"

"Dad's at work," Jen said. "I'll call mom, if you like." She looked curiously at the fireman.

"Please do," said Mr. Thomas.

Mrs. Ashburn came to the door. "Hello, Mark! Haven't seen you in a while."

Mr. Thomas glanced at the fireman.

"It's your son, ma'am," the fireman said.

"The strong looking one, with brown hair, somewhere in the middle," Mr. Thomas added, because Mrs. Ashburn looked confused.

"Oh! James? What about James?"

So the fireman explained, as fast as he could, and in a tremendously short time all the Ashburns—including Mr. Ashburn, who rushed over from his job—were at the hospital. Eleven of them were in the waiting room, and one in the operating room. James had broken both his legs; but all his vital organs were safe.

When James woke up his parents were sitting next to him and the rest of the room was wall-to-wall siblings.

"You're a brave man, James Ashburn," his father said.

"What happened?" he asked. "Is she okay?"

"Yes, Mrs. Evercrest is all right. So is her husband—he had fallen asleep out back and missed all the excitement," Mr. Ashburn answered.

"We're proud of you, James," Mrs. Ashburn said, laying a hand on his arm.

James smiled a little and shrugged. "What's wrong with my legs?" he asked. "—I can't feel very well."

Mr. Ashburn put his lips between his teeth for a second. "I know, son. You—James, you've lost your left leg."

James gasped. In front of him flashed visions of running, biking, swimming and climbing rocks. He sat up abruptly, feeling for the missing foot.

Hannah came and threw her arms around him, sobbing.

"It's—okay, Hannah," James said absently. He caught Essy's eye with a question in it. "No," he thought to himself, shaking his head. "I'll never regret it—so help me God!"

Aunt Clarissa heard about it the next day and told Uncle Bob. "You should have heard his mother," she said, "praising him to the skies—though I could tell she was crying the whole time. It was brave enough, of course, but where's the sense? He was a twelve-year-old kid, healthy as a hunter with a great life ahead of him—losing a leg to save an eighty-three-year-old woman who can't even walk?! I think it's a pity those Ashburn children haven't been taught a bit more common sense."

"What good," Uncle Bob asked, "would the life of a man with two legs be if he weren't man enough to risk them?"

When James got far enough on the road to recovery to come home he was a hero, and everyone bent over backwards to be nice to him. The girls' fit of kindness took the shape of reading books aloud. Hannah read *Anne of Green Gables* and Jen went for *Pride and Prejudice*. After much consideration Essy chose *Where the Red Fern Grows*. Mad read him *Pollyanna*.

James didn't understand the fad, considering that he'd lost a leg, not an eye. Besides, he didn't much enjoy his sisters' choice of books. But once Kyle had said dogmatically, "Any boy who says he doesn't like P&P is either a dunce or just not man enough to admit that he actually does like it." So James said nothing, and fortunately for him the fit didn't last long. Essy was the only one who finished her book, and that was because she read out loud as fast as she did in her head—which was hard to follow.

"Where's Essy?" Roy asked one day when he came into the boys' room to get his favorite pencil.

"Oh, she's playing with Caleb, I think. She finished her book, anyway."

"Oh," said Roy, sitting down. "What about the others?"

"They have better things to do," said James—with obvious relief.

"Oh! —Would you like me to read to you?"

"Um—" James began, thinking to himself, "Now they'll be about pirates instead of little girls. Wish they'd read me something really interesting!"

But Roy picked up James' copy of *The Way Things Work* and flipped to his bookmark.

"Oh," said James, "if you'll read me that—!"

"Sure," Roy said, and plunged right into the uses of the lever.

So in the end it was Roy who kept James company most of his convalescence.

Chapter 11—December 24th

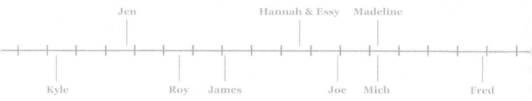

The Ashburn family did not celebrate Christmas. Caleb pitied them very much; and the funny thing was, they pitied Caleb too. The truth was, the Ashburn children were very proud of not celebrating Christmas. They felt like it was a sign of a better education, especially compared to children who believed in Santa. Even on the subject of presents they were proud with a certain independent swagger. Ashburn children didn't *need* presents. They could love their parents anyways. "*We* don't bother our dad for silly little things like Christmas gifts," Kyle said to Caleb, and strutted like a peacock.

If, sometimes, some of the younger ones did not see things quite in this light, at least they saw that not celebrating Christmas was part of what made them Ashburns, and held their heads high in consequence.

To do Mr. and Mrs. Ashburn justice, they were not aware of the airs their children gave themselves. As Mrs. Ashburn explained to her parents, "It's that the holiday has become so commercialized, you know. All this expensive gift giving. Besides, its roots aren't really Christian—the 25th was a pagan holiday first. —Anyway... we decided not to celebrate it."

The grandparents did not appreciate their decision until the fifth or sixth child came along and they realized just how much work it would have been to get presents for each one.

So December 24th was a very different day in the Ashburn household than in the rest of the neighborhood.

"Funny to think other people are bothering about presents and stuff," Jen said the evening of the 23rd.

"What a blessing it is to avoid that," said Mrs. Ashburn.

"Imagine hanging socks up over the fireplace," Kyle snorted.

"And expecting a puffy guy in a red shirt to come down it," James sniffed.

"Is it true that parents always eat cookies and milk after the children go to bed on Christmas Eve?" Hannah asked.

"Um," said Mrs. Ashburn, looking suddenly guilty.

"Do *you* eat cookies after we go to bed?!" exclaimed Essy.

"What are you all talking about?" asked Mr. Ashburn, opportunely walking into the room.

"How nice it is not to celebrate fruitcake day," Kyle said.

"Oh," said Mr. Ashburn, "but I think it's kind of a shame..."

"What!? We never... You can't mean that... We're Ashburns!" the children cried in horrified unison.

"No, no, no, that's not what I meant," Mr. Ashburn hurried to explain. "I just meant—other people take family photos at this time of year. We don't hardly have any family photos."

"Oh," said Kyle. "Well, why shouldn't we take a photo?"

"S'long as we don't have to dress up like elves," Jen agreed.

"Why not?" said Mr. Ashburn. "Go change your dirty shirt, Essy, and put something nice on instead of those torn sweatpants, Joe. Jen—you'd better take the curls out of your hair. Kyle, is that dirt on you, or a tan?"

"My shirt's not dirty," Essy said, "it's just flour." She stood up and started dusting herself off, sending puffs of white into the air.

"*I'm* dirty, though," said Kyle. "I was setting mouse traps under the porch. I'll go shower."

"No you won't," Jen retorted. "I have to shower to get the curls out."

"Mich and Mad should really take baths too," Mrs. Ashburn said. "Suppose we take the picture tomorrow, Jerry?"

Mr. Ashburn stroked his chin. "Yes, maybe that'd be better. I need to shave anyhow."

"All right," said Mrs. Ashburn. "Everyone try to dress nicely tomorrow. No busy and busy. Try not to wear striped pants with your checkered shirt, James."

"I couldn't reach anything else this morning," James explained. He was still in a wheelchair most of the time.

"I'll help you find an outfit," Roy offered.

"Uh-uh," Mrs. Ashburn said quickly. "We don't want *outfits*, Roy. Just nice plain clothes. No sashes or pirate hats. Let's all try to wear a touch of blue, while we're at it. No, Fred, you may not wear your blue pajamas."

The next morning the Ashburn home was a madhouse. Jen, by inflexible decree, had ordered the picture to be taken at eleven sharp, because, she said—and she had spent plenty of time outside taking photos, so everyone agreed she ought to know—the sunlight in front of the backyard trees would be best just then.

"That way we have a good hour before the shadow starts to eat us," she said.

"Wouldn't it be kind of nicer to stand in the shade?" Roy asked.

"It's seventeen degrees outside!" Jen retorted.

"Oh, right."

"Besides, the photo will look better in the light. And it's overcast. Perfect photography weather. Joe, that's busy and busy. Go put a plain pair of pants on."

Jen was dictator today and well she knew it.

"Mich, go wash your hands and don't dry them on your clothes. Mad, you're good except for that stupid hairbow—here, I'll take it. Go wait in the dining room. Roy, grab my tripod and let's go set up. Wait a second, I need to fix my hair first. Bother. I bought myself a pack of fifty bobby pins last week and now I can't even find the one in my hair!" She rushed to her room.

"Where're you gowin?" Fred called after her.

"I'm going crazy!" Jen exclaimed.

"Can I go wid you?" he asked, jumping up and down.

Jen looked down at him, laughing. "Did Essy try to give you a mohawk again? Go get mommy to fix your hair. Roy, let's go."

Jen got her camera set up as the others trooped outside.

"All right," she said. "I don't want us all to have frozen noses in this picture, so let's try to take it quickly. I'm going to come over and stand by you, Roy, when I start the timer. James—oh, are you going to stand up? In that case, you're best between Dad and Essy. Joe, you're not tall enough to be in the back. Okay, everyone, smile when it starts blinking. Except you, Fred. Don't smile. It makes you look like a tiger. Here goes!"

Thirty-eight pictures later and with cold noses after all the Ashburns returned to their living room.

"All those pictures and I look stupid in every one of them," said Kyle. Jen had made him take off his sunglasses.

Jen began to look at the pictures on the computer screen, and the others gathered round. "That one's awful," James said—by which he meant that he looked bad in it—and, "Really? It looks good to me," Mr. Ashburn replied—because he was smiling just the right amount.

In fact, all the pictures looked more or less the same.

Kyle—blue eyed, athletic, average height—stood on the far left. He was eighteen now, and had his father's light hair and his mother's narrow face and a careless ease of manner all his own that shone in the crinkles of his eyes. Next to him was Hannah, with her curly brown hair framing wide, innocent eyes and a dimpled face.

Four-year-old Fred, in front of them, had inherited a cluster of thick red curls from some far-off great uncle. He was frowning hard in an attempt not to smile, but his laughing green eyes contradicted the frown.

The twins stood next to him, their arms around each other's necks. Mich and Mad were soon to turn eight. They both had blond hair, chubby round faces, and wide smiles full of teeth and dimples. Behind them stood Essy and James. Ten-year-old Essy was proud of James' hand on her shoulder, and really thought she was doing most of the work of keeping him up. But James was quite able to stand on his own. Square-jawed and thick-set, he was more strongly built than any of his siblings.

Mr. Ashburn stood on James' left. His light brown hair was touched with grey, but his face would always look young. He had sparkly hazel eyes and eyebrows that dared you not to laugh. Next to him was Mrs. Ashburn; you couldn't very well tell where one blue jacket ended and the other began.

The only person who had noticed any grey hairs on Mrs. Ashburn yet was Mrs. Ashburn herself. She had a long wave of black hair which swept back from her forehead and her delicate but firm jaw justified Uncle Bob's expression, "Sweet, but no nonsense."

Roy, at fourteen, was already as tall as his brother Kyle. He had a serious mouth, dreamy hazel eyes behind glasses, and a scholarly forehead under his dark hair. His smile was rare, but it lit up his face. In front of him was Joe, whose wide smile fit well in his round face, with its dancing brown eyes and straight brown hair, distinguished by exactly one curl in front.

Lastly stood Jen on the right, where she could slip quickly back and forth from the camera. When Mrs. Ashburn laughed, she looked almost exactly like Jen. For Jen was always laughing, and had the jolliest smile. In fact, it was hard to get past her wide smile and notice anything else; but she had Mrs. Ashburn's dark wave of hair, soft eyes, and firm jaw.

Essy was a few minutes late coming to the gathering around the computer to look at the pictures, and when she arrived she said, "I found the cookies. They were under mommy's night table."

"What?!" said Mr. Ashburn blankly. "Cookies? You mean... But those are for..."

"Oh dear," said Mrs. Ashburn. "I guess from now on we'll have to... share..."

"We made it for eighteen years," sighed Mr. Ashburn. "I knew it was too good to last."

"I'll bring the milk!" Kyle volunteered.

Chapter 12—A Challenge

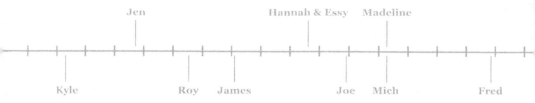

Grandpa and Grandma Ashburn gave the Ashburn children a trampoline this same December, which, they insisted, had nothing to do with the holidays and was just the result of a random whim that might have happened anytime. But all the Ashburns right down to Fred were convinced it was a Christmas present and they made holiday themed jokes when Kyle, Jen, and Roy went to set it up a few months later, once the danger of snow was over.

"We should drape it with Christmas lights and red bows next time Grandma and Grandpa come," Jen said. "Not a Christmas present, indeed!"

Roy unpacked the springs from the box and started hanging them by their hooks on Kyle's back pocket.

"What are you doing?" Kyle asked, turning around quickly and scattering springs everywhere.

Roy looked innocently at the sky.

"Come on, do something useful, boys," said Jen, trying to hold three pieces of the frame together at once.

After they got the frame together Kyle stretched the mat out and put a few springs on different sides. Jen and Roy each got a handful of springs and started to help.

"These are really—umph!—kinda hard to put on," Jen gasped, once she was on her third spring.

"The first ones were easy enough," said Kyle, throwing all his weight into pulling one, "but they're getting harder."

"I haven't even managed to put one on," Roy said, frowning at the three springs he was holding in his right hand.

Just then Essy's voice came across the yard. "Are you all almost done? I brought Caleb to try it out!"

Kyle and Jen looked at each other with the same thought.

"Not quite done yet," said Kyle. "Putting on springs is a job for a real man."

"Yep," said Jen. "This is a job for you, Caleb. We three have to go inside and... read the instructions for setting up the net. Let us know when you're done, Caleb!"

So Kyle, Jen, and Roy went to the kitchen and got a snack.

"Are they coming back?" Caleb asked Essy.

"Maybe, once you've got all the springs on," said Essy, bending over and picking one up.

Caleb looked doubtfully at the tool Kyle had been using to pull on the springs—a T shaped piece of metal with a hook on the long end. He hooked one end of a spring onto the trampoline frame and the other onto the tool, and then pushed out towards the center of the mat until he hooked the spring on.

"Doesn't look that hard," said Essy, sitting down on the trampoline box to watch his progress.

"It *is* hard," said Caleb, frowning and pushing at the next spring.

After he'd got five springs on—each one taking longer than the one before—Essy yawned. "Well, you don't need me," she said. "I'm getting hungry sitting here, gonna go make cookies."

Caleb let the tool slip twice while he was trying to hook the next spring onto the mat and stopped in frustration. He blew on his palms and rubbed them on the cool grass. Then he frowned and said to himself, "I'll do this—see if I don't!"

About an hour and a half later Mrs. Ashburn looked out the kitchen window and saw Caleb, alone, jumping on the trampoline without a net. "Kids!" she called. "What happened? Why isn't the net up, Kyle?"

"The net?" said Kyle, startled. "Oh, the trampoline! I forgot all about that. Jen, Roy! Let's go finish!"

Caleb saw them coming and climbed off the trampoline. Roy said, "You were supposed to tell us when you finished."

"No way—you didn't do them all, did you?" Kyle asked, walking around the frame. "Bet you got your dad to help you!"

"I did it all by myself!" said Caleb, aggrieved.

Jen held up her hand for a high-five.

Caleb slapped it and then winced, because his hands were covered in blisters.

"All right, let's get this net up and then we can play something!" said Kyle.

During the spring and summer that followed the Ashburns played dozens of trampoline games. Their most intense game was monkey-in-the-middle, with three balls to throw around and keep away from whoever was in the middle. Roy always threw balls extra hard, trying to bounce them off someone and into the monkey's hands. Either on purpose or by accident, everyone got their face smashed sometime or other.

Another popular game was barrel rolls. Two or three children stood up while the others rolled across the mat, trying to sweep them off their feet.

Kyle and Roy raced each other to see who could do a full flip first. Roy practiced every single morning, and as soon as Kyle figured that out, he started practicing every evening. In fact, he went one better and got James to coach him. Not that James knew so much about doing a flip, but he watched sharply and could tell Kyle which moves were improving his flip and which ones weren't.

Roy tried to get Jen to coach him. "But don't just laugh," he said, "watch what I do and tell me, is it better to bend down more, or go up straight, and that kind of thing."

"But it looks so funny the way you collapse at the end," Jen grinned.

James' coaching style was more professional. "Gotta get your rear higher up in the air, Ky," he said, "that's what's messing you up."

So Kyle tried three more times and James said, "Nope. Nope. And... nope."

"Do you have anything more... helpful—to say?" Kyle asked.

"Here, get out of the trampoline and come here."

"Okay..."

"Now let me see... put your hands on the frame and keep them as straight as you can. Now just jump up and get your rear end up as high as you can. Again. Keep practicing."

"This feels really silly," said Kyle.

"Do you wanna beat Roy?"

"How many times you want me to do this?" Kyle asked, breathless.

"Oh," said James, looking at his watch, "we'll start with fifty today. A hundred tomorrow."

"How many've I done so far?"

"I don't know. You need to count."

The next morning Jen burst excitedly into the school room. "Roy did it!" she shouted. "He did a flip!"

"*One* flip?" said Kyle. "I've done five or six already. It's gotta come out consistently."

"Well I bet it will, now he's cracked the code. Come see!"

Roy was panting on the trampoline mat, a little dizzy, by the time they all got there. But he jumped up and said, "I did five in a row, Ky!"

"It's not official until everyone sees it," said Kyle.

"Here's how we'll do it," James said. "Roy does one, then Kyle does one, then Roy, and so on. The first person who fails one when the other one succeeds loses."

"Sounds fair," said Jen.

Roy failed his fourth flip and Kyle, nervous at the chance to win, failed his fourth too. Fifth and sixth were mutual successes and Kyle said, "Call it a tie?"

"One more," said Roy, spinning smoothly in the air and landing gracefully.

Kyle climbed into the trampoline and bounced a couple of times, breathing heavily.

"Don't you dare fail on purpose!" Roy shouted.

"All right, I won't," said Kyle, "but if I make this one it's a tie!"

"Deal!"

Kyle jumped high into the air, lost his nerve, and wriggled to the floor.

"I won!" Roy shouted.

Jen crossed her arms and smiled smugly at James.

"Don't give yourself airs," said James. "You had precious little to do with that."

"Anyway," said Kyle, "if today was the first time you did a full flip, then I did one long before you."

"I wanna learn to do that thing!" Fred said, tugging at Jen's arm. "Won't you teach me?"

Essy sat on the trampoline frame and swung her feet. "What's so great about a flip anyway?" she asked, shrugging. "Caleb can do flips."

"What?" said Roy.

"Yeah, he can do a backflip," said Essy.

For a few seconds everyone was stunned, then Kyle said flatly, "We don't believe you."

"Just wait until he gets back from school and you'll see," Essy said.

"Do you suppose Caleb can really do a backflip?" Kyle whispered to Jen.

"Essy probably doesn't know the difference between a flip and summersault," Jen said.

"I heard that!" Essy shouted.

When Caleb came to play that afternoon he found everyone staring at him.

"What?" he said.

"Can you really do a pancake backwards?" Fred asked.

"A what?" Caleb asked.

"He means a flip," said Jen. "Pancakes—flips—kind of the same thing."

"Oh, I can do a backflip," said Caleb, "but I have to cartwheel into it."

"Oh come on! I gotta see this," said Kyle.

Even Mrs. Ashburn stood by the kitchen window to watch—and was impressed.

Chapter 13—They Have Been There Since

"What are you up to, Mad?" Jen asked one evening.

"I'm writing a letter to Unk Bob," Mad said. "How does it sound?"

Jen took it. "Dear Unk Bob," the letter said, "I dropped the last letter on the floor so I washeded it and then it was more dirtier. Ky said that was becase I didn't use soap. The dirty letter said I hope you have a good day, and also Aunt Clissa. And to please paint the truck you make for me green. It is my third favoriet color. It is very sweet of you to make me a truck, mommy says, so I am verry thankful. I know you are very busy so thank you for reading this far. I hope you will read the rest. I hope you will rite me back but you do not have to rite me a long letter unless you want me to spend a long time reading it. Goodbye. Mommy says I should rite love but I like better goodbye. From me Madeline Ashburn."

"Do you think Unk Bob will have time to read it all?" Mad asked.

"Oh yes, I expect so," said Jen. "If not it's certainly his loss. Oh, there you are, Essy. When was the last time you cleaned your dresser, m'dear?" Jen used m'dear in a sarcastic way—as though to say, it's not that I love you so much as all that; only I want you to run along now and do what I say, m'dear!

"Bother! I'm going," Essy said.

She walked into the school room ten minutes later, waving a handful of torn notebook paper. "Look what I found," she chuckled.

"What's that?" asked Roy, swiveling in his chair.

"It's our stories we wrote when we were seven," said Essy, who was ten now. "Hannah and me. She had the ideas and I wrote down the parts I wanted to. They're about all of us. You can read 'em," she added graciously.

"Let's see," said Kyle.

Jen sat on the desk with a pen between her teeth and bounced her freshly curled hair on her hand.

"'Fifteen. Jack,'" Kyle read. "'Born. He wandered of. Then he came back and found noboby there. His mother was there. She was dying. He tried to help her but he could not. He wandered of again. He told the doctor. Then went. Elsa found him. She took him. She was fond of childeren. She made him clean her kicken. He has been there since.

"'Thirteen. Lizy,'" he went on. "'Born. She saw her brother wander of. She followed him. When they got back she tired secertly to help her mother. She did not want Jack to know she was there. Then they Left. They told the docketer. Then went. She Lost sight of Jack. Then Elsa saw her too. Elsa took her home. She feed her well. She gave her water. She has been there since.

"'Eleven. Barak. Boron. Got kicked out. Got rich. Spent his money folishly. Wandered of. Saw his brother Taraka. They saw a Light far of in the distance. They satered towed it. They finally reashed it. Inside was Amy therie sister. She invited them in. They have been there since.

"'Nine. Rabrigo. Born. Got kicked out. Got a hamer and nials. Bilt a little barn. Then Elsa saw him. She new she had to bring him home. She did. She Let him die.'" Kyle paused, momentarily stunned.

"Go on," Roy grinned.

"'Six. Shabataka. Born. Got kicked out. Want Amy all the time. Followed her every ware. When she bilt her palace he satayed outside for a day then nokled. She invited him in. He has been there since.

"'Four. Sussy. Born. Saw everone else go out. The mother stareteret to get sick. The doctor came. The mother died. The doctor took good care of her. Then the doctor Left. Sussy wandered of. She saw a Light far off. She came to the Light. It was Amy her sister. She has been there since.

"'Four. Taraka. Born. Got kicked out. Got rich. Spent his monny on wood and hammer and nials. He wandered into the desessert. He bilt a little barn. He went for a walk. Then he heard Barak running to him. They saw a light. They went on till they reached it. Inside was Amy. They have been there since.

"'Seven. Elsa. Born. Got kicked out. Got rich. Looked around for a place to make a rich house. Found a place. Chose that one. Bought wood. Bought some more wood. Bilted a rich house. Made the rich house out of wood. She found Jack and Lizy. They have been there since.

"'Seven. Amy. Born. Saw her bothers kicked out. Learned marshel arts. Saw her mother start to die. Went out. Got rich. Found a perfact place to make a palace. Made a palace. Made it out of wood. Looked out of the window. Saw her bothers and sisters. She Let them in. They have been there since.'"

"Elsa is Hannah and Amy is me," Essy explained. "The others are the rest of you."

"You two are awful conceited," laughed Jen.

"So is the one who died James?" Kyle asked. "Poor fellow. What'd you do that for?"

"He wouldn't fix my dolly—the one that talks, you know."

Jen laughed. "Let's go read them to James. He was at physical therapy this afternoon so he's resting now."

"And then afterwards we can go round and make up stories until bedtime," Roy suggested. This was one of his favorite games.

Joe started the first story after they were all ready, sitting on the beds around James in the boys' room. "Once upon a time there was a knight," he began, "galloping down the path from France to Serbia in the moonlight. His shining armor bounced back the rays of the sun—I mean the moon—as he flew through the cool air, determined to protect the important—um—message—he was bringing at all costs."

Jen jumped in. "'How much longer till we get there?' the message asked. —You know," she explained, "the 'message' was actually a young princess going to marry the son of the King of Serbia, to make peace between the countries. —The brave knight replied, 'Tis but a stone's throw, my lady. You will be with your fair—er—fiancé—before dawn!' And then..." she paused, at a loss for words.

"And then," Roy went on dreamily, "the lady began to weep. For she liked not the King of Serbia's wicked son, and wished not to marry him. 'Oh, sir knight!' she said pitifully, 'thou art so kind and gentle, I know thou wouldst not willingly grieve a maiden's heart. Would thou couldst take me elsewhere, and let me not ever reach the King of Serbia and his guilty son!'"

"Of course," Kyle said, taking up his part in a very matter of fact voice, "this shocked the knight. He had no clue that the princess didn't want to marry the—the—was it the King of Spain or—"

"Serbia," said Hannah.

"Right, Serbia. She didn't want to marry him, anyhow, and the knight didn't know what to do, for the—King of France I think it was, would chop off the knight's head if he didn't deliver the princess safely. So, not knowing what to do, he stopped to eat his dinner."

"His dinner was awful late," said James.

"Oh! I forgot about the moonlight. Well, he stopped for a midnight snack then. And I'm sure I don't know what happened next, so you take it from there, James."

"All right," said James. "While they were stopped, the clever princess started to take apart one of the carriage wheels, figuring that she couldn't drive to Serbia in a carriage that only had three wheels. So she unscrewed the bolts from the axle hub—she always carried a wrench with her, of course, and she was a strong princess, you know," he explained in answer to a glance from Essy, "anyway she started taking the spokes out of the wheel. Then she took out her pocket knife and whittled away at the spokes—they were made out of wood, obviously—until there was nothing but little shavings that couldn't possibly be put back together even if the knight happened to have three whole bottles of super glue. Your turn, Mich."

"Once she made her carriage so it couldn't move, the princess thought about how she was hungry," Mich said. "So she asked the knight for some of his snack. And he came and spread it out on the... he came and spread it out, and it was brownies and pretzels and a root beer float, and also some corn dogs. The princess was very hungry and she ate it all," he finished.

"Then the knight got up to keep going on his trip," Mad interposed, "and he found the broken carriage wheel. He was mys—mys—he didn't know whatever had happened, but he figured he'd have to get the princess to Serbia some other way. He nobly let her get on his horse and decided to run alongside."

"And then fainted under all his heavy armor," Essy chimed in, "and the princess ran away on the horse, but she was so heavy from all the brownies and pretzels and floats and corn dogs that she fell off the horse and broke her neck. When he woke up, the knight, knowing he was disgraced, tore his hair and stumbled into the nearest forest, where he became a hermit. And when the King of France sent messengers to see what had happened, they only found the broken carriage to tell the sad tale."

"And evewyone lived happily evew after," Fred finished.

"Shouldn't let Essy finish," Jen complained. "They always die instead of getting married like they're supposed to."

"Anyhow her predictability is a virtue," said Kyle. "No one ever knows what your folks are going to do. Of course James' people *always* start tearing things apart. You could maybe have them put something together once in a while."

"James should tell us a whole story now," Essy giggled. "Bet there will be an entire hardware store in it."

"No, thanks," said James quickly. "But I'll start off a new one, if you like."

So they went round again, and three or four stories later Mrs. Ashburn looked into the room. "It's bedtime, children," she said.

"Yes'm. —Can't James tell us a bedtime story first, mommy?" Hannah asked.

"We've been telling stories this whole time," James said quickly.

"But those weren't bedtime stories," Essy said. "We want a *bedtime* story. By you."

"All right," said Mrs. Ashburn. "One last story, and then whether it's a bedtime story or not, it's off to bed for you younger ones."

"Thank you!" said Essy. "Okay, James. Tell us a story."

James growled. "Once upon a time there were two little girls who begged their brother for a bedtime story. And their brother put them in a rocket and—and sent them to the moon. And... and..."

"And," said Kyle slyly, "they have been there since."

Chapter 14—The Toilet Paper Rolls

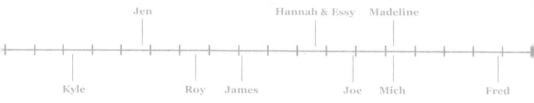

The year Fred turned five the Ashburn children went on a collecting craze. It started with Hannah, who saved individual sized yogurt cups to keep beads in. She had taken up beading a year ago and made bracelets for anyone she thought might wear them.

Essy could not let herself be outdone, so she claimed peanut butter jars; but having nothing to put into them, she began a rock collection. James saved empty ice cream tubs for parts of disassembled machinery; Joe collected used envelopes and sorted them by how far away they had come from; Mich saved kleenex boxes to organize his toys in; but Madeline had hands down the best collection. She saved the insides of toilet paper rolls.

In a household of twelve, the toilet paper roll collection grew quickly. Madeline stacked the rolls on the window sill until that became too much for the light of day to cope with. Then she made a three dimensional pyramid out of them at the end of her bed. It was quite a striking centerpiece for the girls' room.

Mrs. Ashburn did not frequently have the time or the inclination to go upstairs into the children's rooms. Mr. Ashburn put the younger ones to bed, but he was not one to pay close attention to fine details. So it happened that the toilet paper roll collection went unnoticed for several weeks.

Of course toilet paper rolls are rather useless as containers; but they are wonderful for building forts and castles and then seeing who can destroy them fastest. You can also make spyglasses out of toilet paper rolls, and trumpets, and in fact there is no end to the fun you can get out of them.

One rainy afternoon Mich, Mad, and Fred were banished to the upstairs. Downstairs Mrs. Ashburn and the older children were preparing a fancy dinner. Mr. Ashburn was trying to land a new job with a small, start-up company, and had invited his potential future boss and his wife over. Mrs. Ashburn told him it would be wiser to invite them over after he got the job, but it was too late by that time.

James was the chef on special occasions such as these. He measured and mixed ingredients himself, but delegated the chopping and peeling. There were to be five pizzas—with stuffed crust—a crispy lettuce salad, freshly fried ravioli, also freshly fried cheese sticks, and two pizza-shaped danishes for dessert.

Kyle cleaned the dining room and Jen decorated it. "Just give it a slight artistic touch, Jen," Mrs. Ashburn said. Hannah had volunteered, but Mrs. Ashburn did not trust her taste in matters requiring simplicity. Instead Hannah set the table.

Kyle finished his job first and hovered over the others, being annoying.

"The ravioli are starting to get brown, James," he said. "You should probably take them out now. I don't think you should put olives on all the pizzas and those mushrooms should be thinner. Essy, you're supposed to cut red peppers the other way."

"What do you know about red peppers?" Essy asked, and James said, "Isn't there any more dirt for you to scrub?"

So Kyle wandered into the dining room and said, "You should set everyone an extra small fork, Hannah, since we're having dessert afterwards. And the plates need to be turned so the design is at the bottom. You can't fold the napkins in half like a rectangle! They need to be a triangle."

Hannah glared at him.

"Maybe you should go—um—go comb your hair or something, Kyle," Mrs. Ashburn suggested.

"Nobody appreciates my advice," Kyle sighed.

"Advice?" Jen asked thoughtfully. "I would have called that instructions."

"See!" he wailed.

If Mr. Ashburn was to be hired based on the way his house smelled, he would certainly have got the job. Every variety of delicious flavor wafted through the home, and Mr. and Mrs. Elsroth suffered agonies of hunger trying to sustain a polite conversation with Mr. and Mrs. Ashburn in the living room. But finally James stuck his fist around the kitchen wall and put his thumb up.

"Well," said Mrs. Ashburn at the next pause, "shall we go have dinner?"

"Absolutely," said Mr. Elsroth.

Jen went to get her younger siblings, in response to a glance from her mother. She had to lift them one by one over a wall of toilet paper rolls at the head of the stairs, but did not think anything of this.

Mich and Mad came into the dining room giggling to each other, and Fred sat down and clanged his silverware together.

"Fred... behave," Jen whispered.

"I am behaving, only bad," he explained.

Mrs. Ashburn thought about having the three youngest eat in the back yard—a brilliant idea which it was too late to implement.

Mr. Ashburn said grace and Jen served the guests. She only flipped one piece of pizza upside down while doing so.

"So," Mrs. Elsroth asked smilingly, after she'd taken the edge off her appetite, "to which of these young ladies do we owe our dinner?"

"Oh," said Mrs. Ashburn, "um—James—is actually the chef of the family."

"Oh!" Mrs. Elsroth said, glancing between James and the fried ravioli, and back again. "Well it's—very delicious."

"But *I* cut the red pepper," Essy said.

Mr. Ashburn cleared his throat and started talking about architecture. But Mrs. Elsroth didn't find that topic interesting, so she turned to Fred and said, "And are you the youngest? You have the cutest red hair."

Fred pulled a pizza crust out of his mouth, including the part he'd been working on biting off. "Essy says that having red hair makes people angry, but it doesn't make me angry. I like red hair."

Mrs. Ashburn said, "Jerry was telling me how much your husband has to travel. Ever get a chance to go with him?"

"Oh yes, frequently," said Mrs. Elsroth. "I've been in three continents so far. I don't enjoy the plane flights, but there's certainly some breathtaking scenery to discover."

Jen looked envious. "Have you been in the Alps?" she asked.

"Yes, I have. Mason attended an architect's conference there, and I went skiing."

"Jen wants to be a landscape photographer," Kyle said, "she says people take too much patience."

"Landscape takes patience too," said Jen, "but it's a nicer kind."

"The kind where there's no one to yell at," Roy added.

Everyone laughed, and Jen explained, "It's just that with landscapes you know ahead of time. People are either a joy or a terror, and you don't know which."

"Do you do a lot of photography? —I mean, professionally."

"Well," said Jen modestly, "not professionally exactly. It's mostly been friends and so forth, and I haven't earned enough to buy a yacht yet."

Mrs. Elsroth filed that information away for future reference.

By this time Mich and Mad had satisfied their appetites and were ready to participate in the conversation. "Do you like dogs?" Mich asked.

"Yes, I do."

"Thought so," said Mich. "Would you like to be one after dinner?"

Mrs. Elsroth looked at the seven-year-old in blank surprise.

"Mich needs one," Mad explained, "to help him trap beavers."

"Oh!" said Mrs. Elsroth. "I don't think I would really do a good job with that."

"But we use stuffed animals for beavers," said Mich, "so they don't run away. You just have to pick them up with your mouth and fetch them."

Mrs. Ashburn said, "Maybe we should go to the living room where it's more comfortable. Children, you're excused."

"Hurray!" said Joe. He and Mich clanged their plates into the dishwasher and rushed for the outdoors.

"Mich," Mad called after him, in a warning voice.

"Oh, I forgot," Mich said. "Can I go outside to the woods, mommy Mad?"

"You can go to the woods," said Mad graciously. She often played "mom" to Mich. "But you'd better not be eaten by a bear, or I won't be proud of you anymore!"

So the twins and Fred went outside and Mrs. Ashburn breathed more freely.

"If you don't mind," Mrs. Elsroth said, "if I could use your restroom…"

"Oh of course," said Mrs. Ashburn. "Right that way and to your left."

"Ouch!" Mrs. Elsroth exclaimed, picking up her thin sandal and showing a lego block.

"Oh! Sorry about that," said Mrs. Ashburn.

"No problem," Mrs. Elsroth smiled.

Mrs. Ashburn sat down with the husbands in the living room and was just figuring out the topic they were discussing when she heard a sudden quick pattering coming down the stairs.

From the direction of the bathroom came a faint scream.

Mrs. Ashburn rushed to the scene and stopped, exhaling through tight lips. "Oh my," she said.

For, bouncing down the flight of stairs and littering the ground at its foot just in front of the bathroom, were dozens and dozens of toilet paper rolls.

Mrs. Elsroth stood gingerly in a corner and tried not to touch any.

"I am *so* sorry," Mrs. Ashburn said.

"Oh—it's—okay," said Mrs. Elsroth.

James came down the stairs as fast as he could, and scooped them up. "I was trying to step over it," he explained, a little red faced, "and couldn't quite make it."

"It's no problem," Mrs. Elsroth replied politely, picking her way through the path he cleared. She glanced nervously around like she didn't know what might appear next, and took the precaution of feeling the sofa carefully before sitting down.

Mrs. Ashburn couldn't think of anything to say, so she and Mrs. Elsroth listened to their husbands discuss gabled roofs for the rest of the evening.

"Well," said Mr. Ashburn the next day, "I didn't get the job. It might not have been the toilet paper rolls, but then again, it might have been."

Mrs. Ashburn shook her head. "I'll check the kids' rooms from now on before we have guests," she said.

"He did say," Mr. Ashburn said more hopefully, "that if he ever had another opening he'd consider me."

But Jen got her first corporate photography gig out of the dinner, for Mr. Elsroth's company's PR department was just needing some headshots on a budget. Considering the fact that Mr. Ashburn paid for the dinner and all she did was decorate, that hardly seemed fair.

Chapter 15—Jen's Darkest Secret

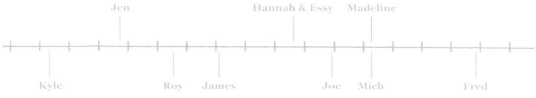

One day Jen finished reading a book and went, as her habit was, to the bathroom to stand in front of the mirror and correct scenes that had left her unsatisfied. Jen usually talked to the mirror as if it were a second person—not because she wanted to look at herself particularly, but for companionship's sake. Besides, it made gestures and expressions easier to visualize.

Jen did not talk out loud, unless she was very sure of not being overheard, but sometimes in the excitement of a dialogue she stopped mouthing words and whispered instead. And sometimes the door made an unnecessary degree of noise when she leaned against it. The door was the perfect place to attitudinize, for leaning against it you could get a good side view of yourself in the mirror.

On the whole it was a wonder she hadn't been caught earlier.

Mich was the first to stop and listen, but then Essy came by and it was all downhill from there.

Jen finished fixing the scene—it was the end of *The Count of Monte Cristo*, and she was getting Mercedes and the Count together as they ought to have been—and then, carefully wiping all traces of her dialogue from her face, she opened the door.

It's never very pleasant to find people gathered around the bathroom door when you come out; but if you've been talking to yourself inside—about a love scene no less—it must be especially disagreeable.

Essy and the twins laughed at her, and Hannah said, "What were you talking about?"

Jen's face flamed. "What do you mean?" she asked quickly.

"You've been talking to yourself for fifteen minutes," Essy said, laughing hard.

"Fifteen minutes baloney," said Jen. "You couldn't know that anyway unless you'd been eavesdropping like a—like a sneak!"

"You're just one person," Joe said. "That doesn't count."

"It's still eavesdropping," said Jen angrily. "You're not supposed to listen to people's conversations when they don't know you're there!"

Essy stuck out her tongue. "Shucks, we hardly even heard what you said. What's funny is that you talk to yourself."

Jen was awfully near losing her temper and knew it. "I don't wanna talk anymore," she snapped. "Get out of my way."

"You're mad!" cried Mich, jumping up and down. "Jen's mad!"

Jen slammed the back door and went to the swing.

By the time Jen had cooled off and come back inside the others had organized a dress-up competition. These competitions started by ransacking the house and ended by seeing who made the strongest impression on Mr. Ashburn when he got home.

The children were busy putting together piles of costume materials in the school room when Jen walked in.

"Jen should be Mercedes," Essy snickered.

"Shut up," said Jen.

"Was I a pirate last time, or a sea captain?" asked Roy.

"Why don't you try something different?" Kyle suggested. "A castaway, maybe."

Roy frowned. "Too messy. I'll be a sea captain."

"I'll be Martha Washington," said Hannah, picking out a flouncy skirt.

"I'm going to find something really unique," said Kyle. "Maybe a giant pinecone."

"Caleb should dress up like an arctic explorer," said Essy, who had just found a winter hat. "I'll go get him."

"Is it true that you talk to yourself in the bathroom, Jen?" James asked.

"If you'd pay more attention to your costume than to Essy's gossip, maybe you'd be able to come up with something better than an inside out cowboy vest," Jen growled.

"Oh," said James, laughing and fixing the vest.

"So it is true," Kyle winked.

"There isn't anything wrong with talking to yourself!" said Jen.

"Nope, it's just embarrassing," Kyle said cheerfully.

"Can we just stop?" Jen said through her teeth.

Mrs. Ashburn passed by the school room a while later and announced, "Dad's on his way home, kids. Better get those finishing touches on!"

When Mr. Ashburn got home he went straight to the couch and closed his eyes as requested. All the children came in and stood against the far wall out of his range of sight. This way everyone could see the show without revealing their costumes prematurely.

Fred went first. Kyle had dressed him up as a castaway, following his own suggestion to Roy. He was dirty and dressed in rags and held a bottle with a rolled up piece of torn paper inside. But Fred spoiled the effect by laughing with his fist in his mouth the whole time.

Mich and Mad were dressed up as twin angels. Jen had rigged them out with a wire halo each and the widest sleeves she could find, with big pieces of styrofoam for wings.

Joe had on a tricorn hat and went arm in arm with Hannah. Mr. Ashburn said, "It's a pirate couple—oh, no," catching sight of Joe's falling face, "it's a militia man and his wife. Oh! George and Martha Washington, to be sure."

Essy had a crown of leaves and a sheet wound around her. Mr. Ashburn drummed his fingers on his leg. "Mm, that's a very nice... outfit... and I can tell you're... not the Queen of England... but apart from that..."

"I'm a Roman Emperor," said Essy.

"Oh! Of course, it's a toga. And the maple leaves are—a crown of laurel, I see. Quite clear once you know what you're looking at."

Caleb did the arctic explorer as Essy ordered him to. He even brought his dog Frankie over to be his husky, though Frankie did not look the part at all and had no idea what to do when Caleb shouted, "Mush!"

James flourished a whip and shouted yeehaw. Besides that he had a cowboy hat on. But he was riding a broomstick, so Mr.

Ashburn stroked his chin and made some comment about a magic wand.

Roy's costumes rarely varied much. He probably had the most realistic outfit, but his glasses were not period appropriate.

Jen hadn't had time to do more than put long boots on and a pair of leather gloves. That, and a knife stuck in a belt. The effect with her dark blue shirt and skirt was good, and she waved her hair half over her face and put on her toughest look.

Kyle found a pinecone too difficult, so he dressed up as an evergreen instead, holding a branch in each hand. He wrapped his feet in brown construction paper and glued pine needles to an old shirt. Of course he couldn't walk, so Jen and Roy dragged him everywhere, and just as he was nearly in place Roy gave an extra shove, and Kyle fell on the floor, dropping his branches and shedding pine needles everywhere.

"So," Essy asked hopefully, "whose was best?"

"Well," said Mr. Ashburn, "some of you had more creative costumes, but Jen did the best job. The rest of you all stand up looking like you're feeling silly, which isn't convincing. It's the acting that sells it," he finished, picking up his bag and going to his office.

"Of course Jen killed it with her acting," Kyle joked, "after all that time she spends practicing in the bathroom!"

"You could have given us a little dialogue too," said James. "About the villain who killed your lover, or whoever that knife was for."

Kyle laughed. "I bet the knife is for taking vengeance on eavesdroppers. Better watch your back, Essy, Jen's a fury when roused!"

That was the last straw. Much to everyone's surprise—including her own—Jen burst into tears.

"You take that back!" shouted Caleb.

Kyle, who hadn't meant anything by it, had been about to apologize, but this confrontation from Jen's little knight was too much to swallow.

"Nonsense. I wasn't tryin' to be mean."

"You'll have to fight me then," said Caleb, white but determined.

"Don't be ridiculous," said Jen, rubbing her eyes hastily, thoroughly ashamed of herself.

"Ky either takes that back or he fights me," Caleb said again.

"I'm not gonna fight you," Kyle said.

"Then say you're sorry."

"But I was just teasing," said Kyle. "You can't make me apologize."

For answer Caleb climbed up on a chair and suddenly landed his knuckles in Kyle's face.

"Caleb!" Jen exclaimed, and Frankie barked excitedly.

Kyle looked angry for a minute, but then he laughed and said, "All right. Sorry, Jen. Now don't you go thinking you beat me, you pesky little fireball. I could land you on your back if I wanted to. — Will you get this yappy dog out of here?"

So Essy and Caleb left to return Frankie.

"You're pretty crazy to try to fight Kyle," Essy said.

"I had to," said Caleb.

"Well Jen *was* awf'ly wimpy anyway, and she *does* act out love scenes to herself," Essy said.

"Esther Ashburn!" Caleb said wrathfully. "I don't ever wanna hear another word about it!"

And he never did.

Chapter 16—Twelve Ashburns on Vacation

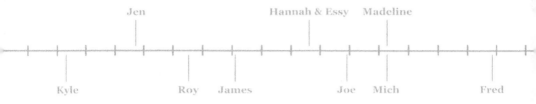

"You know," Mrs. Ashburn said one day to Mr. Ashburn, "some of these children have never seen the beach."

"But some of them have," said Mr. Ashburn thoughtfully, "and ran away screaming."

"I'm sure Kyle's over that by now," Mrs. Ashburn said.

"You don't seriously want to go to the beach, do you?" Gerald asked.

"Yes—no," said Mrs. Ashburn, suddenly remembering how far away the beach was. "But it *has* been a long time since we've had a vacation."

"That's because…"

"I know, last time I complained about how much work it was. But I meant that we could take a break from vacations for a year or two, not for a whole decade."

"Well I wouldn't say you complained exactly. More like you made some good points. Do you have anywhere closer than the beach in mind?"

"No... let me think... Bob said something once about letting us use his cabin at the Lake of the Ozarks."

"That's a great idea," said Mr. Ashburn. "I'll call him right away."

About a week or two later the girls, each armed with a backpack, were in their room packing. "Clothes for four days, children," Mrs. Ashburn had said, "and toothbrushes, and a towel, and your Bibles."

"I can't live without a couple of books," said Jen, trying to choose between three heavy volumes. "That's a lot more important than a towel. You can always air dry."

"Stiffany can't live without me," Hannah said, taking a couple of shirts out of her backpack and stuffing her doll in instead. "Probably two shirts are enough for four days anyways."

"Should I bring my big pocket knife and my small pocket knife, or just the big one?" Essy wondered.

"My clothes are smaller than all yours," Mad boasted. "I can fit clothes for all four days and my truck Unk Bob made." She sat on top of her backpack and tugged on the zipper.

Downstairs, Mrs. Ashburn was staring at a blank sticky note and wondering where to begin. "Four days of food," she said, "but that's not so important, we can always get food there. Let's see, Bob said there were three beds, but no bedding. So how many sleeping bags do we need?"

Mich came into the room and interrupted her planning session. "Is it true that there are bears at the lake, mom?"

"What? Bears? No—didn't I ask you to go pack your clothes?"

"Oh, I'm done," Mich said, holding up a mostly empty backpack.

"Is that all the clothes you'll need for four days?"

"I even packed an estra pair of underwear," Mich said.

"An extra pair? How many did you pack?"

"Just the estra one," said Mich.

"Okay Mich, I'll pack your clothes," Mrs. Ashburn said. "But I just need you to leave me alone for now, please."

"Okay. Are you sure there aren't any bears?"

"Yes... very sure."

When he got back from work Mr. Ashburn looked at the pile Mrs. Ashburn had gotten together and stroked his chin.

"Do we have to bring two waffle irons?" he asked. "And what's this bag?"

"That's everyone's swimsuits," Mrs. Ashburn explained. "And you know how long it takes to make waffles if we don't have at least three irons. Bob said there was one at the cabin."

"We could buy those frozen waffles you just pop in the..."

"Processed food!" Mrs. Ashburn gasped.

Mr. Ashburn finished loading all but the last minute stuff into the back of the van forty-seven minutes after midnight and went to bed with his alarm set for six. "I don't know why I said we should get an early start," he thought. "Really, what does it matter if we get there in the afternoon instead of in the morning?"

But they were all ready to go around seven the next day, thanks to Mich and Mad, who woke everyone up at 5:30.

It would be hard to say which of the children was most looking forward to the vacation. Kyle—who knew nothing about fishing—

was already boasting about the fish he was going to catch, while Jen had packed sandals with an eye to getting unique tan lines while she was lying on the shore reading.

Roy hoped to go boating. The thought of it was making his eyes glitter and Mr. Ashburn secretly decided that he would definitely not let Roy control the motor.

James read up on woodcraft, and told his mother she didn't need to bring food; he'd be happy to go gather roots and leaves and berries. Essy was also into the woodcraft thing, but more along the lines of whittling sticks and starting fires. She had the cord-and-stick method down pat—in theory—and was confident that by the time their stay was out, she'd be able to light a fire quicker with her sticks than anyone else could with a match.

Hannah had her own dreams for the vacation. These involved moonlight strolls on the edge of the lake, early morning hikes in crisp, dewy air, and evenings watching the sunset on a back porch.

Joe turned the idea of a lake over in his mind and was not sure how he liked it. Joe preferred not to get his ears wet. But whenever thoughts of water started to make him nervous he reminded himself of s'mores, and that chased them away.

The twins were excited on principle. It was their rule to be always excited whenever anything unusual happened. They had only vague notions of what a lake was, and even vaguer notions of cabins. "A cabin," Mad said to Mich, "is a house with—honeysuckle on it."

"What's a honeysuckle?" Mich asked.

"It's—um—I think it's a fancy kind of window, but I'm not sure."

"Are there bugs in cabins?" Fred asked.

"Eww!" said Mad.

"I like bugs!" said Fred.

And being assured by Mrs. Ashburn that there would be plenty of bugs outside if not inside, he too was excited.

By the time they arrived at the cabin—after stopping seven times for the bathroom and two more times to stretch their legs, everyone was ravenously hungry.

"But I didn't bring any food," Mrs. Ashburn said to Mr. Ashburn. "You told me that there wasn't enough room for both the box of food and Fred's playpen."

"I had thought you would bring the box of food..."

"And have that octopus sleep with us?!"

"On second thought, you made a wise choice. Well, kids, let's get unpacked on the double and then we'll run to McDonald's."

"McDonald's!" Mrs. Ashburn cried.

"Oh—of course—I—um—I meant Chickfila," said Mr. Ashburn.

"It's still processed—" Mrs. Ashburn began.

"I'll get you a salad, honey!" said Mr. Ashburn, diving into the house with a load of sleeping bags.

Hannah woke up bright and early the next morning, determined to enjoy nature. Essy, who had been distinctly told not to start a fire unless someone no younger than Jen was supervising, did not see the fun of observing nature under any other aspect, especially before six in the morning. She only said, "Don't borrer me!" when Hannah softly called her name. But Joe was ready to go with Hannah to the ends of the earth, as usual, and the two of them snuck out of the cabin carrying their shoes—out of consideration for the people who were still sleeping, not because they were trying not to get caught. If they had been caught, they would probably have been stopped; but Hannah hadn't thought about that.

Hannah sat down on the porch to put her shoes on while Joe hopped around on one foot doing the same thing. "Should we walk by the lake, or in the woods?" Hannah asked.

"I don't know," said Joe. "What's by the lake?"

"We could pretend it was an enchanted lake. If one of us is a prince of the blood a hand with a sword will come up out of the lake as soon as we get near, and then the Lady of the Lake will come and tell us how to get it."

"What if we go to the woods?"

"Then of course we should be millers, traveling homewards with a sack of wheat, until Robin Hood captures us by mistake—because he thinks we're the sheriff—and then…"

"Let's be millers and go to the woods," Joe said decidedly.

"All right. We need to sing something cheery, then," said Hannah. "Millers always do."

Joe began, "Three blind mice! Three blind mice!" and, so singing, they walked across the lawn and entered the tree line.

"When is Robin Hood going to catch us?" Joe asked, after they had fought their way through branches for several minutes.

"When we get to that big tree over there," said Hannah, brushing a spider web aside with a shudder.

Hannah tied Joe up with his own jacket when they got to the tree and explained that Robin Hood was a gentleman and would never tie a lady up.

"Shouldn't we tell Robin Hood that we're not the sheriff?" Joe asked. "Then he might let us go free."

"But he gives the sheriff a feast, remember? Let's have the feast, and then we can tell him."

So they had the feast, sitting around a big rock, and somehow halfway through it turned into a feast given by a Turkish Sultan. Hannah instructed Joe to sit cross legged on the moss—only she called it an embroidered rug—and sip dark coffee out of an acorn.

"This is the kind of feast a Sultan gives to his prisoners in order to fatten them up. Most likely in another three days he'll—did you hear that?"

Joe certainly had heard that, and both children, scared into silence, listened nervously to crackling leaves.

"Something's coming," Hannah whispered.

"Do you think it's the Sultan?" Joe asked, dropping his acorn and staring at the shadow approaching through the underbrush.

"There you two are!" Mr. Ashburn exclaimed, bursting into the open. "Joe, Hannah, we had no idea where you were! Oh boy! This place is full of poison ivy. You two need to shower as soon as we get to the cabin. Next time, Hannah, ask permission before you leave."

Joe got poison ivy bad and had a perfectly miserable vacation. Mr. Ashburn said, "In the interests of poetical justice, it ought to have been Hannah. I'm sure she was the one responsible for that escapade. Nearly gave me a heart attack!"

"I told you they'd probably just gone to the woods and there was nothing to worry about," Mrs. Ashburn said.

"I couldn't help thinking of the lake—oh my! Is that Mad screaming?!" Mr. Ashburn dropped his mug of hot chocolate and flew off the porch.

"It's probably just Fred teasing her with a caterpillar!" Mrs. Ashburn called after him.

The next Monday morning when Mr. Ashburn got back to his office he ran his hand lovingly along his desk. "It's so nice and relaxing to be back at work," he sighed.

Chapter 17—The Ashburn Tea Party

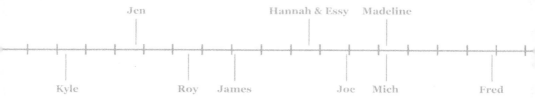

One day in summer before the season had shown its true colors of unbearable heat, Hannah said to Essy, "Let's have a tea party."

And Essy looked up from her book and said, "Go 'way. I'm just at the part where she jumped on the robber's back to capture him and now he's running away with her!"

So Hannah went and said to Jen, "Let's have a tea party."

Jen looked up from her book and sighed and said, "What?"

"A tea party," said Hannah.

"December 16th, 1773," said Jen.

"No, not that kind of tea party. A real tea party with just us girls for drinking tea—only apple juice, because we don't like tea—with crumpets and crepes and ladyfingers and the other fancy things they have at teas. We could have it outside and I'll decorate the table with flowers. Don't you think that would be fun?"

"From what I heard," said Jen, "it sounded like a good idea but talk to me about it sometime when I'm not reading about epistemology please."

"Okay," said Hannah, and went to talk it over with her mother.

Mrs. Ashburn looked unsure, so Hannah said, "We'll do all the work of course," and then she said it was a great idea.

Hannah started by drawing fancy invitations for her sisters. Jen looked at hers and said, "That's neat Hannah, thanks. Did you happen to check the weather for this Saturday?"

Essy put hers in her book as a bookmark without looking at it.

Mad said, "Did you make one for Mich?"

"No, it's a tea party. For girls," Hannah explained.

"But can't Mich come?"

"But it's for girls," said Hannah.

"No, he can't," Essy clarified.

"But..." Mad began, starting to cry.

"He can't come," Essy repeated sternly, seeing that Hannah was about to give in. "He won't want to come anyway," she added.

Hannah nodded. "We're going to have a pink tablecloth and flowers and stuff, Mad," she said. "I don't think Mich would like it."

"We're having a pink tablecloth?" Essy asked.

"Just go make the ladyfingers, Essy, and leave the decorations to wiser heads," Jen said.

So Essy went and cooked up a storm, enough for fifteen people at least.

Hannah coached her sisters on manners on the days leading up to the party. Essy looked disgusted, but Jen said, "All or nothing," and wore a dress with three flounces.

As for Hannah, she made herself a parasol and got the biggest and roundest hat she could tie on.

"I'm ready for a carriage to drive up at any minute," Jen said.

"Sorry Jen, I think you girls will have to walk to the back yard," Mrs. Ashburn replied.

"It's a little awkward," Hannah said as they trooped outside under a load of silverware and food, "to be servants and ladies both."

"Yes," said Essy, "that umbrella will get dreadfully in your way."

"It's called a parasol," Hannah corrected.

"We should do it in stages," Jen suggested. "Once we've set up, we should go inside and put the finishing touches on our toilets before making a grand entrance."

"Go put the finishing touches on our *what?*" Essy asked.

"Before there were toilets in bathrooms," Hannah explained, "toilet just meant getting dressed and clean."

"If you'd read anything besides boy stories," Jen retorted, "you'd have known that."

"Jolly well don't see why anyone needs to know that," said Essy.

Hannah looked at her gravely. "I suppose 'jolly' is okay while we're being servants," she said, "but you'd better put on your company manners later."

Essy found herself a pair of dirty white gloves when she went inside, and came out with an air of killing sophistication.

"What a lovely day this is, Miss Ashburn, don't you agree?" she asked Jen.

"Indeed, Miss Essy, I quite agree."

"Shouldn't you say Miss Ashburn?"

"No," Jen said calmly, "only the oldest gets the last name."

Hannah was the last to arrive, so the others had to wait and admire her table, which was set up on the left of the green lawn, under the generous shade of the maple tree. She'd got a plastic tablecloth, light pink, and cut lace-like patterns in the edges. The table was set for four with the Ashburns' nicest plates, saucers, and teacups—and more spoons and forks than any reasonable person could use in one meal. Trays of goodies lined the middle and in the centerpiece was a wreath of white flowers from the flowerbeds out front. Hannah had paid Roy four cents for them. Altogether it looked fairly elegant for having been designed by a "going on eleven" year-old.

The girls waited patiently behind their seats until Hannah, who had been elected hostess, came and said sweetly, "Welcome to my humble abode. Please, be seated."

Just then a gust of wind blew half of the napkins across the yard and the girls forgot their dignity trying to catch them.

"Well, that's one way to work up an appetite," said Jen, putting the rescued napkins under the floral centerpiece—all except the one that had fallen into the Calhouns' birdbath.

"Hurry up and pray so we can get started, Hannah," Essy said, eyeing the platters of crustless sandwiches and cheese on toothpicks hungrily.

Hannah stopped smoothing her skirt out and said grace.

As soon as the amen was finished Mad grabbed two cookies and crammed them both into her mouth. Hannah stared at her, shocked, and Essy giggled, "That's more unladylike than anything I've done yet."

"We've already lost our company manners," Jen said, with a sandwich in each hand. "But Hannah is so slow, if we waited for her before we started we'd all starve."

Hannah was delicately pouring each girl a teacupful of apple juice.

"And it'd be a shame to starve after all the work I did on this food," Essy added.

"All right," said Hannah, sitting back down and arranging her hat. "Now we can drink our tea properly. —Isn't this lovely weather?"

"Someone said that just a few minutes ago," said Jen thoughtfully.

"I did," said Essy. "See if you can't come up with something more original, Hannah."

"Miss Hannah," Jen murmured.

"What's or—orginal mean?" Mad asked.

"Means that you made it up," said Essy.

Hannah sipped her tea thoughtfully, trying to get inspired. "Life is like—like—like a piggy bank," she said. "The more you put into it, the more you'll get out of it."

Jen laughed and laughed. "Oh my sister, what a falling up was there!" she exclaimed. "You can't talk about piggies if you're going to hold a parasol and drink tea."

"I wasn't talking about piggies exactly," said Hannah.

"Well," said Jen, breaking a momentary silence during which Essy wreaked havoc on the ladyfingers, "come up with a question for us, Hannah."

"How many children do you want?" asked Hannah.

"Lots," said Jen generously. "Ten would do for starters, but I wouldn't mind more."

Essy stared at her. "I want four," she said. "I think ten is good for brothers and sisters but four is good to take care of. I have four now, you know," she explained, "Joe and Mich and Mad and Fred. I don't think I could handle any more," she sighed.

"I would like five or six," said Hannah, "as long as they were all nice calm girls."

Jen grinned. "Well, mom got one in four, and I doubt your odds are that much better."

"You're not supposed to use the toothpick as a toothpick, Miss Essy," Hannah said.

"Such a lot of food left," Jen said after she was satisfied.

"We can't leave any for the boys," said Essy. She frowned and began to eat determinedly. But after finishing the sandwiches she found the plateful of crepes too much for even her, so she left the ruins of the feast and joined the others in a game of badminton.

"Only you can't call it badminton," said Jen. "It's battledore and shuttlecock, like in the olden days."

"That does sound more exciting," Essy conceded.

Mad and Jen creamed Essy and Hannah; badminton was Jen's game.

When Mrs. Ashburn came out to remind them that the sun wouldn't stay up forever and there was the table to clean up, she said, "Girls, it's time to—Jen, why is your dress green?"

Jen looked down and laughed. "Three inches deep in grass stains! Positively medieval. Will it come out?"

"Almost anything will come out—eventually," Mrs. Ashburn said, gathering the forks together.

"All the pretty white flowers have faded," Hannah said sadly. She picked out the nicest one, intending to press it.

Essy looked regretfully at the leftover cookies. "It's a shame to let the boys eat all those," she said.

"How did the tea party go?" Mrs. Ashburn asked.

"Oh, it was beautiful," Hannah said.

Jen and Mad nodded agreement and Essy said as well as she could for the cookie crumbs in her mouth, "Jolly!"

Chapter 18—A Boyfire

It was not fair, the boys all agreed, for the girls to get a tea party and the boys to get nothing. Not that any of them had wanted to go to the stupid tea party—except Fred. But there had been good things to eat and a sense of exclusivity, and Kyle decided it was now the boys' turn.

A bonfire was James' idea. Essy sniffed and called it a boyfire, and so did all the girls—especially the ones who would have liked to be there. Mad made up a song about it to go with her piano exercises: "Boyfire, boyfire, E, D, C, boyfire, boyfire, burn up please." She had cried that Mich couldn't go to the tea party, and now she cried that Mich didn't care to have her go to the boyfire.

James got together a shopping list and Joe and Kyle went and picked up the things. Essy, who had been planning on refusing flatly when she was asked to help, was annoyed when no one asked her. The boys were determined to keep the party their own from start to finish.

"Tomatoes, hotdogs, buns, relish," said James, unpacking the bags. "Chocolate and graham crackers. Where are the marshmallows? Wait, why did you get M&Ms?"

"Oh..." said Kyle. "In my defense, it was Joe who spilled juice on the list. I knew we forgot something that started with an M, but I wasn't sure what it was."

"Well you'll just have to go to the store again then," said James.

"Essy has a bag of marshmallows she's saving for..." Roy said.

Kyle didn't let him finish. "I'm going," he said quickly.

Mich and Fred showed up at the window. "Fred says..." Mich began.

But Fred interrupted, "Mich is getting small sticks! We need big sticks!" He held a small branch aloft.

Mich waved his handful of maple twigs and said, "Fred's stick is bigger 'round than a hotdog!"

"Let's go for something in between, boys," said Roy, and he went outside to start the fire.

They set the food up on an old tarp. Secretly Roy thought this was taking the tough guy act a little too far. But he had offered to bring out his own blanket and been laughed to scorn.

Fred prayed before they ate, "Dear Father, please bless this little food, and please help all the stupid people! Amen."

After this there was an uncomfortable silence, for none of the others quite liked to ask who he was talking about, but they all wanted to know.

"I heard daddy say how there were so many stupid people in the world," Fred said finally. "He said it that day when he and mommy were singing old ads to each other. Oh! My hotdog burned!"

"That's just ashes," said Kyle. "Try to keep it away from the wood."

"Doesn't the way the fire jumps around remind you of how thoughts leap in your brain?" asked Roy.

"Not really," Kyle said.

"I guess it reminds me of my brain because my thoughts pop up in different places on a holographic map. At least, whenever I think about what the inside of my brain looks like, that's what I imagine."

"So your brain looks like a whack-a-mole?" asked James.

"No!" said Roy.

"My thoughts are all stored in cupboards and drawers along the walls of a bottomless hole," Kyle said. "They pop open when the thinking part of me gets near them."

"My brain," said Joe, "is a giant caldron. I stand over it and stir, and ideas bubble to the top. The good ones float over it in a poof of green steam for a while."

"Are you talking about what it looks like inside your heads?" asked Mich.

"Yeah," said Joe.

Mich shut his eyes hard. "Looks like a tree," he said, "and the thinky things crawl up like ants."

"I've never tried to imagine my brain before," James said once they'd all stopped laughing, "but now that I do, I think it's a shooting gallery. Thoughts flip down from the top like targets, and I try to shoot the good ones as straight as I can. —In the other room there's a lounge," he added.

"What's inside your brain look like, Fred?" Kyle asked.

Fred looked rather blank and shook his head. "Don't know," he said. "What's a brain?"

"It's where you think," said Roy.

"I think 'most everywhere," said Fred. "But I 'specially think in bed."

Kyle laughed and then asked, "Anything else in your brain besides the whack-a-mole, Roy?"

"It's not a whack-a-mole," said Roy with dignity. "But I do have a long staircase to nowhere in my brain. I push thoughts I never want to see again down the stairs and watch them go bump, bump, bump, until they vanish into nothingness. It works very well."

"Hmm," Kyle said. "Usually when I'm thinking of something I don't want to think of I pull out a sword and start hacking the pells, with Sir James standing by me to fetch me a smart rap on the crown if I don't hit hard enough, like Myles Falworth in *Men of Iron*—until I've sweated it out."

"How can you think of things you don't want to think of?" Fred wondered.

"When you've eaten a little more of the tree of the knowledge of good and evil," said Roy cryptically, "you'll understand."

"He means," said Kyle, "that when you're older, absolutely everything makes sense!"

"You guys are confusing the kid," said James. "What they're trying to say, Fred, is like sometimes when you see something that's someone else's and you really want it, and you keep thinking about it, but you know you shouldn't think about it so you don't want to think about it. Then you have to do something to stop thinking about it."

"I make it walk the plank," said Joe, "and then it falls into the water and the sharks eat it." He finished by snapping his teeth together.

Kyle laughed heartily. "That's one way to do it. Moving on, what do you boys look like in your daydreams? I mean by default.

Of course sometimes you're in different time periods, but I always start with a top hat and white ruffles, and I swing a monocle in my right hand, and I have a grey cloak."

"In other words, you look like the Scarlet Pimpernel," said Roy.

"Um—well, now that you mention it," Kyle laughed.

Joe said, "I wear a buff jerkin, and gloves, and sit astride a beautiful horse with rich trappings. I'm a duke, you know."

"I have a big sword that has been in my family for twenty generations," Mich began. "It has a huge blue diamond—or whatever the blue stones are called—in the hilt. I wear shiny chainmail with black cloth underneath it. When I put my helmet on I look like a dragon in human shape."

James was sitting next in line, but he shook his head. "I don't look like anything special in my heroic dreams," he said. "I just curl my fists and go for it. Sometimes I dream myself two normal legs, though," he added, looking down and laughing. James had been doing therapy with a prosthetic leg for a while now, and the others frequently forgot all about it. He certainly looked fit as ever. But James never forgot, and was very careful of his good leg.

"I'm a midshipman," said Roy, "and climb the ratlines fearlessly, swinging a saber in my right hand. I love to feel the salt breeze in my hair and see nothing when I look down but foaming ocean waves. Once I decided to make myself seasick, and see if I could be a hero anyways, but it was too hard. I kept throwing up at the wrong moments."

"What about you, Fred?" Kyle asked.

"I'm a prince," said Fred. "I wear 'spensive clothes with gold buttons and I sit in a beautiful chair under a big swingy light and I do nothing all day long."

Even Roy choked on his water at this.

"Well," said Kyle, when he finished stuffing the last of his third hotdog into his mouth, "why don't we play something?"

"Let's play ring-around-the-rosie around the fire," suggested Mich.

"That's dangerous," said Kyle.

"That's a girls' game!" said James, at the same time.

"Oh," said Mich. "I forgot. I 'sociate too much with Mad some days."

"Let's play the slapping game," Joe suggested, holding out his hands.

So the boys got in a circle and slapped each other's hands until they were red as the fire. Then they had s'mores.

Kyle gathered up fragments of hotdog buns as dusk fell. "So much better than that tea party, don't you think, boys?" he asked.

"Yes—sh," said Mich, yawning.

"Me want Jen," Fred gasped sleepily from his chair. Roy picked him up and carried him inside.

James slapped himself. "Mosquitoes!" he growled. "Oh, let's hurry up and go."

So they did, and they were careful to inform the girls they'd had a wonderful time.

The boyfire was the last great activity the Ashburn boys had all together. Three weeks later, in August, nineteen-year-old Kyle went to college.

Chapter 19—Hereafterthis

One wintry day Roy flattened his nose against the window and said, "I think snowflakes are little pieces of clouds that the angels tear off and send to us."

"Is it snowing?" Essy asked. "Oh, mommy, can we have a snow day?"

"Well... I suppose so," said Mrs. Ashburn. "Though homeschooled children really don't need snow days," she added.

Essy ran to tell the others, shouting as she went.

"Do you have to be so loud about it?" Roy exclaimed. He went to put his books away and pull on his coat and gloves.

Roy dressed slowly, buttoning every button and zipping every zipper. He hated getting cold snow into the chinks of his clothes. Long before he was ready he could hear the shouts of his siblings tumbling around in the crisp white snow. "They'll ruin all the prettiness with their muddy boots," he thought. He pulled his sleeves over his gloves and went to the back door.

No sooner had he stepped outside than he was greeted by a furious onslaught of snowballs, pelting him in every direction. "Aw, come on!" he shouted, grabbing handfuls of snow himself. He ran up behind Essy—whose balls were hard packed, half ice, and hurt—and shoved it down her back.

"Ohhh!" Essy yelped, half-laughing and half-angry. "Take that!" She slung a snowball at Roy's cheek, and it burst and trickled down his chin.

"Gotcha!" Mich shouted, sneaking a ball up the back of Roy's coat.

"Little rascal!" Roy growled, picking Mich up and tossing him into the half-finished snowman Hannah was making.

"Mich! Roy..." Hannah groaned.

"Avenge the snowman!" Joe cried, completing the snowman's destruction at the same time by hurling its head at Roy.

"Hurray!" the others shouted, piling on top of Roy.

When he finally came back up Roy looked like a snowman himself—an angry snowman.

"You people are so mean!" he choked, shaking snow off himself. "You know I hate snow in my clothes. Oh fine, I'll go inside. Play by yourselves, children," he sniffed, leaving.

"Aw, Roy!" Jen shouted after him, but Roy ignored her, and Jen loved a good snow fight too much herself to go in after him.

Once warm and dry, Roy recovered his equanimity. "But I'm not going back out there," he said to himself. "They've spoiled the snow anyway. You can't imagine it's pieces of clouds when you're feeling cold in your back."

He got a notebook and lay across the couch, heels in the air, drawing. First he drew an angel tearing off cloud pieces.

"Suppose it was really the angels making snow," he wondered, "how would we know? Maybe it's just a coincidence about the meteorological conditions. A coincidence-on-purpose, you know, so we can predict the weather and make our lives easier. I think it'd be fun to go float around the clouds and tear pieces off. —I wonder if we'll know automatically, in heaven, how all these things work, or if we'll get to do experiments and stuff like we do here. Will there be scientists in heaven?

"Anyhow there won't be any doctors there," he thought. "I mean, no practicing doctors. I wonder if I should take advantage and be a doctor here. I would like to help people. But I'd rather not help them when they're sick. Suppose I did something else, like knee replacements. —Imagine looking at someone's knee from inside..."

Roy frowned. "I really don't know what I want to be—ever since mommy told me I couldn't be a lion. And she had just said I could be whatever I wanted!" He chuckled to himself. Then he looked at his drawing and chuckled again. Thinking about lions had made him draw a tail on his angel.

With all the other children outside, the house was very quiet— and it felt all the quieter for the occasional far-off scream that came through the windows. Roy enjoyed it, until his mom called him to come help fold laundry.

"There's always so much laundry," he said. Then, reverting to his previous train of thought he added, "Mom, if I asked you what God wanted me to do with my life, what would you say?"

"He wants you to shine, Roy," Mrs. Ashburn said. "He wants you to shine by reflecting his glory."

"How do I do that?"

"Well—you be righteous, and holy, honest, loving, generous, joyful... When you were a little boy, you copied your dad and me, and learned to walk and talk. So when you're God's child, you learn about him and you imitate him. —Or were you asking how *can* you do it? You can because of Jesus. He died to pay for your sins so God could forgive you. And God doesn't just forgive you, he also adopts you, and sends his Spirit to change you. So that is how you can act the way a son of God should."

Roy piled his arms full of clean laundry and went to deliver it on his siblings' beds. Then he sat at the window and watched the massive—and rather dirty—snowman that was being rolled together in the backyard.

"I'd like to shine," he thought to himself. "That snow shines because of the sun... but tomorrow it'll melt. —But it will be back next year."

The children outside started a game of knights, on sleds, with James and Jen pulling them, and it looked like great fun. Plenty of times the knights fell off their sleds before they even had a chance to meet in the middle. Roy half wanted to go out and join, but he had visions of being thrown in the snow again, and decided to stay where he was.

After a bit the kids quit the game of knights and went off to make snow sculptures. Joe's was the most ambitious. His sculpture started as a long, fat snow noodle, which he propped up and built a pedestal for. Next Joe packed himself a block of snow to stand on, so he could reach the top of his sculpture. Then the boy took out his pocket knife and started to carve while Roy watched, impressed.

First Joe shaped a few fingers at the top, and then cut out a rough head and body. He gave his sculpture a flat cap, with one hand raised to heaven while the other clasped a book, and he cut waves down the legs and torso, turning it into a robe.

"It's a statue of one of the Reformers," thought Roy, amazed. "A little short and fat, but where did Joe learn to carve like that?"

Roy went back to his own drawing notebook and tried to draw a better statue than the one Joe had sculpted, but after half an hour he gave up. "I can't do a face," he thought. "I can do eyes—lots of them..."

And after he had drawn five eyes he gave his quintops eight legs and the most hideous spider mouth you ever did see. His mother looked over his shoulder and thought to herself, horrified, "Sometimes I really wonder what some of my children will turn out to be. This one might end up a graffiti artist. Well, there are worse things."

Roy looked up and asked, "Mom, is there anything to eat?"

"Lots of food in the kitchen," she said.

"I looked," he said, "but there was nothing but ingredients."

"Hey Roy! Did you see Joe's sculpture?" Jen asked, coming in to get her camera.

"Yeah," said Roy. "How'd he get so good at that?"

"Oh, he does soap sculptures all the time. Have you never seen them? They're in his night table. You gonna come back out?"

"Nah, it's too cold," Roy said, pretending to shiver. After Jen left he went to Joe's night table and opened his drawer. It was full of bits of soap; some with a well-defined shape, others almost complete bars with only a few lines cut in them. There were dogs and cats, cars and airplanes, and even a city skyline. Most intricate of all was the one person Roy spotted. He turned it over in his hand and laughed. "It's Joe himself," he exclaimed, "right down to the curl!"

Then he spotted a piece of paper with a drawing of a cobweb where Joe had written, "A Poem for Mich, who Does not Like History. Ashes to ashes, dust to dust. We study history, because we must."

Joe, in fact, had a whole stash of brief poems under that one. Such as, "A Poem for Grandma, when she Does not want to Play in the Snow with Me. When you are old, you easily get cold. So when you are old, you stay in and behold."

By the time Roy was through with the poems, the short day was already dying and Mrs. Ashburn called the children in for dinner.

"Well," she said, halfway through the meal, "what did everyone learn today?"

That question was the usual price to pay for a day free from normal school activities.

Fred said, "I learned that the white snow tastes better than the brown snow."

Mad said, "I learned how to make a better snowman."

But Mich said gravely, "I didn't learn nothing. Nothing."

Joe claimed he had learned how to pack the tightest possible block of snow. Hannah said, "I don't know if I learned anything today but I learned two things yesterday—how to spell cyclops and the right way to use a can opener."

"Well," said Essy, "I learned that you can make Roy real mad if you stick a handful of snow down his neck."

James said, "I learned that if you start sledding standing up and then sit down halfway through you go a lot faster."

Roy said he'd learned that Joe was an artist.

"I'm not!" said Joe, with his mouth full of chicken.

Jen stroked her chin for a while before she said, "I learned that if you turn your face to the sunshine, the shadows will fall behind you."

"You didn't know that before?" James asked.

"Yes but I noticed it's metaphorical application today," said Jen severely.

Later Joe asked Roy, "Why did you say I was an ar—ar—the person who lights fires?"

"What? I didn't say you were an arsonist, I said you were an artist. How do you even know what an arsonist is?"

"There was one in that book about the German shepherd."

"Oh. No, I was just talking about your sculptures."

"Oh, okay," said Joe, sounding relieved. Then he said, "Do you want to see the one I'm working on now?"

"Sure," Roy said.

Joe got a shoebox out from under his bed and took out half a dozen bars of soap cut into puzzle pieces. "Otherwise," he said, "I can't get a piece big enough." On them he was writing, calligraphy style, "Those who turn many to righteousness..."

"It's part of a verse, about shining like stars forever and ever," he explained.

"Oh yes—I remember that one," Roy said.

And he went to bed thinking that turning many to righteousness, and shining like the stars forever, was a worthy ambition.

Chapter 20—Fight! Fight! Fight!

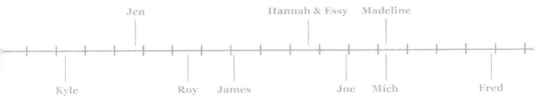

Sometimes fancy is nearly as good as the real thing; but imagination is pretty inadequate when it comes to temperature. When it's hot it's hot, and when it's cold it's cold, and it's not much use trying to imagine it away. You simply have to make the best of it.

The Ashburn children made the best of the summer heat by having water fights. An Ashburn water fight was no paltry affair of a handful of four inch balloons and a few water guns that sprayed a bare sprinkle. They used full size balloons—filled them up at the hose with about a gallon of water, and then carried them, untied, in the crook of one arm while with the other hand they opened and closed the neck to shoot.

The rules of the game were simple: no using the hose to spray other fighters, and no spraying fighters who were in line to fill up their balloons. Both rules were occasionally broken.

Roy came in one day after weeding his flowerbed looking as red as his own petunias. "If anyone is spoiling for a water fight," he said, "count me in!"

"Oh yes!" said Fred excitedly. "Let's go fight!"

Mich and Essy were the first ones ready. Essy brought the balloons and dumped them on the porch.

"Are they new?" Mich asked. "I hate used ones, they always scrunch up and stick together."

"Most of 'em are," said Essy, running toward the maple tree and hoisting the third generation bandana to let Caleb know he was invited.

Fred came and got a pink balloon and Mich helped him fill it up. Then the two boys waited by the backdoor in ambush. Unfortunately it was Mrs. Ashburn who came out, and got two blasts right in the face.

"Oh! Mommy!" Fred cried.

Mich gulped. "S—sorry," he said.

Mrs. Ashburn wiped the streaming water off her face and eyed her sons. "Well," she said, "I guess you two can fill up the bird feeder instead of me. Because now I have to go change..."

Mich groaned, but Essy—who was waiting with a full balloon judiciously far away—said, "Why don't you play, mom? You're already wet!"

Greatly to the children's glee she did play for a few minutes.

Roy was the one to watch out for in a water fight. He was fast and light and showed up behind you when you least expected, pouring water down the back of your shirt. Essy and Hannah banded together against him. Essy took the job of decoy, because that way as soon as Roy was distracted she could turn around and blast him in the face. Since she was shorter than he was, Essy blasted at a low angle, and Roy coughed and sputtered as the water got into his nose.

Essy laughed at him, but then Hannah got her with all the water she had left.

Then Roy secretly filled a bucket with water and snuck behind Hannah for his revenge—but the full bucket cracked as he lifted it over his head, and he drenched himself instead.

"Serves you right for cheating with a bucket!" Essy called out.

"Serves you right," Joe chuckled, "for going after Hannah instead of Essy."

Mrs. Ashburn started a face-to-face fight with Jen. Jen had decidedly the best of it, because she kept her eyes open.

"All right, all right," Mrs. Ashburn said, laughing and coughing and soaked through. "That's enough for me. There's not a dry spot left on me!"

"None of us are still dry," Roy laughed.

"Caleb is," Mad informed everyone.

Caleb ran hard but he was a little outnumbered.

After that they divided into teams and tied up one balloon full of water for each team. Each team threw their balloon back and forth, and they tried to see who could throw and catch the farthest distance.

Once they were done with that—Caleb and Joe won—Jen said, "Time for water fights 2.0!"

"What's that?" Mich asked.

Jen dragged a plastic bucket over to the hose and poured dish soap into it. "You'll see," she said. She turned the water on as hard as it could go, and pretty soon the bucket was full of a thick layer of soap suds.

Essy took a fistful and laid them carefully on Hannah's head. Joe doubled over with laughter.

148

"Wait a second, before we all fight," Jen said. "Let's get another bucket so we can divide into..."

But Joe was already rubbing soap into Essy's back, and Mad, squealing with delight, threw a handful of suds into Jen's face. She gasped and wiped them off with her sleeve, before diving into the bucket for revenge.

Roy, from a safe distance several feet away, watched and laughed, but declined to participate. Hannah lathered James' hair until he looked freshly shampooed, but turned coward and ran for her life when he came after her. James slipped on the wet grass, and lost his handful of suds reaching out to catch himself.

"We need more bubbles in the bucket, Jen," Joe said, and so Jen alternated between spraying Mad—who kept getting soap in her eyes—and spraying into the bucket.

Meanwhile Caleb and Essy dared each other to stick their faces in the bucket. Caleb went first, and Essy shrieked with delight when he came out dripping with foamy white suds.

"Your turn," he said, grinning and spitting soapy water onto the grass.

"Y'all are totally insane," Roy called.

James laughed, rubbing soap into Mich's hair the while. "You should come join us, Roy, it's good fun!"

"It's plenty enough fun to watch," he said, shaking his head.

"Aw come on!" said Essy, who had come out of the bucket looking like a wooly sheep. She filled both hands with suds and ran after Roy, who with shoes on and dry feet, had a considerable advantage. He led her on a chase behind the trees, and Essy came out looking like she had slipped and rolled around on the ground for several seconds—which she had.

"Did you get him?" Jen called.

"No, but I almost died trying," she said, sitting down and rubbing her feet. "And now I'm all dirty too," she added.

"We should try doing this with two buckets and dividing into teams," Jen said, "—which I was actually going to suggest at the beginning, if you all would have let me."

"I've got to go," Caleb said ruefully. "It's almost our dinner time."

Mrs. Calhoun was in her driveway, watering the plants by her mailbox. She looked over and saw Caleb jumping down from the retaining wall.

"Caleb! You're soaking!" she said. "You'd better go change quick before you get a cold." Then she noticed Essy, covered in dirt and mud, and tried not to stare.

"See you later," said Caleb, running off.

After that came the fun part of picking up bits of balloons all over the yard and waiting on the porch for your turn to use the bathroom.

"But maybe we won't have to shower, after all that soap," Hannah said.

"Speak for yourself," Essy retorted, jumping up and down to keep from shivering.

That evening Mich asked, "Mom, why are you and Mrs. Calhoun so different? Aren't you both forty-three?"

"Because, dear," said Mrs. Ashburn, "she's forty-three years old and I'm forty-three years young."

Chapter 21—Far Journey

One day James, poking around in the back of the garage, discovered a box of kites and kite fragments left from when they had moved out of their old house. He put one together, took it to the back yard, and got it stuck in a tree.

After Joe climbed the tree and got it down for him, the boys decided to try kite flying in the front yard instead. James put half a dozen kites together and the children spent the afternoon running across the yard trying to get their kites into the air.

With time, however, they got better at it, and Joe and Fred spent hours watching their kites floating high in the sky. The pastime was much too tame for Mich and Mad, but Essy, Hannah, and James also participated sometimes—and occasionally, Essy dragged Caleb into it.

About a week after kites became all the rage, Jen came home from photographing a wedding and was immediately claimed by Fred, who had been sitting on the living room couch, waiting for her and crying.

"What is it, Fred?" Jen asked.

"Fellow is gone!" he sobbed. Fellow was Fred's pet lizard.

"Where'd he go?"

"He went over the trees and all the way across into The Highway!" Fred wailed.

"He went—*over*—the trees?" asked Jen, wondering for a second if the lizard had molted into a dragon and flown away.

"He rode on my kite," Fred explained, catching his breath. "I was flying a kite and thinking how fun it would be to fly on it, so I tied Fellow onto the kite, and then the string broke and the kite blew away!"

"I'm so sorry, Fred," Jen said, soothing him.

"Sorry? But won't you go get him?" Fred asked.

"Go get him! I don't know where he is, buddy..."

"He's in The Highway," Fred said, "like I told you."

"That's a pretty big place," said Jen.

"I know! Anything could happen to him! Do trolls eat lizards? Hannah says she doesn't think so, acksually she said she didn't think there were really any trolls on The Highway—but Essy said she was just trying to comfort me and lizards on skewers are trolls' favorite snack—" Fred broke down and started to sob again. "Please, Jen!"

"Fred—I'm not going to be able to find Fellow."

"Yes you can! I prayed that you would, so you can. Please!"

Jen blew a long breath between her lips. "All right, I'll try," she agreed. She snapped off three or four ending clauses—such as, "You'd better pray that I find him alive"—and went to the girls' room to put her jacket away.

"Did Fred tell you about his lizard?" asked Hannah, who was sitting on her bed folding clothes.

"Yes, poor Fellow," said Jen.

Essy—from the corner where she was sewing a pocket onto one of her skirts—burst into laughter. "I can't believe Fred thought it would be a good idea to send a lizard up on a kite ride. I'll bet it died of a heart attack at the very beginning."

"Fred is inconsolable though," said Hannah. "—Where are you going, Jen?"

"I'm going to go try to find it," Jen sighed.

"What really?!" Essy exploded.

"What's the deal?" Jen asked.

"She and Caleb have a bet on it," Hannah said with a stifled giggle.

"Serves you right, Essy," Jen replied. "You shouldn't bet."

"I shouldn't bet on you, anyway," Essy said darkly. "There's no way you'll find Fellow and if you do he'll be dead! You really have no common sense!"

"It's the poor boy's first pet," Jen said, "we don't want him to lie in an unmarked grave by the highwayside now do we?"

"We frankly don't care..." said Essy.

But Jen went as promised, and Fred locked himself into the mud room to pray, to the inconvenience of anyone who wanted to go outside.

Jen pulled over on the highway on the other side of the Ashburns' wall feeling that, however heartlessly she had said it, Essy was right. This was silly.

She got out of the car and looked around aimlessly. "If only it were like—a dog, and could bark..."

The side of the highway here was mowed for a few yards, then turned into deep, rank grass for quite a long way before a few feet of dense bushes and tangly undergrowth near the wall. Jen walked to the tall grass, which reached to her waist, and took a survey. The result was a severe disinclination to go any farther.

"I should be scientific about this," Jen said—out loud, for there was no one to overhear her. "It's not likely the kite fell too near the wall. Of course it could have gone straight across the highway—in fact, there's no saying it's not in Canada by now if it caught a real stiff breeze. I'll do the short grass first, anyway."

After five minutes of jogging up and down the side of the highway Jen came back, leaned against her car, and took a chocolate bar out of her pocket. She hadn't found so much as the smallest kite scrap. Jen sucked on the chocolate and looked ruefully at the tall grass. Tall grass is a fun thing to run through in imagination, but in reality it's prickly and full of unsuspected scratchy weeds and things.

So, being stumped, Jen went to the trunk, took out a tripod and a camera, and tried to see if she could frame the tree line on the opposite side of the highway nicely. The sun was just going down and glowed bright orange behind the trees.

Forty minutes later, Jen had quite forgotten Fred's lizard and the kite, and was sitting on her back bumper in the growing dusk, scrolling through the pictures she'd taken and thinking of a photography competition they might be good for, when she noticed a strange artifact in one of them. She zoomed in, wondering what could have caused the red dot. Then Jen remembered Fred's kite with a guilty start and looked across the highway for confirmation with her own eyes. But it was too dark by now to see anything as small as a kite in a tree clearly, so she packed away the tripod and drove to the other side.

There *was* a kite in the tree, after all, and Jen looked ruefully at the lowest branch, at least five feet off the ground. A dozen feet above that, the kite caught the reflection of her flashlight and its tail waved gently in the evening breeze.

"It's my opinion that Fellow definitely probably escaped from that already," Jen muttered to herself—without thinking very hard about what she was saying. "Well, here goes nothing."

Jen held the flashlight between her teeth, grabbed the lowest branch, and swung herself up into the tree. She reached the kite without scraping herself up too badly. Fellow was there, after all. Jen didn't know enough about lizards to know if he was barely alive or hadn't ever felt better in his life; but he *was* alive, so she dropped him into her coat pocket, zipped it up, and made a mental note to avoid squeezing that pocket against the tree as she climbed down.

Then she made it to the lowest branch and sat and waited a second, getting up the nerve to drop to the ground.

"Excuse me—can I ask what's going on?" The voice came from behind a bright flashlight trained suddenly on her.

Jen jumped and came down more precipitately than she'd intended. She gathered her wits and tried to answer the police officer who had startled her.

"Uh—I—I was just looking for a—a—I mean..."

"You're looking for something?" he asked.

"I found it," Jen said, not wanting to admit that she'd been looking for a lizard on a kite in a tree.

"It's not the best time of day to be looking for—something, but I'm glad you found it." The officer's voice sounded skeptical and Jen tried to explain.

"I was looking for my little brother's pet lizard—he gave it a kite ride and it landed in this tree."

He looked as if he weren't quite sure he should believe her, and Jen laughed. "Really," she said, "I found the lizard, too." She took Fellow out of her pocket and showed him off.

"All right," said the officer, laughing himself. "Sorry for having been so doubtful, but I think this is the first time I've found a young lady in a tree catching a lizard. That is your car, I assume?"

"Yes sir."

"Well, have a good evening, and tell your little brother to keep his lizard safely on the ground from now on," he said.

Jen got home with Fellow a few minutes later and Fred was in raptures. But poor Fellow's journey had been too much for him, and he died the next day. Fred buried him with tears and all his siblings—even Essy—attended the ceremony in their nicest outfits.

Chapter 22—James' Revenge

Even in the Ashburn family, there were days when everything seemed to go wrong. Those days frequently started when Mrs. Ashburn woke up with a headache and just went downhill from there. This particular day Hannah and James had both caught a flu somewhere, so they did nothing more than crawl from their beds to the couch and back again.

Then Jen dropped her favorite mug on the way out the door, full of coffee too. She was already running late for an appointment, so she called Roy to clean the mess up. "This is why people shouldn't drink coffee," Roy grumbled.

"I thought it was because it stains your teeth."

"Mostly it's just not an Ashburn thing to do!" Roy said.

"I only did it today because I was very tired this morning—and very busy. So see you!" Jen said, disappearing.

Roy soaked the dark liquid up with paper towels, trying not to cut himself on the shards of broken ceramic, and then Fred came to him with a guilty face. "I axidentally dropped something in the toilet," he said.

"Aw gross," said Roy. "I'm busy, can't you get James to fix it?"

"James is sick," Fred reminded him.

"Of all the days," Roy growled. "Where's Joe?"

"He's in the kitchen making chicken noodle soup for Hannah. He burnt it though."

Roy made a wry face and went to handle the situation.

"Mommy oh mommy!" Madeline came running down the stairs, with Mich right behind her.

"Shh!" Roy said, "mommy's got a headache and is sleeping—or is trying to. What is it?"

"Mich cut my hair and it looks awful!" Mad sat on the bottom stair and sobbed.

"I'm sorry," Mich said penitently, holding a fistful of cut hair in his left hand and scissors in the other.

"Well, it does look awful," said Roy. "It'll grow back though."

Mad wailed.

"Roy!" Mrs. Ashburn called weakly from her room.

"Shh!" Roy hissed at Madeline, before cracking the door open and saying yes softly.

"Please tell the children to be quiet if they can. And, Roy, Joe needs help on his next math lesson. James was going to help him but you'll have to do it. I already talked to Essy, she'll do the cooking and dishes and stuff, but you'll have to look out for the kids, make sure they get their school done."

"But I've got a test tomorrow..." Roy began.

"You can study tonight, Roy, please."

Roy sighed and went to find Joe, saying under his breath, "Times like these, it would be nice to be an only child..."

Unfortunately for Roy, James heard him.

James had been looking out for a good way to prank Roy ever since Roy had decorated his birthday cake with the words, "sweet sixteen." To be fair, James had started the war with a gag gift, but the sweet sixteen rankled in his soul, especially because Jen had caught him with the cake on camera.

He had plenty of time to think over his budding idea while he was lying on the couch sick, and the next day he explained it to his mother.

"What do you think?" he asked when he'd finished. "Will it work? Will dad go for it?"

"It's a pretty decent idea," Mrs. Ashburn agreed. "I'll get your dad on board, but you can do the rest of the work."

"Oh, it'll be a breeze," said James, grinning. "Roy'll be so shocked..."

Two weeks later Roy got up early and drove to a plant nursery a few hours away, in search of a special flower. James seized the opportunity.

First of all he called Uncle Bob.

"Are you and Aunt Clarissa ready for us?" he asked. "Roy is gone for the morning and if I can pull this off we should be on our way to your place in a couple hours."

"I'll let Clarissa know," Bob said. "We've been holding ourselves in readiness. I can't believe your mom signed off on this though."

"You're the one who told me about that time in college when she got her roommate's car and..."

"Now that you mention that, I can believe it. See you all in a few hours then!"

James hung up and rushed over to the Calhouns'.

Caleb opened the door. "What's up, James?" he asked.

"We're on! Oh, I forgot, you don't know anything."

Caleb frowned with his eyebrows.

"—About this, I mean. Where are your parents?"

"At work."

"Oh right. Would you believe me if I told you they said we could borrow your basement?"

"Uh... why?"

"I'm pulling a prank on Roy. I'll need your help too. Come along and I'll explain it to everyone at once."

"All right," said Caleb.

James gathered all his siblings hastily in the living room. "Okay, kids, we don't have much time. I need silence and compliance. Don't ask questions until I'm done."

Jen and Essy exchanged raised eyebrows.

"I'm going to prank Roy once and for all. We're going to all disappear—all of us Ashburns I mean, not Caleb—and we're going to make it look like we never existed. For three days, Roy's gonna be an only child. So, I need everybody's stuff to disappear. Everything. Clothes, books, anything that would give away the fact that you existed needs to go. The extra beds and chairs and stuff go to the Calhouns' basement. We have about four hours, maybe five, to make this place look like a three person home. Any questions?"

"You're crazy," Essy said.

"That's a statement," said James, "not a question. Okay folks, let's go!"

James supervised the move. Nothing escaped his eagle eye. He'd been gradually weeding out books with his siblings' names written in them from the bookshelves. He took extra leaves out of the table, packed the second set of dishes away, backed up his siblings' computer files and then deleted them off the main drive, took all but Roy's bike over to the Calhouns' basement, tore apart beds in record time—four and a half exhausting hours later, he'd done such a good job of rearranging furniture, that it really looked like a single-child family's home.

Jen was in charge of seeing the things moved into the basement. She enlisted Caleb and Joe and got James to lend a hand with the heavier stuff. Twice James almost said he wished Roy were there to help, but caught himself in time.

Mich and Mad were ordered to scrub the wall by the stairs. James didn't really expect them to get much of the excess dirt off, but he figured it'd help keep them out of the way. Actually, they were considerably in the way until the upstairs had been cleared out.

Mrs. Ashburn swept the rooms and gave them a few unusual elegant touches, bringing out some of the breakable decor she usually kept hidden on high shelves. Secretly, she thought having only one child—and one of the quietest too—would be nice for a change.

Essy noticed Hannah writing something at the last minute and glanced over her shoulder. It was a note for Roy. "He's gonna be so lonely," Hannah said. "I'll hide it somewhere, he won't find it right away. Don't tell James."

"I won't," Essy said. "But you really need to hurry, James wants you to look over the rooms. Here, let me hide it."

Hannah handed it to her, and she hid it—down an air vent.

"By the way," Joe asked as they all climbed into the van, "where are we going?"

"We're going to spend the night with Uncle Bob and Aunt Clarissa," James said. "It'll be fun!"

"I can't believe Aunt Clarissa agreed to that," Jen said. "They've never had us over for more than an afternoon!"

"I put it to her strongly that Roy needed a break from us all, for his mental health. She seemed to think that was reasonable. Roy has always been her favorite, you know."

"I wish I were Caleb," said Essy enviously, waving good-bye. "Won't he get all the fun of seeing what Roy thinks!"

"And of pretending like he's never heard of us before," Joe giggled.

"Wait, why should that be fun?" Essy asked.

James honked twice and Caleb and Mrs. Ashburn waved from the driveway.

"Did my parents really say James could use our basement?" Caleb asked.

"Oh yes, they're all in on it—I wonder how Roy will take it," Mrs. Ashburn mused.

Roy got home fifteen minutes later and unloaded his precious plants. Something struck him as funny and then he noticed that the row of bicycles in the garage was gone.

Mrs. Ashburn was on the couch reading when he came in.

"Hi mom!" he said.

"Hi Roy, did you get the plant you were looking for?"

"Yes, though they were a little older than I had hoped. They'll probably do well anyway. Did the others go biking?"

"The others?" Mrs. Ashburn asked, looking at him funny.

"Yeah—you know, James and Essy and Fred and the rest."

Mrs. Ashburn stared at him. "Roy, who are you talking about?"

"My brothers and sisters, of course!" Roy said.

Mrs. Ashburn revolved that in her mind, keeping up a blank stare up in the meantime. Conscience suggested that the difference between pretending not to know he had siblings and actually saying so was virtually negligible. This made her question the rights of pretending it, but she said, "Roy, are you okay? Here—sit down—I'll get you a glass of water."

Roy looked around and suddenly noticed that there were only two couches in the living room, instead of the usual four. On the coffee table was a fancy vase he'd never seen before. The end table was home to a china figurine he'd often spotted on top of the highest bookshelf. He'd heard his mother say it'd stay there until Fred was fourteen.

He caught sight of the dining room next. The table had shrunk; the chest full of old blankets he was used to seeing at the foot of his parents' bed was against the wall. He opened it; there was nothing inside but the fancy glasses the Ashburns never used.

Roy flew up the stairs and stopped at the door of his room in breathless surprise. One bed—one desk, his own school books neatly arranged. The girls' room, when he checked it, looked like it hadn't been lived in for months. He pulled open all the drawers of the one remaining dresser. Empty—empty—empty.

"This is definitely a dream," he thought to himself.

Mrs. Ashburn called for dinner eventually, wondering how she and Jerry would get through it. Fortunately, Roy was too sensitive—both for himself and for them—to bother his parents much with questions that obviously made them uncomfortable. But after dinner he went back to wandering around the house, looking for something his siblings had left. Then he tried different ways of waking himself up—even a cold shower.

Caleb came over and enjoyed himself thoroughly. Roy pretended to be oblivious, although he spent his whole time laying word traps for Caleb, who in his turn pretended to be equally oblivious. Neither got any admission out of the other, that anything was in the least out of the ordinary.

In the gathering dusk he went out and planted his new flowers. The dirt certainly looked real—felt real—tasted real, although it occurred to Roy that he didn't recall ever tasting dirt before, so he didn't really know. But it *tasted*, so that was a point in its favor.

"Aw, snap out of it!" he said to himself. "I'm just—hallucinating, or something. Soon as I finish these plants I'll go inside and they'll all be there."

But the house was silent and empty, and Roy determined to himself that this was just some big joke. "Joke will be on them," he decided. "I can get along just fine!"

Still, when he lay down in his solitary room he felt nagged by a terrifying doubt.

"Poor boy," Mrs. Ashburn said to Mr. Ashburn, "I think it's really kinda rough on him."

"Don't feel bad, he'll appreciate his siblings more after this," Mr. Ashburn said.

"I still feel like some kind of criminal," said Mrs. Ashburn, shaking her head.

Roy spent the next morning thinking over all his most vivid memories—which all involved at least one sibling—and convinced himself again that this was a joke. But then he remembered all the times he'd wished—and the few times he'd said—how nice it'd be to be an only child—and the terrifying doubt came back.

"All right," he said to himself, staring moodily out his bedroom window, "if it depends on me saying that it's lonely without them and I miss them, I'll say it."

Nothing happened, and he went back to the joke hypothesis.

"We're going to visit Bob and Clarissa this afternoon, Roy," Mrs. Ashburn said at breakfast. "Be sure you do all your chores before we leave."

"Is that where the others went?" Roy said, before he thought.

Mr. and Mrs. Ashburn exchanged glances.

Roy excused himself quickly and went to his room, where he did a victory dance.

But when he got to Uncle Bob and Aunt Clarissa's house and there was still no sign of his siblings, Roy looked as disappointed as he felt.

"What's gotten into you, Roy?" Uncle Bob asked. "You can get 'em back, you know," he winked. "All you have to do is..." He paused dramatically.

"What?" asked Roy, excited. "Come on, Uncle Bob, tell me! I'll do anything!"

"You just have to admit that James' prank is unbeatable and that he won," Uncle Bob said.

"Really?!" Roy exploded. "A prank! Oh, where is that boy..."

"I think you'll have to say, 'James won,' if you want to see him," Mrs. Ashburn said, laughing.

"Oh—fine—James won," Roy grumbled.

"Whoop!" James shouted, bursting into the room, followed by his laughing siblings, all eager to see Roy's face.

"Sorry if that was a bit of a mean prank," James added, slapping him on the back. "I didn't mean it to be. You didn't miss us too bad did you?"

"Miss you! All this and you expect me to miss you?! I don't know why anyone ever wants siblings, it'd be nice to be..." Roy caught himself suddenly and grinned.

"Okay," he said, "maybe I missed some of you a little bit."

Chapter 23—The Housing Project

Kyle came home for a winter break and James asked him what he'd like to eat. "A gingerbread house," Kyle said, and Essy wrinkled her nose at him.

"An entire house?! You little pig," she sniffed.

"We'll make a quadruple batch of dough," James said.

It sat in the fridge overnight, and when the Ashburn children gathered around the table the next day to shape it, they found they had to chisel the dough out of the bowls with butter knives.

"It's supposed to be thoroughly chilled," Essy said defensively. "That's what the recipe said."

"It's so thoroughly chilled," Jen said, "you have to knead warmth into it just to get it to stick together."

"Kneading is good exercise," Essy retorted. "You need something to get rid of all these calories you're about to eat anyway."

"You *knead* something to get rid of calories?" Kyle said. "Oh, Essy, Essy..."

"Anyone who would make a pun would pick a pocket," quoth Jen.

Essy loftily ignored Jen and said, "Be sure you vultures save enough dough for me to make the house pieces."

"No fear of that," said James. "There's enough here for an entire city."

"Don't underestimate Fred's ability to eat raw dough," Roy warned.

"Eww..." Mad made a face.

"Ish good," said Fred, with his mouth full, and Kyle decided to try a bite.

Each child got a ball of dough and the rolling pin flew around the table as they all tried to roll theirs out at the same time.

Kyle made what he called inverted cookies. He rolled out coaster sized bits of dough, cut a shape out of the middle, and put the rest on the cookie sheet.

Jen found her favorite cookie cutter and made dozens of cute little gingerbread men, all exactly the same. "If it ain't broke, don't fix it," she said.

Roy shaped his cookies into the letters of his name. "That way everyone knows they're mine," he explained.

"The Y could be from my name or Essy's," Kyle said.

"Are you two making Ys?" Roy asked.

"Eh—no," Kyle admitted.

"Objection overruled as frivolous, then," Roy said.

James made three castle walls out of his ball of dough, and then borrowed some from the common stock to make the fourth one. He first had to promise to share.

Hannah cut hers into flower shapes with a knife. Mrs. Ashburn took a picture of the frosted flowers and sent it to the grandparents with the line, "We made cookies!" And later Grandma said, "I don't think anyone else has so many talented grandchildren. Look at these! Do you think Fred made the dandelion? I'm sure Essy did the rose... beautiful red frosting."

But actually Essy stuck to making gingerbread houses. She rolled out huge balls of dough and cut walls and roofs for three houses. She also made three chimneys, but Mr. Ashburn thought the little chimney bits were scraps and ate most of them before the houses got put together.

Joe cut pictures into square cookies by pressing the edge of a knife into the dough. Unfortunately, only the deepest lines kept their shape after being cooked.

Mich forgot to flour the table underneath his dough, so after making a dozen cookies that wouldn't come off the table, he scraped everything together, flattened it into a large pancake, and baked it. It came out a little raw in the middle, but he didn't care.

On the other hand Mad was particular about not having raw dough. Essy told her that rolling her cookies out thin would avoid that problem, and she rolled them out so thin, they turned out very crunchy and rather brown.

Fred ate most of his dough, but saved just enough for one big gingerbread man.

Everyone was too tired—and full—to build the houses that same day. But the next morning they divided into teams and sorted out the pieces. Essy had picked three different house designs. She teamed up with Kyle and James and they took the most realistic looking house, a rectangle with two stories of windows and pieces for a small attic window with a gabled roof.

Jen, Roy, Caleb—against whom there was a conspiracy to not mention the big batch of cookies that had been eaten yesterday— and Fred built a fantasy style house, with slanted walls and round windows.

Hannah, Joe, Mich, and Mad took the traditional looking gingerbread house, square with a high peaked roof.

"There's a prize for the most beautiful, right?" said Hannah.

"Prize is for the fastest," James said.

"No, it's for the coolest," Jen said.

"There's no prize," said Essy.

"Fred!" Jen exclaimed suddenly. "No snitching! What are we supposed to do now with a finger-sized hole in the wall?"

"Put a mouse trap in front of it?" Roy suggested.

"This frosting is really good," said Kyle, preparing to dip his spoon into the bowl a second time.

"Kyle!" Hannah, Mad, and Roy exclaimed in unison.

"What?"

"Double-dipping," said Joe, shaking his head.

"Oh. Sorry. What'm I supposed to do with this spoon now?" Kyle asked.

"Throw it away," Essy said. "It's not good for anything now that you've licked it."

"Oh!" Kyle exclaimed, surprised. He walked to the trash can and dropped the spoon in.

Essy gasped and Jen burst into laughter. "Not in the trash can!" Essy exploded. "You're so jolly literal. I meant throw it in the sink, of course."

After all the houses were done the children agreed that they were too pretty to eat.

"Let's admire them for a day or two," Kyle said.

"They'll get stale," Essy warned.

"We can let them sit for an afternoon at least," Jen said. "Come on, let's go play something."

Mr. Ashburn got home around five thirty and found Fred in the kitchen.

"Hullo, Freddie," he said, and Fred jumped. "What're you up to?"

"Um..." said Fred, looking from the half of a roof he held in his hand to the structurally compromised gingerbread house on the table.

"Are you supposed to be eating that?" Mr. Ashburn asked suspiciously. "Why are you here by yourself?"

Fred gulped. "The others didn't want to eat 'em," he said.

"Oh! Huh," Mr. Ashburn replied. Then he sat down next to Fred and took a wall. "Who decorated this house?" he asked. "These crushed peppermints are so delicious."

"I did this one—I mean, me and Jen," Fred said. "Hannah did that one and Kyle—" Fred chopped his sentence off suddenly. He'd already eaten Kyle's house.

"Hannah and Kyle did a really nice job," Mr. Ashburn said, not noticing Fred's abrupt ending. "I never thought candy corn would make such nice shingles."

"It looks nice," Fred said, "but it's too sweet to eat."

"How would you know? —Oh, I see, there's a piece missing on the back." Mr. Ashburn finished his piece of wall and stood up. "That was a yummy house. Good call on the peppermints. Don't eat too much now, Fred," he said as he left the room.

Fred kept going for another fifteen minutes and then found that he couldn't eat any more. He put the ruins of the houses back on the pantry shelf and went to lay down on the couch with a book, too full to be interested in the game of king of the mountain that the others were playing outside.

Mrs. Ashburn called for dinner a while later and the children came in arguing about whose house to eat first. They'd worked up too much of an appetite playing to care anymore about admiring the houses.

"You have to eat your dinner first," Mrs. Ashburn reminded them. "—Has anyone seen Fred?"

Fred was upstairs in his bed, and when Mrs. Ashburn called him from the top of the stairs he said in a small voice, "I'm not hungry. My belly hurts."

"You don't have to eat," Mrs. Ashburn said, "but if you don't have dinner you don't get any dessert."

"I don't want dessert," Fred said, groaning.

"Oh! Are you okay?" Mrs. Ashburn asked.

"My belly hurts!" said Fred.

"Oh. Okay. Hope you feel better soon," she said.

Mrs. Ashburn came back to the dining room and found the atmosphere stormy. Everyone turned in her direction, glaring.

"Where is that little rascal..." Kyle growled.

"Fred?" Mrs. Ashburn asked blankly. "He said his stomach hurts."

"I'll bet it hurts!" James exclaimed.

"It's gonna do more than hurt..." Roy began, rubbing his fist in his open palm.

"What happened?" Mrs. Ashburn asked.

"He ate two. entire. houses." said Jen gloomily.

"He didn't eat them *all*," Mr. Ashburn said cheerfully, sitting down at his end of the table and helping himself to a spoonful of macaroni. "I had a wall. He told me you guys didn't want to eat 'em. Was that true?"

James started to laugh. "Yes... it was true, but not like that," he grinned.

Essy sat down and sighed loudly. "He's such a little pig!" she said, with the air of having closed the subject.

But Mich gave the last word by snorting through his nose.

Chapter 24—From One Queen Mother to Another

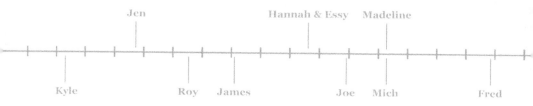

Mrs. Ashburn's ten children certainly kept her busy, but somehow she made time every few months to email her old highschool friend. The two had corresponded ever since Allie and her family took a trip to Europe when she was in twelfth grade.

Jennifer wrote a new subject line—From One Queen Mother to Another—a few weeks after Kyle was born. Seventy-nine emails later Allie said, "I've been assailed by a sudden doubt—are we Queens who happen to be mothers, or are we Queen Mothers in the sense that we're regents for our sons?"

To which Mrs. Ashburn responded, "We're Queens in our own right, of course!"

But that was a long time ago. Now the queens were somewhere in the three hundreds. In one of those Allie said, "By the way, I always enjoy your breezy descriptions of ordinary life, but you outdid yourself in the last one. If you ever apply for a job writing some famous person's correspondence you should put it on your resume."

Mrs. Ashburn's complimented email read as follows:

To my valued correspondent—how's everything going?

I'm in a mood today—not sure what kind of mood, judge for yourself—caused by Mich, who thought he was being a responsible young man, using my nicest towel—one of the set Aunt Rosa gave me for a wedding present—to clean up a bottle of sauce that fell out of the fridge when he opened it. I found the now red towel while I was taking the laundry out of the dryer this afternoon. I feel like I have lost the last connecting link that bound me to the good old days—although, by the way, my precious vase (the one your grandmother used to bribe me to weed the poison ivy out of her garden) is still intact—or was last I checked—packed in a box under the attic stairway. Oh, and I also have that toy ghost I bought for twenty cents that day we wandered around the mall together. I had forgotten about that. Now that I've remembered it I'll be more cheerful directly.

Let me see... re: the pickling rage—fortunately that turned out to be just a phase, though it was smelly while it lasted. Essy's last batch of pickles turned out bad (they had a sort of carbonated fizz to them, which tasted kind of good on the first try, weird on the second, and revolting on the third; I have no idea where the taste came from) and since then she seems to have given up.

After your scathing remarks, I feel bound to justify my opinion on rolly-pollies. I suppose someone who has only ever seen two or three under a rock in the great outdoors where they belong might think they are cute. If you had had three or four hundred, dead and alive, infesting your house, climbing onto the ceiling, and dropping into anything and everything, you might change your mind. Just because we left a pile of bricks on our porch over a rainstorm! They're pests. In fact, I wouldn't be surprised if the dictionary definition of pest is, "Three or four hundred of anything that moves."

Also on the subject of your last email, I love the way you remember exactly what you had for lunch most every day, but the rest of the events are frequently beyond your recollection.

Last time I emailed you we had just had a birthday party for Fred—that was a long time ago, but yesterday was such a crazy day that I can't remember anything that happened in between (and certainly not what I had for lunch every day).

First of all Joe fell down the stairs. He gashed the back of his leg bad enough to need three stitches—three stitches of which he is very proud. I never quite got what really happened out of them, but Joe generously said it was his fault—and then damaged the generosity of his assertion by adding, "for being stupid enough to argue with Mich!" It wasn't intentional on Mich's part, anyway, but he felt bad enough to hug Joe when he came back home and offer him a bouquet of dandelions, which Joe had no idea what to do with.

A few weeks ago Jerry got the kids wiffle balls and a plastic bat. He showed them how to run a string through the ball, tie it to a tree, and practice their swing. This was much too tame an exercise for my children; next thing I knew they were hitting it back and forth to each other with tennis rackets. I think you lose a point if you miss a swing. After a three or four day tournament, Essy and Roy had a match yesterday morning and got so violent that the wiffle ball split in two. One half flew into the kitchen window where I was washing the wooden cutting board and the impact was hard enough to chip a visible crack in the glass.

We had guests for lunch—and orange chicken; which I remember because Fred got the sauce all over his hands and then all over his hair. He needed a haircut anyway. I didn't realize how much sauce he'd gotten in his hair until I started cutting it and then in the heat of the moment I just buzzed it all off. Poor boy, he looks rather forlorn without his red curls!

Later in the afternoon Hannah came to me, almost crying, because she had made Essy mad. In fact, I think it was Caleb who made her mad—he said Hannah deserved a medal for having lived with Essy for so long. But Hannah laughed, and later on that troubled her conscience. To do Essy justice, I think she was more amused than angry, but she saw fit to chase Caleb up a tree and bark at him until Jen finally opened the upstairs window and shouted, "Undignified!"

Only a few minutes after I'd succeeded in convincing Hannah that her sister's skin was thick enough to take Caleb's rudeness (of all people, Essy is the last anyone need worry about offending), James gave us all a scare by accidentally causing a machine he was working on to explode.

Taken altogether, our house is really a bewildering place, where you might be called upon to juggle spoons, give your opinion on unemployment benefits, or duct tape a broken door handle at a moment's notice. Spoon juggling was a big thing here last week—because one day I had to handle an emergency related to the washing machine just at dinner time, and when I came back to the dining room I found that instead of starting dinner, Jerry had got all the children spellbound watching him juggle spoons. Trying to find enough clean spoons for breakfast was difficult for the next three days.

The children have a new game; cowboys and indians. I asked which were the bad guys, and Roy said it was shades of grey. But Essy told me that whichever side Roy was on was the bad guys. It seems to me like the goal of the game is to see which team can shout loudest. But there is also something about kidnapping each other. When the indians catch the cowboys they tie them to trees and hoot in their faces. When the cowboys catch the indians they take them down to the basement and chase them with wet towels until they're tired.

Mich scalped Mad's doll the other day—literally cut the top of its head off. Of course Mad was devastated. She stoned Mich's horse in retaliation; but Mich's horse is a broken broomstick, so it didn't make much of an impact. I wanted to throw the doll away, but Mad protested that "mommy loves her dolly just as much without hair!" and goes to bed with the gruesome spectacle beside her. I did stop Mich from dangling the scalp from his belt.

Fred has a new pair of lizards, which he's named Goodness and Mercy, pursuant to a suggestion from Hannah, I believe. He has a jar of honey by the maple tree and stands by with a fly swatter. I don't know why he can't show the same kind of patience when it comes to math!

You were asking how we manage to host dozens of people for our birthday parties. That's Essy's line of expertise, and she says she has two pieces of advice; toss the salad in a trash bag, and don't let anyone see it. She wouldn't tell me if she actually tosses salad in a trash bag, but she has certainly never let me see it.

This reminds me that at our last party one of the visiting children wandered into the tree line behind our house, and fell into a pit my enterprising children appear to have dug, for purposes into which I have not dared enquire too closely. It had rained the day before, and she came trooping into the house looking like something a tornado left behind. She went straight for Roy, crying like a fountain, and he had no choice but to pick her up and try to soothe her. Her parents thought it was a great joke; I don't know what Roy thought, but he took it with a better grace than I had expected.

Well, that's enough excitement for one email. Also I told Roy I'd come give him my opinion on unemployment benefits in a minute—and that was twelve minutes ago, so I'd better go.

Pardon the very prompt reply (just when you thought you were done emailing me for a while!). After not having written you for five months my fingers were itching to get to it. After all, I find that many of the hilarious things said and done have now vanished from memory leaving nothing more than a vague trace of golden laughter across the tapestry of life to prove that they were more than just a dream... though we had the Calhouns for dinner, three days ago, and Mad asked Mr. Calhoun very seriously whether he considered himself a Whig or a Tory.

Anyways, the typing conclave shall adjourn for now, wishing you a happy Thursday and a merry May. Until next time—love,

Jennifer

P.S. Say hi to the rest of the Hansons for me, but *don't* punch them all and then say I sent it.

Chapter 25—Ahoy the Ship!

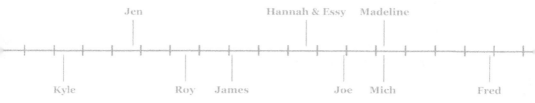

Back when Joe, Fred, and the twins were little, Roy frequently "impressed" them—in the sense of taking them by force and making them sailors. He bribed Hannah and Essy to participate in his game by naming them first and second mates. Then they would all sail the ship—the house—until they safely landed on the treasure island—the back yard—where James had buried cookies before the game started.

Roy divided the treasure very fairly—half for himself, because he was Captain, and then he split the other half into eight shares, of which Hannah and Essy got a double portion.

This game got a little old when Joe started to question Captain Roy's right to half of everything. Roy was tenacious of his power, and also owned all the pirate hats (he'd collected them gradually, mostly second hand from garage sales), so the game fell out of favor. But the children kept referring to the north side of the house as port and the south side as starboard for a long time.

One day when Fred was nine he came and asked Roy if he could borrow a pirate hat. Roy generously gave him his shabbiest one, and Fred refused to take it off for two weeks.

Of course this reminded Roy of the good old pirate game. "We should play again," he said to Joe.

Joe said, "I think I'll mutiny this time."

"I'll make you walk the plank if you mutiny," Roy warned.

"More likely everyone'll mutiny with me and you'll have to walk the plank," Joe said.

"We'll see about that," said Roy, and he brought all his pirate hats into the school room and dumped them in a heap.

Joe found his favorite hat, and then ran to call the others.

"Hurray," said Essy, "I'll be second mate again."

"You can be first mate," Hannah said. "I don't really want to play."

"You have to play, Hannah!" said Joe, so Hannah sighed, put her beads away, and went to put on the least piratical pirate hat she could find in the heap.

Jen was out working, Kyle still at college, but James baked enough cookies for all the others, put them in a box, and buried them under the maple tree. Then he drew a map.

Captain Roy took the map and went to his cabin—the mud room—and kept Hannah and Essy busy running back and forth carrying orders to Joe, who was helmsman.

Joe, standing in the living room and using a spinning chair as a steering wheel, sang pirate songs to Mich and Mad while they clambered around adjusting the sails—that is, the curtains—according to Essy's directions. Fred was cabin boy, and kept Roy supplied with apples. Essy caught him bringing Roy a fifth apple and said, "You can stop stuffing the Captain with apples now, picaroon. Get a mop and swab the deck in your spare time!"

"Why does everyone get to order the cabin boy around?" Fred asked, finding a broom and starting to sweep.

"A pirate's life for me!" Joe shouted out. "When's this watch over, Essy?"

Hannah came into the room saying, "All hands on deck! Furl the topsail! Heave the lar overboard!"

"Heave the what?" Joe asked.

"Something about lar and overboard and tack," said Hannah, who was not up to Roy's detailed nautical orders.

"Hard a-port!" Essy shouted, taking her orders for granted. "It's blowing great guns! Another reef in the mainsail—shake a leg, you lubber there, you!" she said, taking the broom from Fred and poking Mich with it.

"It's a gale," Joe exclaimed. "We'll be torn to shreds if we don't get those sails down! Shiver me timbers! 'Tis like the Captain to lead us into such dangerous waters. And he snug in his cabin!"

"He's trying to figure out James' map," Hannah said.

"Aye! And what for? You know's well's I that the Captain snitches mor'n his fair share of the goods. Divvy fair, say I! Why should the Captain get half, when we do all the work?"

"Is that the way pirates talk?" Fred asked, putting his head on one side.

"The point is," said Joe, "let's mutiny!"

Hannah and Essy looked rather blank. "Roy's always the Captain," Essy said.

"Not anymore! I'll make him walk the plank, see if I don't! Who's with me?"

"Me!" Mich shouted.

"Me too!" added Mad.

"Sounds jolly," said Essy. "Count me in."

Hannah looked doubtful.

"First mate is too loyal," Joe said. "Get a hold of her, Essy, don't let her escape and tell Roy. We'll maroon the two of them together and you'll be first mate."

Essy got a hold of Hannah with a will, and tied her to a chair, though Hannah protested that the rope was not necessary.

"Are you going to give Roy the black spot, Joe?" Mich asked eagerly.

"Of course!" said Joe. "Hand over a scrap of paper." He broke a pen open on the back end and poured ink onto the page.

"You could have just drawn the spot," said Essy.

"That wouldn't have been authentic," Joe retorted. "Now you keep an eye on that ex-first mate there, and I'll go serve the Captain his demotion. What say you, mateys?"

"Hip hip hurrah!" Mad said, waving the end of a curtain in the air.

Just then Roy's voice was heard in the hallway. "I figured it out!" he called. "James used lemon juice to draw the real map. Here's the... what's this? Aren't you scalawags supposed to be battling a storm? And here I find you spinning yarns around the capstan? You deserve the cat's end for this, every man jack of you!"

"We'll not take the cat's end from you anymore," Joe said boldly. "You've been served, Captain!" He handed Roy the paper with the black spot.

"Well if you all aren't a low down set of—"

"Running out of piratical epithets, are you?" Joe asked. "Better say your prayers instead, Captain-that-was, because you and your loyal little first mate here are being marooned! Hand that map over!"

"Never!"

"Fight!" Fred shouted. "Fight, fight!"

Essy rushed up with a pair of toy swords. "First one touched in the face loses," she said. "Hurray for Captain Joe!"

"Captain Joe!" Mich yelled.

"Captain Roy!" Hannah retorted from her chair.

Roy's sword bent at the first blow, and Joe's rebounded and caught Roy on the cheek. "There's for you, Captain no longer! Hand over the map, and we'll divvy the treasure up fairly!"

Roy took the map from his pocket and in another second would have eaten it, but Essy caught his hand and tore most of it away from him.

"Look at that, mates! Trying to cheat us out of our share in the treasure! We'll serve you, won't we?!"

"Aye!" Mich shouted.

"We'll make him walk the plank!" Joe said.

"Aye! Aye!" the twins said, banging their fists on the coffee table.

Essy untied Hannah and started to tie Roy up instead.

"Oh, don't mutiny!" Hannah said. "England will catch you and..."

"And make you all swing from the yardarm," Roy roared, struggling against Essy's bonds. "Your carcasses'll rot in the salty winds..."

"You're a pirate captain," Joe said, holding his toy sword to Roy's throat. "England doesn't care if we mutiny."

"Oh snap, he got you there," Essy chuckled.

"Now what are we going to do for a plank?" Joe asked.

"Did I hear someone say plank?" asked James, sticking his head around the corner.

"Yay, James built us a plank," said Fred, running to the dining room window, which overlooked the small pool in the back yard.

James' plank went from the porch to the edge of the pool, which made it slope upwards, and Roy rather expected it to break in the middle once he got on it.

"Say good-bye, Captain!" Joe said, dragging Roy over to the plank while Essy pushed him from behind.

Roy turned at the head of the plank and addressed his former sailors. "You'll regret this one day, mates. This here lubber you've let wheedle you into the act of mutiny against your lawful Captain'll make you rue the day you ever served me the black spot."

"Plank! Plank!" Mich chanted.

Roy sat down and took his shoes off before he ran across the plank and jumped into the two feet of water that was in the pool.

"Now for the first mate," said Essy with a relish.

Hannah looked at her blankly. "I don't want to get wet!"

"Then you have to mutiny with us," said Joe.

"But..."

"Cast your lot in with us, or walk the plank!" said Essy.

"I guess it's okay to mutiny against a pirate," said Hannah.

"Where's your loyalty?" Roy shouted from the grass, where he was shaking the water off.

"Normally I'd be loyal," Hannah said, "but today it's cold."

"You can keep being first mate if you stay with us," Joe said as they all turned to go inside.

"Wait what?!" said Essy.

"The map, the map!" Mich said. "Let's find the treasure."

"South by southwest," said Joe. "Reef the topsail, Mad. Ho for Cartagena!" He glanced at the map. "It looks like it's under the maple tree."

"Land ho!" Fred said, standing on tip-toe to look out the kitchen window.

"What's Roy doing?" Essy asked. "He better not be digging up the treasure."

"I can't see him," said Fred. "He's not under the maple."

"All right, there might be natives on this island," Joe said, "so arm yourselves to the teeth, mates."

Mich flourished one of the toy swords and Mad grabbed a little chair to use as a club. Essy put a stick under each arm and a butter knife over her ear. Fred brought a fork.

"I guess you could stab someone with that," Essy said doubtfully.

"I can grab more cookies with a fork," Fred said.

Essy rolled her eyes.

Joe got a shovel from the garage and they went and found the recently disturbed earth under the maple tree. He uncovered a bucket full of cookies and held them up for everyone to gloat over.

"Now back to the ship, and we'll divvy up the loot," Joe said.

They went to the dining room and he spread the cookies out on the table. "One, two, three—six of us," Joe counted, "and twenty-four cookies. That's four each."

"But you have to divide it into more shares," Essy objected. "Hannah and I get extra for being mates."

"No you don't, that's why we mutinied. We're divvying fair now."

"What?" said Essy. "That wasn't why I mutinied!"

"I came back on the understanding that I'd be first mate and get a double share," agreed Hannah, who planned on saving some of her cookies for Roy.

"Well, that's too bad. We're dividing the cookies into six," said Joe.

"Hurray for Captain Joe!" said Fred.

"Captain Joe, forsooth," Essy sniffed.

Mrs. Ashburn came into the room suddenly and said, "Children!"

Everyone looked at her. She was holding a very dirty version of Caleb's dog Frankie by his collar. "What have I told you about Caleb's dog?"

"Caleb's dog stays outside," said Essy. Once she'd had to write that out a hundred times on a sheet of paper.

"Who's Captain of this here sinking tub?" Mrs. Ashburn asked.

"I am," said Joe, in a small voice.

"So how'd the dog get in here?"

"I don't know," said Joe. "I guess one of us left the door open."

"Probably Roy put the dog in here," Essy whispered to Hannah, "but Joe's no good as a Captain. He's too plebeian. Let's make him walk the plank. —Got anything to say for yourself, *Captain* Joe?" she said aloud.

"Back down, you scalawag of a second mate. We'll have no more mutinies aboard this ship."

"Dog got into the house on your watch! What's the verdict, mates?" Essy asked.

"Plank?" asked Mad.

"Plank!" said Essy.

"Plank, plank!" Fred and Mich shouted gleefully.

"Yes, make him walk the plank," said Roy, climbing through the window Hannah had opened for him.

"Captain Roy!" said Essy, seizing the moment.

So ended Joe's moment of glory as Captain. Fred threw a toy shark into the pool after him and then the children all went back inside to eat the cookies.

Chapter 26—The World Gets Older

Jen came back from a road trip to the beach where she had met with some photography clients for family photos and sat down to talk with her parents.

"Mom—Dad," she said, "I want to go get a photography degree."

Mrs. Ashburn raised her eyebrows and blew on her cup of hot chocolate.

"I'll pay for it myself, of course," Jen said. "I've been saving for a while. With the two years I did at the community college here, I can finish in another two."

"But," said Mr. Ashburn, a little confused, "if you're making enough to pay for college, why do you want to go to college?"

"I'm tired of shooting people," she said.

"Well, if you put it that way!" Mrs. Ashburn exclaimed.

Jen laughed. "I mean, I'm tired of portrait photography. I like doing it once in a while, but I can't make a living off once-in-a-while. And I've come to the conclusion that if I want to break into the landscape photography industry a degree will really help. Besides, there's a lot I don't know about landscape photography. I could learn on the job like I did with portrait, but I don't have the money to travel the world for practice and no one will hire me to learn on the job."

"Well," said Mr. Ashburn, "that makes sense. And you're almost twenty-two. Where were you thinking of going?"

So Jen brought out her list of colleges. She had pros and cons neatly arranged in bulleted lists for each one. Generally you could judge how much Jen wanted something by the degree of effort she'd put into the list she presented for it.

All the children were surprised to hear of Jen's plan. "I didn't think you wanted to study anymore," Roy said.

"I wouldn't have thought you needed to make *more* money!" said Essy.

"You're not going to go off and marry someone you meet at college who we don't even know, will you?" Hannah asked.

"Oh!" said Essy. "Is *that* why you're going!"

"Of course not," Jen exclaimed, coloring with annoyance.

"Makes sense now," Essy added, shaking her head.

Jen frowned tremendously, which made everyone laugh.

"I'd like you even if you were married," Fred announced.

"Relieved, I'm sure," said Jen.

When Caleb next came over he found the household abuzz with excitement. Jen had been accepted and was formally enrolled, with a date for leaving and everything.

"What's up?" he asked. "Where's Jen going?"

"She's going to college to find a husband," said Fred, repeating the family joke with dead seriousness.

"Oh!" gasped Caleb, and fell silent.

Fred went back to the cars he and the twins were playing with and Caleb wandered around trying to find something to do.

Roy was in the school room with headphones on, surrounded by books. One was open on his lap, another was in his left hand, and he was using his elbow as a bookmark for a third while trying to type a quote in. He was working on a paper for one of his correspondence courses.

He looked up when Caleb came in and said, "What's better— 'this leads us to the inevitable conclusion'—and so forth—or, 'after considering the evidence it becomes clear'—?"

"Why don't you just say 'so'?"

"That's only one word!" Roy exclaimed.

Next Caleb went to the kitchen, where James pounced on him. "Try this sauce for me, would you?"

Caleb gingerly licked the tip of the spoon James handed him.

"Would it go better with fish or chicken?"

"I think it'd be good on top of ice cream," said Caleb, sticking the rest in his mouth. "Can I have more?"

James looked puzzled. "I started with a ketchup base and then added vinegar and... oh, that was the wrong spoon. Here, try this."

Caleb tried it and choked. "Is this the kind of stuff people eat at that gourmet restaurant you're doing an internship at?"

"So what do you think, fish or chicken?"

"Dog food," Caleb said.

"Aw come on! Get along with you. No appreciation for the finer things of life," James said.

Next Caleb came upon Essy. She was seated on the floor of the girls' room, with an entire drawer in her lap. "Threadbare," she was saying, holding up a skirt. "Totally ruined hem," she said of the next one. "This shirt has holes under both arms. Jen, do you have even one piece of clothing in decent shape?"

"Probably not," said Jen cheerfully from the other side of the room, where she was packing the odds and ends in her night table. "I photograph other people, not me."

"Wanna play boggle or something, Essy?" Caleb asked.

"Can't," Essy said. "I'm going to have to sew nonstop all month so Jen doesn't disgrace the name of Ashburn."

"Where's Hannah then?" he asked.

"Hannah? Oh, she's dropping off a bunch of orders at the post office," Jen said. "That girl has a booming business, if anything as small as beads can boom."

"You can't turn around these days without stepping on a bead she's dropped," Essy grumbled. "I found one in my glass the other day and almost drank it."

"Why is everyone in this house so busy all of the sudden?" Caleb asked.

"Try Joe," Essy suggested.

It took Caleb a while to find Joe—who was in the laundry room, sobbing his heart out.

"What is it?" Caleb asked, surprised.

Joe looked up and said, "I'm trying to get in the mood," in a perfectly natural voice.

"The mood for what?" Caleb asked.

"For an artist," Joe said. "It's called mel-and-something."

"You don't have to be melancholy to be an artist," Caleb said.

"You do to be a really great one," Joe replied.

"Well, how's it going?"

"Not very well," said Joe, shaking his head and looking gravely at Caleb. "People keep interrupting me."

So with all the Ashburns busy Caleb found himself with some extra time on his hands the next few days, which he spent thinking. For now that Jen of all people was going to college it had suddenly come upon him that the world was getting older. Caleb realized that he'd be going to college himself soon—very soon, in fact, because his mom had decided he would do dual enrollment.

Essy, when she could spare a moment from reworking Jen's wardrobe to think about him, found Caleb strangely serious. For Caleb was calculating how long it would take him to study, get a job, and be ready to marry.

And he was still boy enough to wonder what a knight was to do now that his princess had grown up and gone to college.

Chapter 27—Rite of Passage

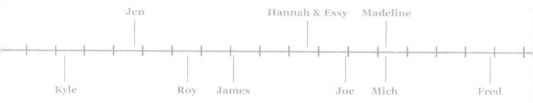

Jen Hannah & Essy Madeline

Kyle Roy James Joe Mich Fred

Mr. Ashburn owned a motorcycle—a relic of his "cool" days—and starting with Kyle, every Ashburn child took turns driving it on their sixteenth birthday. The family made a holiday of it, took a trip to a friend's field, and all watched to see whether or not the birthday child was really ready to be sixteen.

Essy had looked forward to her turn for years, and started reminding her dad about it in June. She helped him check the engine and rode behind him when he test drove it around the subdivision.

Hannah cringed every time Essy mentioned it. She was scared of the motorcycle itself, and even more scared of losing her nerve and making a mistake. She started riding her bike for thirty minutes a day, hoping it would help embolden her for the motorcycle. Her siblings were all a little surprised at her sudden obsession.

"I never thought the day would come when I'd see Hannah fly by on her bike like that," Roy said.

"I caught her nearly killing herself on that curve by the Thomas' house," James said. "She was going nineteen miles an hour. Last person I'd have expected to be a speed devil."

"Nineteen? So precise," Roy said.

"I was behind her in the car," James explained.

Mr. Ashburn took the birthday girls out to pick their own helmets the week before their birthday. Kyle, Jen, Roy, and James had all used his old helmet, but last year Fred had worn it while he was climbing trees, and dropped it several times. Mr. Ashburn was kind of hoping Hannah and Essy would like the same helmet, but Essy picked a black one that wouldn't have looked wrong in a first-person-shooter video game and Hannah found a white one with floral patterns.

On Friday all the Ashburns got up early and packed into the van. Mr. Ashburn loaded the motorcycle into the back of the pickup truck and had Jen drive it. Hannah had some thoughts about hiding in the basement, but Essy, who guessed Hannah wasn't very keen on the motorcycle ride, didn't let her out of her sight.

Fred sang happy birthday the whole thirty-three minute car ride, and Joe told Essy that he thought she was a wonderful older sister every time he confused her with Hannah.

"Complimenting two birds with one stone," said Roy.

"I don't know about the complimenting part," Essy retorted.

The weather was perfect, although it had rained a couple days before and the ground was a bit wet and muddy. Mrs. Ashburn had come prepared with a tarp underneath the picnic blanket, and James hurried to empty the basket onto the four corners so it wouldn't blow away.

"Are we going to eat first?" Mich asked.

"Are you kidding?" James asked. "We just had breakfast. Time for the motorcycle rides!"

"Essy's not ready to be sixteen," Mad said. "Look!"

Essy had both feet in a puddle and was splashing in Joe's direction.

"Hannah may be ready to be sixteen, but I'm not sure she's ready to drive the motorcycle," said James, glancing at Hannah who was sitting on the tailgate of the truck looking pale.

"She'll do a good job," Mrs. Ashburn said. "It's Essy's head that I'm worried about."

Mr. Ashburn had explained how to drive the motorcycle for each of the four older children's sixteenth birthdays, so Hannah and Essy only needed a brief refresher.

Hannah got to go first, because she was the oldest. Kyle and Jen had taken great pains to impress this on Essy when she was little, to save Hannah from her bossiness. So Essy never forgot that Hannah was older—and was respectful to her on that account, but also sometimes pushed her forward when Hannah would have preferred the background.

The rest of the family stood a safe distance away, and Jen, who would be leaving for college in a week, set up her tripod at about the middle of the intended route.

Mr. Ashburn started with Hannah on the motorcycle behind him, explaining how to drive. Then they switched places. Mrs. Ashburn never understood how her husband could stand riding behind a brand new learner.

Hannah was so nervous her knuckles turned white when she gripped the handle bars. "Hey look," Mr. Ashburn said, "Jen did it—you can do it."

"It doesn't necessarily work that way," Hannah said faintly.

"Okay," said Mr. Ashburn, "Roy did it. You can do it."

"Hey!" said Roy.

"Key—brake—gas pedal—and everything else I've told you. You got this, Hannah," Mr. Ashburn said encouragingly.

Hannah drove forward a few inches, then another few inches, then a few feet, amid wild cheers from her siblings.

"Give it some gas," James shouted. "Pedal to the metal! Go make Jen's pictures blurry!"

Hannah drove at an even twenty-five miles an hour, and was just starting to enjoy herself when she got back to the starting point.

"All right sweetheart!" Mr. Ashburn said, climbing down from the bike. "You did great. Ready to go by yourself?"

"I—I guess so," said Hannah.

"Go Hannah!" Joe yelled.

Hannah snapped the visor shut on her helmet and revved the engine.

Mr. Ashburn winked at Mrs. Ashburn.

"Where'd she learn how to do that?" Jennifer whispered to him.

"Oh, I may have shown her a thing or two last week..." Jerry said.

Hannah pulled off to a clean start, accelerating quickly and taking the curves in stride. "Born with a silver motorcycle in her mouth," James joked.

"I knew Hannah could do it," Joe yelled. "Bet Essy won't be able to go so fast!"

"Let's not bet on how fast Essy can go," Mr. Ashburn said quickly.

Hannah did the loop twice and then came skidding to a stop that left all her siblings amazed.

"Eat her dust..." Roy muttered.

"A thing or two, huh?" said Mrs. Ashburn. "How many hours did that take?"

Hannah got off the motorcycle and took off her helmet shyly while her siblings applauded. "Daddy showed me how to do that," she said, catching his eye. "Where's Essy? It's her turn now."

"Where *is* Essy?" James asked.

"Esther!" Mr. Ashburn called. "Essy!"

"Don't tell me she got cold feet," said Roy, chuckling. "If Essy of all people chickens out, she'll never hear the last of it."

"It's not like Essy to run away," said Mr. Ashburn, looking concerned. "I know she was in the van—has anyone seen her since then?"

"Shh," said James, "I'll call her. Essy! Essy—halloo!"

A faint "Ohh!" came over the breeze.

Roy and Mich took off running, while the others followed more slowly.

Essy was down by the creek, up to her waist in mud, holding onto the trunk of a small tree with both hands.

"Yow! Essy!" Mich said. "What happened?"

"I came here to clean the mud off my shoes," said Essy, "and now I'm jolly well stuck. So much for that!"

"Have you been here long?" Roy asked, looking around for a stick or something to help her with.

198

"Oh, I don't know, just the ten longest minutes of my life," said Essy. "Tell everyone else to watch out."

Mich yanked his shoes out of the oozing muck and ran back to warn the others. Mr. Ashburn and James picked their way carefully.

"Are you at the bottom, Essy?" Mr. Ashburn asked.

"Don't know," said Essy. "Don't want to know. I got this far and then decided to stop moving."

"Have you stopped sinking since then, or are you still going down?" asked James.

"I've stopped sinking. Been measuring it by this seam," she said cheerfully, pointing to the bottom of her shirt.

"You'd better hold tight then while we go for a rope. Roy, there should be something in the pickup," said Mr. Ashburn. "I'll stay here. Mich—back up, we don't need another one stuck."

Mich retreated quickly to higher ground, slipping as he did so and covering his arm in dirt.

"What's happened?" Mrs. Ashburn asked, trying to see without getting too close. "Fred, stay with me."

"Essy got stuck in the mud," Mad called from the third branch of a willow tree, where she had an excellent view.

"It's a slimy situation," said James, "but we're not freaking out. If *I* were in there I'd be freaking out... but it's Essy. She has nine lives."

"Yes, but don't forget I've already used three of them," said Essy, "falling out of trees and stuff like that."

Roy came back with the rope, breathless.

Mr. Ashburn tossed it to Essy. "Tie that around you as well as you can."

Essy tied it, and he and the three boys each got a hand on it.

"On three, boys," Mr. Ashburn said. "One, two—three! Oh!" All four slipped on the slick ground and Roy, who was in front, barely managed to scramble out of the mud with James' help.

"Can't get any traction here," said James.

Mr. Ashburn stroked his chin.

"No hurry on this end," said Essy, "but things would be more comfortable if you all could pretend like you know what you're doing."

"This will be another of your nine lives for sure..." said James, laughing, but not very heartily.

"The motorcycle has good traction," Roy said thoughtfully.

"The tires are good for dirt but I don't know about this much mud," said Mr. Ashburn. "Maybe we should try it..."

Mrs. Ashburn didn't wait, but sent Hannah to drive it over.

Hannah came, and Mr. Ashburn tied the rope to the bike. She moved to get off, but he shook his head. "You've come this far, you can do the honors. Ready, Essy?"

"No, let me tie my shoelaces first," said Essy sarcastically.

Hannah gave the engine a good gulp of gas, and the bike leapt forward—the wheels spun for a second—James, Roy, Mr. Ashburn, and Mich all got a hand on it and pushed—and Essy came slithering out of the mud.

"Whew," Mr. Ashburn said.

"We'd normally hug you after a life-threatening situation like that," Jen said, "but—um..."

Essy laughed, and looked ruefully at her mud soaked clothes.

"Does this mean you won't get to turn sixteen?" James asked. "You can't ride the motorcycle like that."

"I can't!?" Essy exclaimed.

"Oh—Essy—I really don't think you should," said Mr. Ashburn.

"Aw dad!"

"We can come back tomorrow," he said.

"How is she going to ride home?" Mrs. Ashburn worried.

"Wrap her up in the tarp," Jen suggested.

And much to Essy's disgust, that was what they did.

Chapter 28—The First to Fall

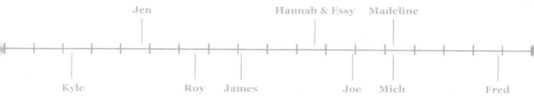

Kyle came home the summer before Jen left, but he only lived with his parents a few weeks. Then he rented an apartment of his own, closer to his new job—but he spent the weekends at home, to tide him over five days of his own cooking.

He enjoyed his bachelor life for about a year, and then he got a new coworker, a forty-year-old who'd never married. "Boy," he thought to himself, "not marrying really does something to a man. I wonder if I could ever get that bad?"

So Kyle began to cast a critical eye upon girls of his acquaintance. One and all failed somehow. Either they had no sense of humor, or didn't know how to cook, or didn't like little children, or else they were too lazy, or too energetic, or weren't sufficiently well-read—or were a little too well-read. Snooty was the word Kyle used for that last one.

One day he said to himself, "I'm really getting old and need to make up my mind." (He was almost twenty-five.) "But it's hard to pick one in cold blood like this. Of course I don't really want to pick one in... in warm blood, or whatever—that'd be sure to be the wrong one..." Here his thoughts trailed off into a foamy substance that he tried to shovel away as fast as it came. In fact Kyle had a specific wrong one in mind.

"No," he said to himself, "nope. Forget it. Not even going to think about her. —All right, I'll make a list of why not. And then we can wipe it clean and find someone else."

So he wrote down: "Paula. 1. Her family is a mess. 2. No it's like, seriously a mess. 3. Actually that's about it because personally she's really nice."

Kyle sighed. "I think that was a failure," he said.

Paula Jordan had started going to the Ashburns' church about three months earlier. She went by herself, for her mother was not interested, her brother was a militant atheist, and she'd never known her father. Paula talked about her "dad" every now and then, and once she said he was a roofer, and the other time she said he had been a computer programmer. When someone looked at her funny she explained that she'd had three step-fathers.

But Paula herself was cheerful, bright, and compassionate. She'd been a Christian for two years, and you couldn't be around her long without noticing how much it meant to her. Also, by the way, she was pretty.

Kyle noticed her every smile the next week, and decided to see if his parents thought he was totally crazy.

"Well," Mr. Ashburn said, stroking his chin, "I like her. I don't suppose she knows much about raising a family, but she can learn—if you're humble enough to teach her."

"Humble enough?" Kyle asked.

"You'll find out, if you haven't already, that you know lots of things she doesn't know. But don't forget that the lessons she's learned, she learned the hard way. She knows them a lot better than you do."

Kyle had long since formed his plan of what to do when he decided on a girl. He wanted a marriage that would last his entire life, and figured that he should lay as good a foundation as possible. First he'd talk to her father. Then—if no objections were raised—he'd talk to her, and they could start by making sure they were on the same page about critical issues, and so forth. Only after that point was he supposed to really start liking her.

Under the circumstances this protocol was difficult to follow.

Kyle explained the difficulty to his mother and she said, "You're trying to get to know her, right? The girls were already talking about inviting her to the next game night—and you can see if she wants to play frisbee with you all on Fridays. Make sure she gets invited to whatever group activities you're going to."

That worked for starters, but Kyle got tired of group activities surprisingly fast. So after consideration, he decided to ask her out on a double date with his parents. Paula thought that was a very interesting arrangement, but she accepted it with a good grace. In fact, she and Mrs. Ashburn got on the subject of birdwatching, which Mrs. Ashburn had done a lot of when she was younger, and Kyle and Mr. Ashburn found themselves out in the cold.

Afterwards Paula thought to herself, "I don't think I've ever been on a date where I talked so little to the guy who asked me out. But I haven't been on that many dates. I wonder if this was to be considered extra serious because his parents were there. It's very interesting. The Ashburns always struck me as nice, but I never particularly noticed Kyle before—except to know that he always wears sunglasses outside of church."

Meanwhile Kyle sat at his apartment table and groaned. Then he called his mother.

"Hi Kyle?"

"Hey, mom. You don't have it on loudspeaker do you?"

"I do, but I'm alone in the room. This about Paula?"

"How well do you have to know a girl before you can start talking about—you know, how many kids she'd like to have and..."

Mrs. Ashburn laughed and laughed.

"What?" Kyle asked.

"Let's not start with that question," said Mrs. Ashburn.

"Well, where do I start?"

"Hmm—well—maybe start by explaining that you want to get to know her better... and ask... whatever..."

"You want me to just sit in front of her and say, 'Miss Jordan, I'm looking for a wife and I rather like you but I don't know you quite well enough, so if you don't mind, please let's get together a few times to discuss some questions.' —That'll go over big!" Kyle said, half-laughing.

"You could try writing..."

"It wasn't saying it out loud so much as just saying it at all..." Kyle said, but he took his mother's advice. At least he was spared seeing Paula's face as she read it.

On the whole it made a good impression. "His honesty is nice," she said to herself. "His tact—not so much. 'Doing my best not to fall in love with you until I'm sure you check all the boxes.'" She laughed. "But I suppose it's sensible, if not very romantic. Well, I don't see why we shouldn't talk."

The next difficult thing he had to do was tell his siblings. This he postponed as long as he could. Perhaps a little too long. Paula was already wearing a ring by the time he got around to it.

His excuse was that he'd decided to announce it while Jen was home for winter break. But it wasn't until her last Saturday that he said at lunch, "By the way, a friend of mine is coming for dinner."

Roy nodded casually, and Joe said, "Yes, Ky, and I've asked you three times for the salt, if you don't mind…"

Essy said, "Is it a very important friend? I was just going to scramble eggs with those leftover potatoes and peas from that strange casserole Mich made on Tuesday."

"Um," said Kyle, "yes—I'd rather it were a little more—nicer. It's a—she's a pretty important friend."

Suddenly you could have heard a pin drop.

"She?" said Essy, posing her fork at an interrogative angle.

"Um, yes," said Kyle.

"So it's like—a—*girl*—friend?" asked Jen.

"Yes," said Kyle, slowly getting red.

"When were you going to tell us about this?" Roy demanded.

"I just did!"

"How long has this been going on?" Essy asked, as though she was personally insulted.

"Um," said Kyle.

"And you're just now telling us?" Jen demanded.

"Well, I…" said Kyle.

"Who is it?" Hannah asked.

Kyle was a little taken aback. "But you know all about it, Hannah."

Hannah stared at him. "Well of course I know I knew all about it, but I *thought* you didn't want anyone else to know."

"You—told—*Hannah?*" Jen said.

"You haven't got much taste in confidants," Essy grumbled.

"I would have told you, Jen, if—if you'd been here, of course, but—but I needed to tell someone, you know, who could help me with plans and things, and keep me in countenance—and so, you know, I told Hannah. —As for you, Essy," he went on, recovering his natural tone, "I'd never have told you. You have no discretion."

Essy huffed. "This is what comes of keeping secrets so well that no one knows you have them," she sputtered. "If I could only tell you all the secrets I've been entrusted with…!"

"But you can't," said James, as everyone laughed.

Essy growled in the bottom of her throat.

"Well! You haven't told us who yet!" Jen exclaimed.

"Um," said Kyle. "Paula."

"Paula who?" said Jen, who had just recently met her. "Not the one from church—she wears an engagement ring."

"Yeah…" said Kyle. "I—I know I shoulda told you guys earlier."

"That's it," said Essy, putting her fork down. "You're disinbrothered. I hope you don't expect me to be your sister anymore after this."

Jen looked to be of the same opinion.

"Paula, really?" said James meditatively. "She's awful good-looking. However did she fall for you?"

"I guess she was smitten with his sunglasses," said Roy.

About a year later—six months after Jen came home from college—Kyle and Paula were married. There was nothing particularly unique about their wedding, itself, but afterwards they had a reception, and it was very unique indeed.

"You know," Paula had said to Kyle, a little hesitantly, "that verse in the Bible about inviting people to your feast who can't invite you back?"

"Yes?" said Kyle, who didn't see the connection to anything in his life.

"Well—what if we did that for our wedding reception?"

Kyle looked at her carefully over his sunglasses, and then he laughed. "I had no idea you could be so impractical. But it's not a bad idea. —As long as we don't invite *too* many. Actually, it's a pretty good idea. I hope you have some thoughts on implementing it though, because I sure don't."

"There's a soup kitchen I work at sometimes," she began.

"I didn't know you worked at a soup kitchen!" said Kyle.

"Well, you never asked me," Paula smiled.

"Did you expect me to ask you, 'Paula, do you work at a soup kitchen?'"

She laughed. "You asked me every other question you could possibly think of!"

Kyle chuckled. "All right. Go on—there's a soup kitchen?"

"Yes—I think they would be glad to host it—or anyways they could find somewhere to host it, and they'll get the word out, and—"

"And my sisters can make all the food. —It's a great plan."

"Well I'll help of course, as much as I can. That is, if we're not going to do catering. I had thought we were doing catering."

"No, Essy volunteered—although she might not have known what she was getting into."

Essy certainly had not known. Paula's idea involved about four hundred more people than she'd been counting on. But she enlisted James' help and pulled it off, though she declared afterwards that she didn't want to see another kitchen for a month.

The bridal party and immediate relatives all went to the reception, and Kyle stood up—and made Paula stand up next to him—and gave a speech to the guests.

"You might be wondering," he said, "why we—why Paula and I—why my wife and I—" (cheers from the bridal party) "—decided to do this. So I'll read you a verse from the Bible. 'When you make a feast, call the poor, the crippled, the lame, the blind—and you will be blessed, because they cannot repay you: for you will be repaid at the resurrection of the just.' Long before Paula had this idea," he went on, clearing his throat, "God made an even bigger feast, a feast not of good things to eat, but of eternal life, of righteousness, and of friendship with God. And he invites the poor, the miserable, and the sinful. He invites you and me. God's feast was made possible because of what Jesus, God's own Son, did. He died so that we could be invited, so that we could be forgiven, so that we could be made new, and made fit for heaven. —I hope you'll walk away from this reception with more than just a piece of cake. I hope you walk away hungry for God's feast." Kyle paused and bowed his head. "God," he prayed, "please bless this food and this time. Make us hungry for you. —Amen."

Kyle smiled slowly as he raised his head and looked at Paula, who smiled back at him with tears in her eyes. "Dad was right," he suddenly thought. "There are some things she knows a lot better than I do."

And everyone clapped except Essy—and the reason everyone clapped except Essy was because they kissed.

Chapter 29—Not Fred's Fault

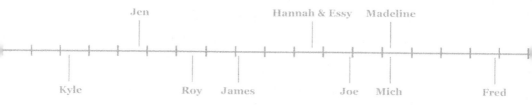

A general feeling of about-to-happen hung over the Ashburn household after Kyle's wedding. Jen couldn't walk into a room without someone raising their eyebrows. This, thought Jen, was perfectly ridiculous.

"I'm twenty-five and a confirmed old maid," she avowed.

Her siblings snickered, not knowing how many potential suitors she had turned down. Her parents knew, and looked concerned.

"It's not that I want her gone, of course," Mrs. Ashburn said to Mr. Ashburn. "It'd be terrible having to adjust to life without Jen. But it's just—well it's just a pity. I really thought Parker Lane would have been her type."

"I think," Mr. Ashburn began.

"Come on, Jerry. We've been over this before. You know Jen is far too sensible to object to a poor guy just because of his name."

"Well," said Mr. Ashburn. He stroked his chin. "Would you have married *me* if my name had been Parker Lane?"

But after all it was Fred who diffused the tension by having an adventure—not, of course, in a matrimonial way.

Birthdays in the Ashburn family were generally celebrated according as the child to whom the birthday belonged was willing and able to do more or less work towards a party. Essy threw herself and Hannah magnificent parties, and sometimes Mich and Mad convinced her to do theirs too, since they were in the other half of the year. James was always up for making anyone a cake, but he wasn't insatiable in the number of guests, like Essy was. Essy said that in no other family would anything be considered a party if the guests didn't at least triple the amount of people in the house. "So having over less than thirty-six really doesn't count!"

For his thirteenth birthday Fred asked for a sleepover. James started to plan dishes, until he realized that Fred wanted to go to his friend's house, not the other way around.

"We can't exactly ask them to host..." Mrs. Ashburn began.

"But they've already invited me," Fred said. "It won't be a birthday party really, just a sleepover."

"Well," said Mrs. Ashburn, "I guess if your dad says yes..."

There were a few grumbles from the other Ashburn children. "When *we* were little," they said, "*we* never got to do sleepovers!"

"Fred's thirteen," Mrs. Ashburn pointed out.

"When I was thirteen," Essy began.

"We know, we know. You had to walk to school in the snow and it was uphill both ways," Jen said.

"I had to go to bed at ten o'clock, sharp!" Essy said, ignoring Jen's sarcasm. "And no whispering, or reading on a tablet, or any of this—"

"Take care, Essy," said Jen. "Your speech savors strongly of bitterness..."

So Fred went to spend the day and the night with his friend Matt—and Matt's little brother Benson.

Matt's most vaunted possession was a lake in his back yard. In fact, it was more like a pond, but his parents had installed a filter system to keep the water moving, so it made a good pool in summer—and in the winter when they turned the filter off and it froze over it was perfect for skating if you weren't bothered by an occasional bump.

After lunch Fred asked Matt, "Can't we go skate now?"

"Sure," Matt said, "but we'll have to hurry and sneak out without Benson. He's not supposed to skate unless there's someone older."

The boys watched their opportunity and ran for the lake as soon as Benson's mother took him to clean his face.

"It's still a little thin in the middle," Matt said, tying his skate laces, "so stay to the edges. Catch me if you can!"

Fred, who hardly knew how to skate at all, took one wobbly step onto the ice and landed sitting down. Then he grabbed a chunk of loose ice and shot it across the lake, catching the mocking Matt's blades and stopping him in his tracks.

"This would make a good puck," said Matt, picking up the block of ice as he got back up. "We need a pair of sticks. Take your skates off and get 'em."

"Take *your* skates off and get 'em!" Fred retorted.

"Let's race for it. Loser gets the sticks. Ready?"

Fred wiped out after four or five steps and went to get two sticks.

"That's your side of the lake, and this is mine," Matt said. "Gotta knock the puck off the lake to score a point. You can start with the puck, since you're not very good. Start in the center," he added, forgetting about the thin ice.

Fred looked like he disagreed with one of those statements, but instead of saying anything he sent the ice puck cleverly through Matt's legs and all the way past the edge of the lake.

"Ha! Beginner's luck," Matt said. "—Oh brother."

He pointed, and Fred turned and saw Benson running toward them, shouting, "Wait for me! Wait for me, boys!"

"You're not allowed on the ice unless there's someone older," Matt said.

"I'm older," Fred said. "I'm thirteen now."

"That's true," said Matt thoughtfully. He was twelve.

"Thirteen is very old," said eight-year-old Benson.

"Much older than twelve," Fred said, with his chin in the air.

"I brought my real puck," Benson added ingeniously. "If you let me play..."

"Well," said Matt. "But Fred is responsible to save you if you fall through."

"Okay," said Fred, eyeing Benson as though he were trying to figure out where'd be the best place to grab him in case of rescue.

So the game went on, with Benson sometimes on Matt's team and sometimes on Fred's, depending on which one thought he was losing.

Mostly what Benson did was talk, anyway. He said, "And Matt started with the puck, and Matt passed the puck to himself, and he passed it to him again, and then Fred fell down! And goooaaaal Matt!"

"You be on my team now," Fred said.

"So now Fred and Benson started with the ball—I mean puck," Benson said, "and Fred passed it to Benson who missed it! And Matt went and got it! And now—gooooaaal Matt! Also Fred fell down—again."

"If you'd pay a little more attention," Fred said, picking himself up.

So Benson went on a spurt, and knocked into Matt, and said, "'Foul!' Matt shouted." ("Didn't!" Matt interjected, from where he was lying on the ground.) "But the refs missed it and now Benson has the puck and Benson goooaaaaaaaaaal! Goooooaaaaaaal! Have you ever—! 2—0 Fred and Benson!" He flew around the pond's circumference, waving his stick in the air.

"What?!" said Matt. "I have two points too."

"Well I don't see them on the scoreboard," Benson said. "And now—Matt starts with the puck! And he is furious! And he wants revenge! Oh, Fred fell down again..."

"I'm not angry," Matt said.

"And the puck is about to go into Fred's goal—but no! A piece of goalie ice stops it and sends it flying to the middle of the field—pond—and Matt goes to get it and—watch out Matt!"

A crack like a shot came from the center ice and Matt jumped backwards quickly.

"My puck!" said Benson.

"It didn't break," Fred said.

Matt tried again, crawling. But the ice creaked and Fred said, "It's not my particular responsibility to rescue you so watch out."

"You try, Benson," Matt said. "You're lighter."

"I don't think that's a good idea," Fred said.

"Oh, I'm very light," Benson said, and skated fearlessly out to the center.

He got the puck and then the ice shattered. Screaming—because of the cold—he splashed into the water.

"Matt, grab onto my legs!" Fred said.

But Matt was at the edge, yanking his skates off. "I'm gonna get help," he shouted. "You can't pull him out by yourself!"

Fred didn't try to argue. He just grabbed his stick and lay down, edging slowly toward the hole.

Benson, to his credit, did not lose his head. He trode water at the edge and when the stick came, he tore his gloves off and grabbed onto it.

Fred felt the weight on the other end and wondered how he was going to pull. His legs slipped on the ice and he was afraid to stand up for fear he'd break it more.

"It's very c-cold," Benson chattered.

"All right," Fred said determinately. "You hold onto the stick and do your best to climb up with the other hand. I'm gonna stand up and pull as hard as I can."

"Be sure you t-turn your skates sideways," Benson said.

That was a fortunate thought, for Fred would probably have gone skating straight into the hole without that reminder.

Just as Matt's mother came flying toward the ice Fred yanked Benson out and they tumbled toward the pond's edge.

Mrs. Wilsea was so relieved to see them both safe that she immediately became sharp, even as she carried the soaking and shivering Benson into the house. "Boys!" she said. "You know perfectly well Benson is not to be out on the ice without supervision. And you also knew perfectly well that the middle ice was dangerous. I can't believe you'd let your little brother get into that kind of danger, Matt. Benson is in trouble too—you knew better! Both you boys'll be grounded as soon as your guest leaves."

She made Benson a cup of warm sesame-seed-and-lemon water, and made him drink it all. But she gave Fred as much hot chocolate he wanted, patted his curls, and told him he was a brave boy. Fred did not appreciate the pats, but he enjoyed the rest.

Mr. Wilsea also had nothing but praise for Fred when he came back from work and heard about it, and after all that Fred was rather disappointed to find that he was no sort of hero when he got back home.

"You let that little boy go out onto ice you knew was dangerous just to get a puck," Roy said.

"I told Matt it was a bad idea!"

"You were the oldest one there," Essy said. "Anything that happens when you're the oldest one around is your fault."

James grinned at Fred. "You've said that to Essy plenty of times, I bet."

Fred frowned. "Well, I did save him," he said. "And it wasn't *really* my fault."

Chapter 30—School Day

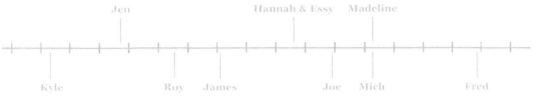

Five days out of every Ashburn week were school days. At first, school had been a well-structured thing of fifteen minutes of this, half an hour of that—a chapter of one book and two pages of the other one. The children may not have found it easy to say what they had learned on any given school day, but they always knew what they had done.

School was a little different by the time Kyle had married, Jen had started "landing photography gigs" around the world, Roy had hidden himself under heavy university level studies and a pair of earphones, and James had started work as a chef at a local restaurant. Mrs. Ashburn used the word "self-directed" when explaining things to Mr. Ashburn and made comments about personal responsibility and learning to make wise choices. Mr. Ashburn stroked his chin and signed the report cards.

There was a basic highschool curriculum the children were expected to follow, but substitutions were welcomed and no one cared about the pace. Joe preferred to read more literature and less history. Mich and Mad powered through their math book in two months and ignored their French lessons for that same period of time. Mrs. Ashburn hardly even noticed, though she did cringe a little when Fred substituted his biology textbook for a tank full of lizards and snails.

Hannah and Essy having graduated a year ago were in charge of grading papers. This used to be Jen's job, and the children were sorry for the change. Essy was obnoxiously strict and Hannah conscientiously so.

On one particular school day Essy came into the school room waving a physics test in the air. "Well Joe," she said in a disapproving tone, "I couldn't find anything wrong except one misspelled word. You got an A."

"Goodie!" Joe said.

"So as a prize," Essy continued, "here's an oreo."

"Thanks!" said Joe, surprised. He took a bite and then spit it out. "What's it got inside, toothpaste?" he sputtered, rushing to the bathroom.

Essy sat down and laughed hard.

"O Esther, master of the magicians!" Fred said, "will you listen to me say my verses?"

"All right," said Essy. "You're on Daniel 4, I take it."

"When was the battle of Hastings, Mich?" Mad looked up from the laptop where she was writing a history report.

"October 14th, 1066," Mich said.

Fred interrupted his repetition of Daniel 4 to ask, "How did you remember that, Mich?"

"I make the dates I want to remember my passwords and tell Google not to save them," Mich said.

"Oh. But why did you want to remember about the battle of Hastings?" Fred asked.

"William of Normandy conquered England then," said Mad. "So the rough Saxons became civilized and started building castles instead of longhouses with cracks in the walls."

"Life must have been so hard in those days," said Hannah reflectively. She had brought a fishing tackle box full of beads into the school room and was making a bracelet.

"Nothing doing!" Essy exclaimed. "They never had to plug in their chargers in the dark."

"They didn't have so many dates to remember, either," Mich added. "They couldn't possibly have had so many dates to remember a thousand years ago as we do today."

"Feel sorry for the people in 3012!" Joe said. He'd brushed the mess of cookie and toothpaste out of his mouth and was now back in the room, trying to finish a poem.

"Can we get back to King Nebuchadnezzar, Fred?" Essy asked.

So Fred went back to his verses and Mich—who was stalling over his French lesson—cast an eye over Joe's poem.

"I wouldn't end a line with 'catalyst' if I were you," Mich said.

"There's got to be something that rhymes with it," Joe said, pressing his hands into his forehead.

"Activist?" Hannah suggested.

"Just glancing over the poem and without really knowing where it's going," Mich said, "I don't think that's going to work."

"Joe, if you want to say that something is in the back yard, should that be one word or two?" Mad asked.

"Two words. It's only one word if it's an adjective," said Joe.

Essy said, "Why are you using the word—I mean the words—back yard in your history report?"

"Oh!" said Mad. "I'm taking a break and writing an email now."

"What's something I could learn instead of French?" Mich asked Hannah. "If I learned morse code, would that count for a foreign language?"

"What good will morse code ever do you?" Hannah said.

"What good will French ever do me?"

"It's the principle of the thing," Hannah began, "you learn—"

"You learn to appreciate English better," Joe said.

"I was going to say that you learn grammar better and it helps you with English," Hannah corrected.

Then they all went back to their work for a bit. Once he was done with his verses, Fred pulled out his terrarium. "I got something new," he said proudly.

"A snake, I'll be bound," Joe said.

Hannah got up quickly and left the room.

"Yes," said Fred. "I've been saving for three months. I put the lizards in a smaller jar for now, so this is just for the snake. Got some baby mice too—wanna see me feed him?"

Mad suddenly remembered that she needed to start cooking lunch. "No, really," she said. "When you said 'feed him' it reminded me..."

Mich stuck out his tongue at her and the boys and Essy gathered around the terrarium.

In the afternoon the twins and Fred had writing class while Joe went and practiced cello. The writing class today was mostly brainstorming for a short story—it started out with the time period of Alexander the Great but ended with a discussion on whether or not colonizing Mars would be worthwhile.

Then Mich and Mad, still arguing, walked up the street to take a plate of cookies to Mrs. Wimpole. But by this time they were arguing about a slightly different subject.

"It seems to me," Mich said, "that it's pretty stupid to fall in love if the other person doesn't care at all about you."

"That's so mercenary!" Mad said. "Not loving someone until they love you!"

"We're not talking about love, we're talking about falling in love. Where's the sense in falling in love all by yourself? You're asking for a broken heart—or whatever."

"How on earth is anyone supposed to fall in love if they have to wait for the other person first?"

"Well—I guess that's where arranged marriages come in," Mich said.

Mad stared at him. "Come on!"

"Well, think about it," Mich said argumentatively. "After all, what business do two people who aren't married have falling in love with each other?"

"So you're going to ask mom and dad to just find you a girl and then marry her?! Before falling in love?!"

"Well no! Okay, okay, I'm not prepared to accept all the implications of that question," Mich laughed. "I guess you can fall in love before you marry. But... oh, I don't know. Here we are, anyhow."

When they got back home Mich looked again at his French lesson and then went to talk to his mom.

"Mom, you remember when I wanted to buy myself an xbox?"

"Yes?" said Mrs. Ashburn.

"Remember how I had to write a five paragraph persuasive essay on why it would be a good thing?"

"I remember."

"So... how about you write a five paragraph essay on why I should study French? I think it would really help me understand. Right now it just—doesn't make sense to me."

"Would you like to keep your xbox?" Mrs. Ashburn asked.

"Of course!" said Mich.

"Well then, how about *you* write the five paragraph essay on why to study French?"

"Oh!" said Mich, "I don't really need the essay."

"Sure you do," Mrs. Ashburn said. "And you'll remember the reasons so much better if you write them down yourself."

Mich sighed.

That night while Essy was turning off the school computer and putting a few loose books back into their places, Joe came into the school room and asked, "Want a cookie Essy?"

She laughed. "No thank you!"

Joe stood there and ate it in front of her. Then he said smugly, "It was a perfectly good cookie."

Chapter 31—Mich's Surprise

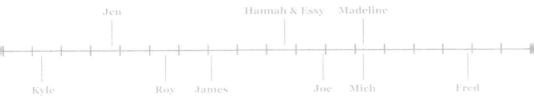

One day Mich found his mother in the laundry room and looked around mysteriously. "I want to do something, mom," he said.

"What kind of a something? Does it have to do with this load of laundry?" Mrs. Ashburn asked.

"Oh! It's nothing to do with clothes. At least not particularly. I want to throw Mad a surprise birthday party."

"You!" said Mrs. Ashburn. "Throw a *surprise* party?"

"I know!" said Mich. "Everyone will be shocked. I don't think I've ever kept a secret from Mad in my life."

"Or anyone else, for that matter. What's your plan?"

"I'll get up really early Tuesday morning to cook and decorate."

"By yourself?"

"It's *my* surprise party. How hard can it be to bake a cake, anyways?"

"Okay..."

"But I need you to buy the food and decorations and stuff."

"Oh, I see, I was wondering where I came in," said Mrs. Ashburn.

"I got a list ready," said Mich, "but maybe you know some things I've forgotten."

Mrs. Ashburn glanced over the list. "Wait, you want me to buy you a cake mix?"

"Of course! How else would I make a cake?"

"Hmm—well, I suppose I can get these for you," Mrs. Ashburn said. "Are you sure you can pull this off?"

"Sure I can!" said Mich.

So bright and early on his birthday morning Mich dragged himself out of bed. He was still so sleepy that he curled up on the floor and only when he reached for his covers did he suddenly realize that he was about to go back to sleep again. He bounced up, washed his face, got dressed, read a chapter of the Bible, and went downstairs to the kitchen.

Mrs. Ashburn had hid the bag of groceries she'd gotten for him in the darkest corner of the pantry. Mich spilled the bucket of oats trying to reach the bag, but got it out at last.

"I wonder," thought Mich, "if I should decorate first, or make the cake first. I want the cake to be warm, don't I? No, maybe I don't want the cake to be warm. Do people usually eat cakes warm or not?"

After splashing his face a little more with cold water, Mich remembered having seen Essy put cakes in the freezer in order to cool them quickly. "But I don't know why she does that," Mich said to himself. "In fact, a fresh warm cake sounds really good. But I guess I'd better not innovate today. Besides, it'll probably take me twice as long to make the cake as the box says."

So Mich cracked the eggs, milk, and oil into a bowl, poured the cake mix in—after treating himself to a generous spoonful of the powder, which stuck his mouth together and was hard to swallow, but tasted delicious—and mixed it by hand with a soup spoon for three minutes. Only after that did he realize that the recipe had told him to beat the liquid ingredients separately first.

Then Mich remembered to turn the oven on, and while he left it to preheat he arranged the decorating materials on the table and started blowing up balloons.

Mich blew several dozen balloons up and started tying them together—taking a break to put the cake in when the preheating was over. Red was Mad's favorite color—at least it had been for the past four or five months—so Mich had red streamers, red balloons, and a pack of red construction paper to cut letters out of.

The balloons he taped up in an arch on the dining room wall. Then he sat down and started cutting out letters for "Happy 17th Birthday Mad!" He'd gotten as far as the second P when the alarm sounded—and sounded terribly loud in the early morning silence. Mich jumped up, knocking over his chair and stubbing his toe on it. He caught his breath and lunged at the timer, dropping it on the floor. That effectively silenced it by breaking the battery case open. The battery went in one direction and the rest of the timer in another.

Mich scrambled to pick them up, and then pulled a beautiful, golden brown cake out of the oven. He smacked his lips over it and spread red frosting generously over the top. Then he wrote 17 in M&M's, pushed his masterpiece to the back of the counter, and went back to decorating.

By the time he had finished the sign and the streamers, the light of a grey dawn was streaking in through the windows. Mich stuck the last few letters onto the wall in feverish haste. Then he rushed for the cookbook. Cake was not a square breakfast even in

Mich's book, so he had planned on bacon, egg, and cheese biscuits to supplement it. "Biscuits only take twenty minutes," he said to himself, under his breath. "Essy says that every time Hannah asks her why she didn't start supper earlier. Biscuits only take twenty minutes. Plenty of time, Mich."

Probably biscuits took even Essy more than twenty minutes; anyway, it took Mich twenty-five minutes just to have them ready for the oven. Then he realized that he needed to fry ten eggs and cook twenty strips of bacon in the fifteen minutes the biscuits would take to cook. Sounds of awakening siblings were already making themselves heard, but Mich took a deep breath, brought out two griddles, and started cracking eggs as fast as his fingers would go.

Of course he dropped eggshells into two of them, and spent three precious minutes fishing them out—turning those two particular fried eggs into scrambled eggs in the process.

The next few minutes were a whirlwind of jumping back and forth from the bacon griddle to the egg griddle. Mich lost one egg down the crack between the oven and the wall, but he finished the replacement one just as the timer for the biscuits beeped.

"Oh boy," he said, "I haven't even set the table yet..."

"Whoa, what's going on in here?" Hannah asked, coming into the room.

"Shh!" said Mich. "It's a surprise for Mad. Oh Hannah, can you help me set the table?"

"Wow, did you do all this?" Hannah asked, obligingly gathering together forks and plates and knives.

"Yep!" said Mich proudly. He started slicing the hot biscuits, exclaiming, "Ow! Ow!" meanwhile.

After each plate had a piping hot biscuit on it with an egg and two slices of bacon inside Mich stood back and wrinkled his forehead. "I'm missing something," he said. "I know I'm missing something..."

"Vegetables, maybe?" Hannah suggested.

"What?! No... it was something for the sandwiches..."

"Do I smell bacon egg and cheese biscuits?" James asked, sticking his head into the room.

"Oh that was it!" Mich exclaimed. "Cheese..."

"Is Mad up yet?" Hannah asked.

"Yes," said James, eyeing the sign, "and she's making the rounds, getting happy birthdays from everyone. Do you want me to stall her?"

"Please!" said Mich. "Hannah'll tell you when it's all ready."

He flew from the fridge to the table, peeling slices of cheese off of each other.

"I'm still missing something—Hannah, what is it? Oh my, oh my..."

"Calm down, Mich," Hannah said. "Just think for a moment and it'll come back to you."

"The cake!" Mich cried. He went to the counter and grabbed it. "Whoa!" he exclaimed.

"What?" asked Hannah.

"Someone ate the frosting off it!" Mich exclaimed in disbelief. "Look!"

Sure enough, only patchy blotches of frosting and a general greasy appearance were left.

"Did you put the frosting on while it was still warm?" Hannah asked.

"Yeah!"

"It melted," said Hannah.

"But it didn't just melt, it disappeared!" Mich objected.

"It got soaked into the cake. —What are those round brown spots?"

"Those were M&Ms," Mich said ruefully.

"Well, it'll still taste good," said Hannah encouragingly.

So Mich put the cake in the center of the table and brought out a new handful of M&Ms to write 17 on it again.

"It doesn't look—too—bad..." said Hannah encouragingly. "Here—" She got a knife and smoothed out the melted frosting. "Should I go tell James he can let Mad come?"

Mich took a deep breath and surveyed the room. "Does it look okay?" he asked.

Hannah hesitated for the briefest of seconds before she said, "Mad is gonna love it!"

James' voice carried from the other room. "Wait up Mad, where are you going? I haven't finished saying happy birthday yet—"

"Why, what else were you going to say?"

"Um—and many more? Wishing you loads of presents and... that your hair would straighten. Guys, she's coming and I can't stop her!" he hollered.

Mich suddenly dove under the table.

"Mich!" Hannah exclaimed.

"Oh my!" said Mad, bursting into the room.

"Happy birthday, Madeline," Hannah said.

"Surprise!" Mich shouted, jumping out of his hiding place with a very red face.

"Did you do this, Mich?" Mad gasped. "Even the cake?!"

"Yeah," said Mich, gulping. "I got you a present too," he added quickly, trying to distract attention from his cake. "See!"

Mad stuck her hand into the paper-filled gift bag and came out with recording software. She sat down suddenly, looking a little blank.

"It's for when you get that electronic piano you've been saving for, so you can record yourself when you play," Mich said.

"Oh... thank you, Mich!" said Mad. "It's just that—" she started to laugh. "I used the money I had saved so far for the piano to get your present. —I'll be right back," she said, running to get it.

Mad brought in a carefully wrapped box in a minute and Mich tore it open. Then it was his turn to look blank. "Oh—Mad—rechargeable batteries! But I didn't buy that remote control car after all... I bought the recording program instead."

Hannah left the room and astonished Essy by throwing herself on the living room couch and laughing until she cried.

Chapter 32—The True Knight Again

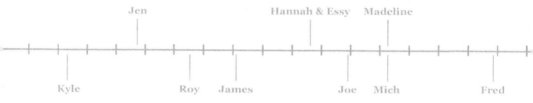

There came a day which Mrs. Ashburn had long warned Mr. Ashburn of. It did not quite fall out exactly as her prophecy had stated, but she took so much credit for it afterwards, you would have supposed she had been right to a T.

Mrs. Ashburn's prediction began something like, "Caleb shall come speak unto thee in thy office..." and that *was* how it started.

"Mr. Ashburn?" Caleb asked, pausing at the half open door.

"Come in! Oh, Caleb. What is it?"

"Can I... talk to you?"

"Of course. Have a seat."

Caleb sat down.

"Well?" Mr. Ashburn asked.

A few seconds later he had to ask again. "Well, what is it, Caleb?"

Caleb cleared his throat twice and sat down. "It's—I—I'll shut the door," he said, standing up again.

Mr. Ashburn raised his eyebrows. "This is awfully suspicious," he sighed to himself. "Let's see, Caleb did dual enrollment and just graduated, didn't he. Some kind of journalism, if I recall correctly. Oh, and he got a job a month ago. Dear me," said Mr. Ashburn, beginning to run over the list of his daughters in his mind.

Caleb closed the door behind him and sat back down.

"Flag's nailed to the mast," thought Mr. Ashburn. "Burning the bridges. Look at that red face. If he didn't come for one of them, I'll be..."

"Mr. Ashburn, I..."

"Go on, son—" Mr. Ashburn cleared his throat quickly. "Caleb."

"You know I graduated a couple months ago," Caleb began very quickly, "and I have a good job now, and a car, and no debt, and I think... I mean I hope... I mean maybe I..."

Mr. Ashburn waited calmly, thinking, "If you want one of 'em, the least you can do is say it yourself."

"I would like," he said with a flaming face, "your permission to... to marry..."

"I'm not your father, Caleb," Mr. Ashburn said calmly. "I don't think you need my permission."

"Oh! But I—you know—I want to marry—to marry—one of your daughters," he blurted.

Mr. Ashburn laughed a little. Caleb's face was too much for his sense of humor. Then he tried to be serious. "Caleb," he said gravely, "you're both still very young."

"Oh," gasped Caleb, turning, if possible, redder than ever. "I haven't said which one yet."

"That's—true," said Mr. Ashburn, sounding curious.

"You'll laugh at me," he said.

This Mr. Ashburn promptly did. Then he asked, "Well?"

"I—I know that she's older than I am," he began, "but I—and—I mean, I always—I'm not such an idiot," he said, making an effort to speak clearly, "that I don't know that she's never thought of me—that way—and of course I know—that I'm much younger—but I—love her. I made up my mind—when she went to college—I wanted to say something then, but of course that would have been silly. I've waited for five years now, and I have a good job, and I can provide for her. I know I'm very young, but—she isn't—so very, and I'm scared... I've been scared all this time and I—it sounds silly, I know!—but six years isn't much, really it isn't—and I love Jen—and oh Mr. Ashburn, won't you give me a chance?"

Mr. Ashburn had listened to this speech with his mouth open. "Yikes," he finally said.

Caleb stood behind the chair, breathless, pale, mouthing the word, "please."

"You had better go now," said Mr. Ashburn a little thickly, for he was trying hard to suppress an almost irresistible laugh. "I'll—I'll have to—think about this. —Wait until Jennifer hears of it," he thought to himself, turning as red in the face as Caleb had been.

"Yes sir," said Caleb meanwhile, and left.

"Well," said Mr. Ashburn to Mrs. Ashburn, after he told her the story, "what do you think?"

"Are you *sure* you understood him right?" she asked.

"Absolutely positive."

"What a shame," Mrs. Ashburn said. "I mean, I like Caleb—I thought he would have been good for—boy oh boy. Was he really *very* serious? It's just too bad."

"So you don't think Jen would—"

Mrs. Ashburn looked astonished. "You don't mean to say you do?!"

"Oh—no, no I don't, not really. She'd laugh, I suppose. But it's kind of a shame—I've half a mind," Mr. Ashburn went on, "to give him a chance. At first I was thinking I'd spare him, but that might be a cruel kindness. Suppose I talked to Jen about it?"

"What good would that do? Another notch in her belt of victims, I suppose," said Mrs. Ashburn sarcastically.

"At least," Mr. Ashburn reflected diplomatically, "she likes Caleb well enough to be sorry—a little. Maybe it'll—you know, seem more serious. I never noticed her giving anyone's feelings much consideration before."

"Ain't that the truth," Mrs. Ashburn groaned.

"Oh—uh—just to be prepared—if by some miracle—you wouldn't object to him as a son-in-law, would you?"

"Oh, no, not at all—well, you'd better run over the questions you always ask first, but I'm sure he'd pass," said Mrs. Ashburn. "You really are going to talk to Jen about it?"

"No," said Mr. Ashburn suddenly, after thinking about it for a minute. "No, I'll let him ask her about it."

Mrs. Ashburn raised her eyebrows. "Going to lay it on thick, are we?"

"We'll give him a chance," said Mr. Ashburn, "we'll give him as good a chance as we can."

Poor Caleb paced his bedroom for hours over the next few days.

"I—I just don't know how to say it," he said miserably, every time Mr. Ashburn asked if he was ready.

After that had gone on for about a week, during which Hannah and Joe talked and came to the conclusion that Caleb's job was much too stressful for him, Mr. Ashburn gave up waiting. He took Caleb and planted him in his office.

"Now," he said. "Faint heart never, and so forth. I'm bringing Jen in here and you'll have your shot. This waiting is not helping you get inspired."

Caleb looked like he would have enjoyed being stuck alone in a rowboat on the Pacific just then.

Jen had learned to recognize her father's "it's about a young man" look, and came into the room looking as innocent as possible. But Caleb took the train of her thoughts right off its tracks.

"Oh! Caleb! I didn't—good afternoon."

"Have a seat, Jen," Mr. Ashburn said, smiling at her bewilderment.

Jen sat down. "Maybe it's not about me at all, or maybe it's not about that at all," she thought to herself. "But I was sure I recognized the look. What *is* wrong with Caleb? He looks like he's been tormented by ghosts for several weeks. Or... he did a second ago. Now I think he's blushing. Goodness, why *am* I here?"

"Go ahead, Caleb," Mr. Ashburn said cheerfully.

"Jen," Caleb said, summoning his courage from some far planet, and speaking tolerably evenly, "I know this will probably—surprise you. I—you know how I used to be your knight long ago. I—um—I'd like to be your knight for the rest of my life. I don't think you've ever—I know you've never thought about it. Jen—let me pretend to be your knight for a little bit longer, and—just—if..." He stopped.

Jen stared at him. "Um... Caleb... I—really," she tried to laugh. "What are you, twenty? I'm five—six years older than you! Don't be—silly..." She looked him in the eye, felt her face get hot, and standing up retreated to the window.

He didn't say anything.

"Caleb—I," she tried again. "You're not—actually—serious, are you?"

"Won't you—think about it, Jen?"

There was a silence, and Mr. Ashburn nervously twisted his shirt corner. "I didn't think it would be this intense," he said to himself.

Finally Jen said, in a very low voice, "Yes."

A wave of relief swept over Caleb, and suddenly he was across the room, holding her hand. She was never very sure if he kissed it, or only squeezed it hard before he ran away.

Mr. Ashburn smiled and stroked his chin. "I begin to think," he said, "we might marry you off yet."

Jen, crimson, fled the room.

"Wait a second you two, aren't we gonna talk about the... rules... of your courtship... well I guess—tomorrow..." said Mr. Ashburn to his empty office.

Essy found Caleb flying around on the tire swing and called his name three times before he heard. Essy had got a confession from Caleb long ago. In later years she said, "If it hadn't been for me, Caleb would have made an idiot of himself telling Jen he loved her when he was fifteen. In fact..." But Caleb growled and said, "I only thought about that for a second! I would never have been such a—!"

"Well!" Essy exclaimed as Caleb stopped the swing. "Don't knock me over, but calm down and talk. I'm a genius at plan Bs."

But Caleb only grinned.

"Jolly!" Essy said breathlessly, "you don't mean to say she said yes?!"

"Yes—no—not completely," said Caleb.

"But she didn't say no?"

"No, she didn't."

"You're busy counting chickens already, you conceited child. You're not out of the woods yet!"

"I know, I know. But I have a chance now—I really—I really think I do!"

Essy looked musingly at the ground. "Well, this is going to be jolly you know, watching you try to make Jen fall in love with you," she said, giggling heartily. "How are you going to start, Mr. Knight in Shining Armor? I hope you'll bring her flowers tomorrow."

Caleb wrinkled his nose. "Jen would think that was silly."

"Actually you know," Essy said musingly, "I'm not sure. Jen is a softy at bottom. Go ahead and make a fool of yourself, she'll be impressed."

"Oh, come on!"

"Really!" said Essy. "Don't be *too* stupid of course, but—look here Caleb, I'm being serious. You gotta sweep her off her feet. She's always kept 'em all at arm's length. Don't let her do that to you. I'm being serious, not *literal*," Essy added, glaring at him.

"Okay," said Caleb doubtfully. "So..."

"So I really think you should bring her flowers tomorrow," said Essy, fighting to keep a straight face. "No, really! It'll make her take it seriously."

"But... how..."

It would be nice to explain how Essy and Caleb, with the help of a few dandelions, spent the afternoon practicing, and how annoying Essy was to Jen all evening—especially when she sang, "I'm an old maid, an old old maid, twenty-six and an old old o-old maid!"—and how Caleb brought Jen the most expensive bouquet he could find the next day, and how desperately Jen tried to hide it but could not quite bring herself to throw it away, and how Mr. Ashburn and Mrs. Ashburn exchanged glances and raised their eyebrows, and how Essy chased Fred out of the house with genuine fury and a broomstick when Fred said, "But I thought Caleb liked—" and how Madeline was caught writing "Jen Calhoun" on a napkin, to see how it looked—and all the hundred and one other things that happened, but then the rest of the book would be about Caleb and Jen.

Jen tried. She got out the piece of paper where she had written, "Things I would have to give up if I married," and the list seemed shorter than usual. She thought about all the solo trips she'd taken and the beautiful times she'd had photographing breathtaking scenery by herself—and pretty soon she was imagining how nice it'd be if Caleb had been there too. "And I know I'd *like* to have children," she thought in despair, "so it's no use thinking about that. Oh dear, I'm slipping fast."

Caleb bought a ring three weeks later. Essy thought that was a little premature, but he said, "What if the perfect moment comes along and I haven't got it?"

"Then just propose and tell her you'll buy the ring later, of course," said Essy.

"But—but that would look so—unprepared!"

"Well, yes, I suppose it wouldn't quite jibe with the illusion of calm maturity you've been trying to foist on us lately," said Essy, referring to the sudden grown-up airs Caleb had been putting on. "Still, you might just possibly have wasted two thousand dollars. I mean, you definitely wasted it, because that's a ridiculous amount to spend on a ring, but you might have *completely* wasted it."

"Do you really think so?" asked Caleb, worried.

"Well..." said Essy, and did not get any further.

Jen had a photography gig at the Grand Canyon, and spent a whole two weeks traveling the area and taking pictures. Essy said to Hannah, "I'm jolly well never letting her leave that moonstruck boy on my hands again! Do you know he'd rather sit and reread their old texts than go out and rollerblade?"

"Well," said Hannah, "I don't see why he shouldn't sit and read texts if he wants to."

"But *I* wanted to rollerblade!" Essy sputtered.

Caleb went with Roy to the airport to pick Jen up. They got caught in traffic and Jen was waiting for them when they arrived.

"Oh, hello!" she exclaimed, a smile breaking over her face. She jumped up and hugged Roy—very much to his surprise.

Roy picked up her tripod and Caleb offered to take the suitcase. "Thanks," said Jen briefly, without looking at him. She walked to the car next to Roy, talking about her trip, while Caleb trailed behind.

He loaded the suitcase slowly into the trunk, feeling silly for having thought Jen might be particularly glad to see him there and wondering if she would sit in the passenger seat.

She did not. She sat in the middle back, and Caleb buckled in next to her.

"Oh!" Jen said. She started to add, "I thought you'd want the passenger seat—" but then she shut her mouth, for that wasn't quite true.

Caleb enjoyed the next few minutes, and then his spirits slowly sank again as Jen looked only out the far window and said nothing. He was ready to conclude in despair that she didn't care and never would, when he suddenly realized that he was holding her hand—though he was not at all sure whose fault that was.

"Jen!" he said.

She tried to look at him casually but, failing, took back her hand and leant forward to cover her face.

"Jen, are you glad to be back?" he asked.

"Yes!"

Caleb hesitated for an instant, his hand in his pocket. Then he turned to face Jen—as well as he could with a seatbelt on—and said, "I meant to go on one knee, after a romantic dinner or something—really I did, but—I can't. Jen"—he took the ring box out of his pocket—"Jennifer Ashburn, will you marry me?"

"Yes," Jen gasped.

Roy honked twice and they both jumped, and Roy laughed the rest of the way.

Chapter 33—The Inseparables

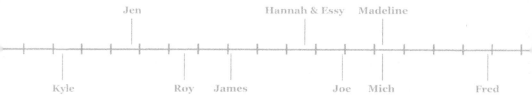

Among the guests at Jen's wedding were, of course, her grandparents. Not Grandpa and Grandma Waring; they had passed before this story began, after first spoiling the older Ashburns as long as they could and then retiring to live with their son Bob. Clarissa's well-ordered housekeeping was much easier on their nerves than even a one week visit to the Ashburns had been. "It's not quite as homelike," Grandpa Waring had observed, "but more peaceful-like." Both died, within months of each other, a year before Fred was born.

But Grandpa and Grandma Ashburn were still hale and hearty, and quite as young as any couple with ten grandchildren could possibly be. They visited their son and daughter-in-law once every three months, regular as clockwork. Then there were three days of candy and parks and bedtime stories, followed by three weeks of recovery before the children settled back down.

A few days after the wedding they had a conversation with Mr. and Mrs. Ashburn that went like this.

Grandpa Ashburn, looking desperate, like a gambler about to make a risky bet: "We have a—a request."

Mr. Ashburn, very curious: "Let's hear it, dad."

"Well. We would like to—well, you see. We're planning a trip to Europe in a few months, just to see some sights, you know, and, well, we thought we'd like to invite Mich and Mad to come along."

Grandma Ashburn nodded, slowly, as if to say, "And we hope we won't regret it."

"Oh!" said Mr. Ashburn. "Well, I'm sure they would enjoy that!"

"We thought it would be a fun graduation gift," Grandpa Ashburn nodded. "And we can use a bit of excitement in our old age, anyways."

When Mich and Mad heard of it—which was not until it was settled, of course—they went wild.

"Europe!" Mich shouted. "Knights and cathedrals and Napoleon and the Alps!"

"Cobblestone roads and Queens and Swiss chocolate! Oh my!" said Mad.

"And guillotines and escargot and the Pope," said Joe, who wished he could have gone.

"I remember lots of French," Mad said. "Bonjour, monsieur!"

"Je mons France is all I remember," Mich said, "and I don't know what it means."

"You'll both have to brush up on it," Hannah laughed.

"And we'll have to walk like this," said Mad, taking Mich's arm and prancing up and down the room.

"And dance like this," said Mich, clicking his heels together and spinning Mad around with one hand.

"Do you suppose they still have balls? Will you sew me a gown, Essy?" Mad asked, stopping in the middle of a spin and making Mich waltz her up and down the room instead.

"You two are so silly," Essy said.

"First the heel and then the toe," Mich sang. "Spin around and then let go!"

Mad landed breathless on the couch. "I wonder if I should learn German too," she said. "Just imagine! We're going to Europe, Mich!"

"And until then we'll get no peace," Essy grumbled.

"Didn't someone once say that one of the responsibilities of being an American was fighting against a superstitious valuation of Europe?" Hannah mused.

"Mich and Mad are not patriotic," Joe agreed.

"We'll sing the star spangled banner in the airport at Paris, see if we don't," said Mad.

"I dare you to!" Essy said.

So of course, when they got there, they did. Grandma and Grandpa hurried to get the suitcases and leave the scene as quickly as possible.

But the twins horrified their grandparents even worse in England.

After having been dragged around to far more sights in and around London than he had bargained for, Grandpa Ashburn decided it was time to send Mich and Mad off for a little journey of their own. He booked them a hotel for a night in Canterbury, bought their train tickets, handed them each a hundred and fifty pounds, and told them to enjoy themselves. Then as soon as he and

Grandma had seen their train safely off they went back to their hotel in Rochester and to bed.

The twins toured the cathedral, checked into their hotel, got a guided boat tour, ate, and shopped. Mad found a whole load of souvenirs but since she'd left her wallet in the hotel, Mich had to buy them.

"We'll have to be more careful tomorrow," Mich said, when he counted his leftover change that night. "I've got less than twenty pounds left and to be safe we need to save at least fifty for our return tickets. Where's your wallet, Mad?"

Mad looked uncomfortably at a very disordered backpack. "I don't—know—exactly," she said.

"Well, it's in there, right?" Mich asked.

"It was the first thing I packed," Mad said, "and I put it in one of the pockets."

"Well it's obviously not in that one."

"Let me think," Mad said, shutting her eyes. "Grandpa gave me the money, and I put it in my wallet, and I opened the suitcase... Oh," she said.

"What?" Mich asked.

"I put the wallet in my suitcase, not my backpack."

"The suitcase—which you left in Rochester?"

"Yeah," said Mad.

"Twenty pounds," Mich said, "is not good for much more than our meals tomorrow—not even that much, if we eat as fancy as we did today. You haven't got any money of your own on you, do you? —I sure don't."

"Me neither," Mad sighed. "What do we do?"

"*We* don't do nothing, but *you'll* have to call Grandpa."

"Just when he was hoping for a break from us!" Mad said regretfully. "Where's the phone?"

"Well, hold on a second," Mich said, picking up the phone Mr. and Mrs. Ashburn had given to the twins for their trip. "Maybe there's something cheaper than the train that we can take back."

"Well?" Mad asked, after a few minutes.

"If only you'd spent a little bit less, we could probably have taken a bus. But no, you had to get that fancy picture frame."

"You're the one who bought the most expensive meal on the menu," Mad retorted. "Oh never mind," she added quickly, seeing that Mich was about to mention her wallet.

"Hey," Mich said, fiddling around with the phone, "looks like it would only take about nine hours to walk there."

Mad laughed.

"Well, what do you say?"

"You can't walk for nine hours! You complained about walking through the art gallery for three hours last week."

"Sure I can walk for nine hours!" Mich said. "It was the art that bothered me, not the walking. Maybe *you* can't walk for nine hours."

"Of course I could," Mad fired.

"Let's try it," said Mich. "We can get our lunch on the way. The directions are right here, it's not like we'll get lost."

"We'd have to get an early start," Mad said doubtfully.

"We've seen enough of this old town anyway," Mich replied. "It'll be great fun to walk like in the old days!"

"Tell me that after you've walked ten miles."

Fortunately for the twins—who had not thought about the weather at all—the next day was perfect, just overcast enough to be shady but no threat of rain. So they swung on their backpacks after breakfast—Mad secretly regretted that heavy frame—and got going.

At first the walk was pleasant. The twins enjoyed the scenery, made believe they were returning pilgrims, and argued about ice cream flavors. But after an hour and half, ice cream flavors became too dangerous of a subject, and they couldn't find anything to replace it. Trudging along in silence, Mad found her backpack getting heavier and heavier and Mich felt his feet becoming sorer and sorer.

"It's really fun to walk like this, isn't it?" Mich said after they'd gone eight miles.

"Oh yeah," Mad replied, tightening the straps of her backpack. "It's such a beautiful day too."

"I am getting hungry for lunch though," Mich said.

"It's only ten," Mad replied.

"Oh," said Mich. "I thought—never mind."

They had lunch at twelve sharp, and then stopped for a snack at three, and spent the last four pounds on a painfully small dinner at five. Then Mich got his reserve stubbornness together and said, "Well, just an hour of walking left. I'm glad you left your wallet behind, otherwise we'd have missed all this fun."

So Mad, not to be outdone, nodded and said, "I'll almost be sorry when we get there!"

And it was only when the whole trip was over and the twins told their siblings the full story that Mich admitted he'd suffered agonies getting his socks off that night and Mad said that her backpack straps had rubbed three inches of skin off on either shoulder.

Chapter 34—A Day of Hallowed Peace

Someone once asked Fred what his family did on Sundays and he said, "We spend it in the public and private exercises of God's worship—except so much as is to be taken up in works of necessity and mercy." (This was a quote from the Shorter Catechism.) The person who asked him the question went away wondering what the exercises of public and private worship—not to mention the works of necessity and mercy—looked like.

Sunday—or the Lord's Day, as the Ashburns knew it—started with Mr. Ashburn, in his slippers, going and getting a violin from the music room and playing all the rousing hymns he could think of, standing at the bottom of the stairs. By the time he was tired, Mrs. Ashburn was up and scrambling eggs. A bit later James would join her in the kitchen to fry bacon.

Then the other children trickled down, dressed in their best outfits, and began to set the table and put the clean dishes from last night away, and Essy took stock of the fruit left in the house and arranged it on the table as nicely as she could. Sometimes—like when there were only lemons, or only two half moldy pears—that took a lot of talent.

During breakfast Mr. Ashburn often read Psalm 92, which Hannah enjoyed because it mentioned unicorns and Mich liked because of the phrase, "fat and flourishing."

After breakfast they all piled into the van and went to church. Sometimes other people thought that their large family was the reason the Ashburns were occasionally a minute or two late. But the truth was, Mr. Ashburn was the one still standing in front of the mirror making sure his hair was combed the right way after all the others had already buckled up.

One of the distinguishing marks of being an Ashburn, besides not celebrating Christmas or watching TV, was singing out at church. Fortunately they all had fairly tuneful voices. On the few occasions when travels or sickness kept them from church, the congregational singing felt unusually soft.

Roy and Hannah took notes during the sermon. Roy's notes were short and his handwriting was small; he had used the same notebook for ten years. Hannah's notes deserved to be framed. Sometimes Mrs. Ashburn wondered if Hannah could pay attention while she was drawing fancy flourishes to each letter. She talked to Hannah about it, but left the decision up to her. Hannah kept drawing, so it is to be hoped that she was sure she could listen at the same time.

Mich and Mad had also taken notes when they were little; Mich's notes were long lines crisscrossing his paper and Mad's were hundreds of circles.

On the ride home Mrs. Ashburn always asked, "What did you get out of the sermon, children?"

Fred went first. When he was very young, he used to say, "Amen!" But by this time he could do better.

"That we shouldn't ever give up praying," Fred said one Sunday.

"Not even if it takes 400 years for the answer to come, like between the end of the Old Testament and the beginning of the New," Mad supplemented.

Mich said, "I heard him say that none of us should ever think we can't do something for someone else, because we can always pray for them." Then he drew a long breath. He'd been repeating that to himself every couple of minutes since the sermon had finished.

"There was something about waiting for God's timing," said Joe.

Essy thought for a long time and finally said, "Prayer is a privilege. I'm not actually quite sure that was in the sermon, but it sounds like it might have been."

Hannah had her point down word perfect. "We don't just pray because we want things from God, but because we want to talk about things to God."

James said, "Mich said what I was going to say, and then Hannah said my other thing. Sometimes sermons don't have enough points for all of us."

Roy glanced over his notes. "That when we pray, we need to remember to trust in the wisdom of God who made all things."

They ate a lunch Hannah had gotten ready the day before, and afterwards Essy, Mich, and Mad went for a walk while Hannah and Joe played music together. Fred read a book about escaping Huguenots and Mrs. Ashburn sat at the dining room table with a pen and her prayer journal. Mr. Ashburn tried to read a book too, but it wasn't as exciting as the escaping Huguenots and he fell asleep.

On their walk the twins and Essy took turns reciting the Sermon on the Mount—Matthew chapters 5-7. Since none of them had brought a Bible with them, they sometimes argued for a while over exact verse order.

After they were done Mad asked, "So how did you go the extra mile last week?"

"I cleaned under Fred's bed for him," Essy said. "What about you?"

"I framed one of Joe's poems," Mad said, and they both looked at Mich.

"I... well I'm going the extra mile right now, walking with you," Mich grinned.

"I think it's debatable as to whose extra mile this is," Essy said.

"Surely you did something nice for someone last week," Mad added.

"Probably," Mich said virtuously, "but I didn't make a note of it like you two. And it also says not to let your left hand know what your right hand is doing when you're giving things away, so..."

When they got back home there were two other cars in the driveway.

"Looks like Jen and Kyle are here," said Mad cheerfully, "and their wi—husb—people."

"There goes our peaceful Sunday," Essy said.

"Nephews," Mich said, shaking his head and referring to Kyle's little son Kenny.

Kenny was definitely a handful. Paula wondered how on earth Mrs. Ashburn had raised ten children, and Mrs. Ashburn wondered how on earth Paula was raising Kenny. When the three came in from their walk, Kenny was sitting on his dad's lap, throwing his shoes at Mr. Ashburn who was only half awake. Kyle watched and laughed, while Caleb sat by and made wise resolutions about not encouraging his future children to do silly things by laughing at them.

Paula was in the kitchen with Jen and Mrs. Ashburn, and Essy joined them just in time to hear Paula say, "and then he flushed the toilet. It took Kyle all day to get the toothbrush out. I just never thought about telling him not to put a toothbrush in the toilet before."

Jen looked sympathetic and a little worried as she put the dessert she'd brought on the counter.

"Well, I guess boys will be boys," Mrs. Ashburn said, "although Kenny..."

"Has a good imagination," Essy suggested. "Most kids wouldn't think about dropping their toothbrush in the toilet."

"It was actually my toothbrush," Paula said, tossing the salad ingredients she'd brought together.

Mrs. Ashburn turned away from Paula and exchanged raised eyebrows with Essy.

After dinner all the Ashburns went to the Sunday evening service. This was Joe's favorite time of the day in summer, for he loved to see the sun set through the stained windows of the church. "Sunday is such a refreshing day," he thought, just before Kenny crawled under the pew behind him and pulled on his shoe.

The Ashburns were usually the last family to leave church. There were always so many people to talk to and so much to say, that even on the longest days of summer it was dark by the time they left. Then on the way home they sang. In the dark, with the windows down and a cool night breeze blowing through the car, even a hymn you've sung a thousand times before has a fresh meaning. At some point or another, every single child said to themselves, "I'll remember this even when I'm sixty"—and they all did.

Everyone made good resolutions about getting to bed on time, but they usually stayed up until eleven or twelve anyways, with the lights out, discussing difficult points of doctrine with vigor.

"It seems to me," Joe said, "that a sequence of events is a necessary concept—like the law of non-contradiction. It doesn't have to involve time, but without a sequence of events you can't have events at all, and since you do have events—for instance, creation—you have to have a sequence of events, i.e. before creation, and after creation, and…"

"What does i.e. mean?" Fred interrupted.

"Latin for 'that is,'" Hannah explained.

"Oh," said Fred. "And what did the rest of the sentence mean?"

"But," said James, ignoring Fred's question, "how can you have a sequence of events without time? And if you have time, then you're in time, and limited by it, and not in eternity."

"Well… no, not really. The point is," Joe began.

"The point is," Essy interrupted, "that in heaven, for instance, which is in eternity, you'll still be able to do things. Which means that there is a before you did it, and an after you did it. Ergo, a sequence of events."

"Another Latin word," Hannah explained in an undertone. "Ergo means therefore."

Mad said, "Can't we talk about something a little less confusing? Say supralapsarianism, for a change?"

"What's that?" asked Fred.

"Has to do with the order of the divine decrees," said James. "Personally I think it's pretty confusing but..."

"I was being sarcastic, obviously," Mad explained.

"Remember that time we argued over whether Mad's hair was curly or kinky?" Mich asked. "Now there was something I could understand."

"It's not really kinky," Joe said. "I've seen a lot kinkier."

"It is kinky," said Mad, "and you'd know it if you had to comb it."

Finally Mrs. Ashburn, having woken up for the third time from a light doze, came out of her room and called up the stairs, "Children—it's really time to get some sleep now..."

"All the same," Joe hissed as he went to get in bed, "Mad's hair isn't kinky and there's obviously a sequence of events in eternity."

Chapter 35—Just a Friend

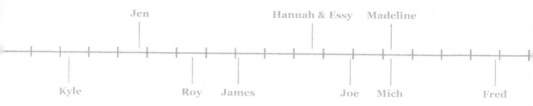

There was a park within easy biking distance of the Ashburns' house, and the Ashburn children often went there to play Ultimate Frisbee with a group of young people. They all enjoyed it, but Essy was a die-hard. So even though thunder had been heard in the distance this Friday and the wind was gusting at about 35 miles per hour, Essy got on her bike, hooted at her siblings for staying home, and went to the park.

"No one else'll show up!" Roy shouted after her, but the wind carried his voice away.

Sure enough, no one was there when Essy arrived.

"It's not even raining," she complained to the trees. "Wimps!"

Essy took the frisbee out of her backpack, set it on the grass, and sat down moodily in front of it.

Someone walked by her—no one she recognized—and then turned and walked by the other way. Then he coughed a little and said, "Are you here to play frisbee? Peter Heath invited me to come some Friday. I guess," he zipped his jacket up a bit more, "I didn't pick the best Friday."

"Just like Pete to invite someone and then not show up!" said Essy.

"Oh, but he didn't know I was coming this week. In fact, I told him I wasn't sure I'd ever make it. I usually work on Friday afternoons."

"Well, I'm Essy Ashburn," she said, standing up and brushing off the grass.

"Andrew Leland," he said.

Essy twirled the frisbee on one finger. "I was just wishing for people," she said, "but one person is awkward. You didn't bring a chauffeur, by any chance?"

Andrew laughed. "No, I'm by myself."

"Well, we'll give them a few more minutes. What are you, anyways?"

"What am I?"

"Profession, you know," she explained. "Baker, butcher, candlestick maker. Is a candlestick maker a goldsmith, I wonder?"

"I'm a fireman," he said.

"Oh!" Essy exclaimed.

"I just recently moved here," he added, "but I was a fireman for years in West Virginia."

"I got stuck in a tree once and firemen came and rescued me," said Essy. "By the way, do people call you Andy or is it always Andrew?"

"Actually, I go by Drew for short," he said. "Um—I don't mean to be rude, but how did you get stuck in a tree?"

"Oh," said Essy, "it was because I climbed from a tree with low branches to a tree with high branches, and I broke the branch between them when I did it." She looked around and sighed. "I really don't think anyone else is coming."

"Well, another Friday then," Drew said, smiling a little.

"But I wanted to play frisbee," Essy said. "If you follow me home I'll get those kids to play. Our backyard is kind of tree-y but it does in a pinch. Only I'm on a bike, so you'll have to go slow."

"I'd be glad to, if you like," he said. "But really, I can come another Friday."

"Thought you worked most Fridays?"

"Well... yes."

"Then you'd better take advantage of today," said Essy. "So come along!"

"All right," said Drew, laughing.

With the game coming to them like this, nearly all the Ashburns still at home were willing to join in. The wind was wild, and Joe bragged terribly over making the only goal catch of the game.

Eventually it started to pour, and they went inside. Mrs. Ashburn said, "Kids, I need you to make sure everything breakable is at least two feet off the ground. Kyle and Paula are coming for dinner and you know how Kenny is. —Oh!" she said, catching sight of Andrew.

"Hi," he said. "I'm Andrew Leland."

"I invited him to play frisbee," Essy said.

"Oh!" said Mrs. Ashburn. "Where did you... um... meet?"

"Found him at the park," Essy called over her shoulder, her arms full of books she'd scooped off the table.

Mrs. Ashburn looked a little blank and Andrew hastened to explain. "I'm a friend of Peter Heath's, and he invited me to the frisbee game."

"Oh, right, it's Friday, isn't it. You'll stay for dinner?"

"Oh no, thank you though. I really should go," Drew said.

"You should come again sometime," said Essy, who would have scorned to be shy. "We're having a game night next Tuesday evening, if you're free."

"You'd be welcome," said Mrs. Ashburn, turning back toward the kitchen.

Drew did come. After a bit Jen asked James, "So who is the fellow who looks like a misunderstood hero in disguise?"

"Who? Oh—you mean Drew."

"Yes, Drew. With a name like that I hope he's an artist. He doesn't have a twin, right?"

"A twin? No—why—what are you talking about?"

"What's his real name, anyway?"

"Andrew Leland," said James. "He's a firefighter, not an artist. I think he's a captain, but I'm not sure. He's got a degree in fire science or something, anyway. How do you like him?"

"Oh, he's handsome enough," Jen said carelessly, "if you like that slick villain hairstyle and the tough just-barely smile. Of course, I prefer curls and I never did believe in a smile if you can't see the person's teeth."

"You really should stop comparing everybody to Caleb," said James. "Of course they'll all lose. I meant how did you like his personality? Just by itself, leaving Caleb out of it."

"Seems nice," said Jen. "Also seemed a little too deep for me to fathom during one game of Black Hole. But how'd he get here, anyways?"

"Oh," said James, shrugging, "he's a friend of Essy's."

"What!" Jen exclaimed. "Really?"

"Yes—why, what is it?"

"You don't see anything—interesting—about that?" Jen asked.

"About him and Essy? No. She's been bringing home friends for years, starting with the neighbor's dog when she was four—and including a certain young man whose initials are CAC. I wouldn't get excited, if I were you."

"Hm-m," Jen chuckled. "We'll see. This is good raw material, anyhow... good raw material," she repeated. Jen had not quite forgiven Essy for the torture she'd inflicted on her during her courtship.

Despite what he'd said, James watched Drew closely the rest of the evening, weighing him in a very fine scale. For instance, Drew didn't say thank you when Jen handed him his cards. He didn't make extra room next to himself on the couch when Mad tried to sit down there. The one joke he ventured on was a bad pun.

These were grave shortcomings, no doubt. But on the other hand, he brought the lemonade pitcher around and filled up everyone's glasses, he got up from a game to help Kenny reach a toy on a high shelf, and he said amen after the prayer.

"He *might* do," James thought. "We'll have to see."

On her way out the door at ten Jen said to Essy, "I see you've made a new friend."

"Are you talking about Drew?" Essy asked, provokingly calm. "Yes, picked him up in the park that day no one else showed up to play frisbee. I do like a person who isn't scared of a little thunder."

"You know it was Mrs. Calhoun's birthday," Jen said, "so Caleb and I couldn't come."

"Oh, right," said Essy. "Do you still call her Mrs. Calhoun? Shouldn't you say mom?"

"I do, just not to you. Anyway this conversation is about Andrew, not me."

"What about him?"

"You sure he's just a friend?" Jen asked meaningfully.

"Of course," said Essy. "What more do you want?"

Chapter 36—The Tithe

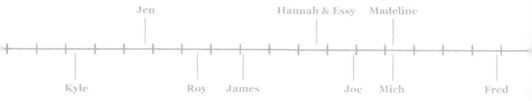

Roy Ashburn graduated from college and then from seminary "summa cum laude." He hadn't left home for any of his studies, since he'd done correspondence courses for college and attended a seminary in his home town. So when he graduated from seminary at the age of twenty-five, his whole family was able to come to the ceremony.

Somehow Roy's graduation was different than Kyle's or Jen's. Afterwards Hannah asked Essy, "Were you the only one of us girls who didn't cry? Why did everyone cry, anyways?"

"You tell me!" said Essy. "You were the ones doing it."

"I cried out of sympathy," said Hannah. "But I don't know what I was sympathizing with. Only I know mom and dad both cried, and I think you're heartless not to have any sympathy."

Essy shrugged. "You're perfectly welcome to think I'm heartless," she said. "If mom and dad want to cry because their third baby graduated, that's their business."

Hannah looked doubtful and shook her head. "It wasn't just that," she said.

The family had a late celebratory dinner after the ceremony, and Roy stood up, once everyone had finished eating.

"I want to say something to all of you. I—I'll try to be an Ashburn," he went on, grinning and steadying his voice, "and not betray emotion. For years and years I've had the dream—the desire—for God to use me to bring the good news about Jesus to places that have never heard his name before. Now that I've finished college and seminary I'm going to go to a missionary school in California. God willing, I'll be leaving in a couple of weeks for several months of training. If all goes well in a year or so I'll be on the mission field. I don't know where yet for sure, but somewhere where there haven't been hardly any missionaries before."

Roy paused and twisted his cup around, glancing at his dad, who nodded. "Part of my training," he said, "well—because—since I'm not likely to be able to communicate with you all regularly when I get to the field, part of the training is getting used to that. So you won't be hearing from me while I'm at school. Of course I'll come back for a few weeks after the training is over and before I leave. But—I'll miss you all," he said. "Jen—mom—dad—" he caught his breath and went on, looking around the table, "Caleb, Kyle, Paula, Kenny, Hannah, James, Essy, Mich, Mad, Fred, Joe. I couldn't imagine a better family. One day we'll all be together again—if not on earth then in heaven," he finished, sitting down.

"You're our tithe, Roy," Mr. Ashburn said, "one of ten. Your mother and I are glad—God go with you!" he said.

So Roy went to the mission school he'd chosen, and his family looked forward to, and at the same time dreaded, the brief return he'd planned.

Kyle missed Roy; he'd always been a quiet word at the right time to Kyle. Jen missed his rare smile—which no one had been better at getting him to smile than she. Roy was Jen's baby brother to the exclusion of all her other brothers, and deep down she was always a little surprised to come home and not find him there.

James never said he missed Roy. Neither did he ever say he missed his left leg. But long ago he had written in the front of his Bible, "Earth is not my home," and when Roy left, he went over the fading pencil marks in ink.

Hannah and Essy were both surprised to find that they missed their quiet older brother. "I didn't think I would, really," said Hannah. "I mean, not in a particular sort of way. I didn't miss Kyle much when he moved out."

"Kyle didn't go so far," said Essy, in a sulky voice. Talking about anything emotional tended to put Essy in a bad mood.

"I miss Roy like a... like a pine tree, I think," Hannah mused. "Tall and strong, and standing straight and pointing to the sky."

"You miss people like... things?" Essy asked.

"Yes—no—I mean, that's what the feeling feels like. I mean, the feeling thinking about a pine tree gives me is like the feeling missing Roy gives me."

Essy was so confused she forgot to be in a bad mood. "That's not—what does that mean?"

"Don't you ever imagine landscapes to go with a certain feeling?"

Essy gaped at her.

"Oh well," said Hannah. "I guess if you don't do it, you probably can't understand. Roy would have understood..."

Joe found writing poems hard work after Roy had left, partly because he'd lost his most appreciative audience. He noticed things Roy used to do that now went undone—like dusting the books in the school room—and took the tasks on himself.

The twins and Fred missed Roy in the non-particular way Hannah had referred to. Fred sometimes regretted not having someone to talk about biology with, it took Mich two weeks to remember not to set him a place at the table, and Mad got confused when she tried to count how many Ashburns were around to accept a friend's birthday party invitation.

Roy came home as promised, and stayed for twenty-three days. He was going far into the interior of India, not necessarily a dangerous area, but certainly one where he'd have very limited communication. So the Ashburns made the most of having him home, always with the ghost of the twenty-third day hanging over them.

One Friday night they all sat around in the living room. Kenny had fallen asleep on Paula's lap, so conversation was possible.

"Remember the time I hid you in the laundry machine when you were six and you broke the tub, and we went a week and a half without washing clothes?" Kyle asked.

"*I* remember that," Mr. Ashburn said. "I had to wrestle that laundry machine out the door and into the truck."

"Remember that time we went sledding at one o'clock, after everyone else was in bed?" Jen said.

Roy nodded. "I remember having to yank you out of the mound you crashed into."

"You're the one who dared me to use it as a ramp!" Jen laughed.

"I remember when Roy dropped his entire ice cream cone on my shoe," Essy said.

"You were being awfully annoying, sticking leaves in my face," Roy retorted.

"How about that time you and me and Essy scared Caleb out of his wits?" James chuckled.

Caleb pretended to be mad and Roy grinned.

"We should do one last crazy thing!" Mich exclaimed. "Come on, Roy, think of something."

"Well," said Roy, hesitating, "I've always wanted a zip line from the upstairs window to the trees..."

James put his ingenuity to work and a week later everyone got together to try out the zip line he set up. Climbing through the window was a bit of a tight squeeze, especially for Mich and James, but all the Ashburn children went down it at least once—even Hannah, though it took three minutes of cheering on Essy's part to get her to take the plunge.

They played that the tree was a marooned pirate's raft, and the house was a man-o-war sent to bring the pirate to justice. Roy lasted longest as the marooned pirate, keeping the others from landing on his raft. Mad caught him eventually by springing a water gun on him when he least expected it.

Jen got hundreds of pictures, and Kenny loved the line—but Kyle, who had to stand in the tree and catch him so he wouldn't smash into the trunk every time, ended up rather bruised.

Of course on the last day of Roy's stay the whole extended family met together. Roy looked at the lunch Essy and James had made and shook his head. "Boy am I going to miss you two," he joked.

"Eat up!" said James. "It'll be all curry and lentils after this."

"First you'll get synthetic tasting beef and zucchini on your plane ride," Jen said.

"What time does your plane leave?" Caleb asked.

"Six," said Roy, "so I need to be at the airport around three. Did you make this sweet and sour chicken, James?"

"No, just gave Essy some tips," James said. "I did the crab rangoon."

But after all, more than half of the meal didn't get eaten. Jen and Mrs. Ashburn didn't even try to eat and Essy looked regretfully at a half-full plate. "Can't eat another bite without choking," she thought to herself. "Why do people have to grow up and leave?"

"Who's going with me to the airport?" Roy asked.

"We all are," said Hannah, "of course."

Essy wasn't the only one who was disappointed to see that Roy's flight was on time.

After Roy had checked in, the family gathered together one last time before he went through security. Roy stood between both his parents, and Mr. Ashburn prayed. "Our God, from whom all blessings flow, thank you for Roy—for all he has been to us and all he is. Go before him, go with him, be a shady cloud to him by day and a fiery pillar by night. Bring us together again on earth if that is your will, but if not, may the day come soon when we will be praising you together in heaven. Oh God—bless Roy!"

Then Roy went on, "Father, you've given us so much—it's only a little of your own that we could ever give back to you. Help us all gladly give our lives to you—I by going, the others by staying. Take our lives and use them—let us shine a little before we melt. For your love to us, we love you—let us praise you forever, wherever we are! Amen."

So Roy left. All the flowers in the Ashburns' yard died that year, and Mr. Ashburn planted the flowerbeds with grass.

Chapter 37—Essy's Romance

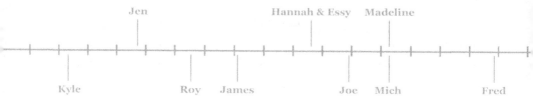

Jen

Hannah & Essy   Madeline

Kyle   Roy   James   Joe   Mich   Fred

Andrew Leland got into the habit of dropping by the Ashburns' house after work a couple times a week. Mr. Ashburn nodded sagaciously and made remarks about seeing through brick walls to Mrs. Ashburn. But she said noncommittally, "It *seems* that way," remembering how things had turned out with Caleb.

"Well," Mr. Ashburn said, "I'll tell you one thing: he does not come just to play chess with James."

Whether that was true or not, James and Drew did often play chess anyways, and James usually won by distracting Drew with long discussions. At first Drew enjoyed talking to James and catching only occasional glimpses of Essy as she flashed in and out of the room on different errands, but eventually he began to find the situation mildly irritating.

One day when he came he found Essy on one couch grading Fred's history paper, while James at the other was reading a book.

"Chess?" said James, looking up cheerfully.

"Let's play a three player game," Drew suggested, "Monopoly or something."

James sighed, but Essy took to the suggestion—or part of it.

"Let's play something that's *not* Monopoly," she said.

So they taught Drew Catan instead and James thought, "Well, that's the end of chess."

But he was wrong. The next time Drew came James was late from work, and he found Drew and Essy over a chess board. James did notice that she'd only moved three pawns, though he was a full hour late—but maybe they were on their second game.

"Thought you didn't like chess," he said to Essy.

"Oh, it's a fine game," Essy said.

"That's actually not how a knight moves," James said to her a minute later.

"Okay," said Essy laughing, "so I don't know anything about chess. Just trying to amuse the lonely boy while you were gone."

"Yeah, sorry to keep you waiting," James said. "We had a small kitchen fire. What time'd you get here?"

"Oh," Drew said, glancing at his watch, "um—a while ago."

"An hour or so," Essy clarified.

"Oh!" James said. "I'm sure Drew must have been very entertained watching you move three pawns."

"Essy plays chess fairly well," said Drew. Then, seeing in James' face that he had missed something, he corrected it to—"at least, she knows how to move the pawns."

Essy laughed half a laugh before she caught it.

"You're not a very avid player," James said, "if a three pawn game is enough for you."

"What's a three pawn game?" Drew asked, confused.

James grinned at him. "Was work particularly stressful today? Had to run through a burning building with three people on your back?" he asked.

"Yes," said Drew absently.

Essy laughed outright.

"Oh!" said Drew with a little start. "What did you say?"

James put on his most serious face and said, "I said, 'Is it because you're lovestruck that you're not paying any attention?'"

Drew froze—except for his blood, which rose slowly to his face.

"Don't worry," James grinned, "that's not actually what I said."

"But you said it now," said Essy, who was laughing so hard she couldn't sit up straight.

Drew pulled himself together and laughed. Then he said, "Let's start over and this time I'll pay attention to avoid such accusations—though..."

"What?" James asked.

"Nothing," said Drew.

Essy was still laughing heartily. But she was in an inexplicably good mood the rest of the day.

After thinking about it Drew decided to make a confidant out of James. James said, "Well you should talk to my dad about it," so he did.

When it got to her Essy said, "Sure, Drew can court me"—so he did.

So in the calendar of Ashburn events the next big thing was Drew's proposal. Hannah said it was very romantic—because there was a sunset somewhere in the background—and she is probably a good judge; but it was certainly boring, and all you need to know is that Essy said yes, calm as a cucumber.

That over with, Essy immediately began to make wedding plans. "When were you thinking?" she asked Drew.

"As soon as possible," he said.

"Well, I think you're supposed to send out invitations six weeks in advance. Suppose we found the wedding venue today and designed the invitation tomorrow—and made a list of people to invite somewhere in there—we could send it out Wednesday. Six weeks from Wednesday is—March 5th. Should we have it that Saturday?"

Drew had not expected to be taken so literally.

Mrs. Ashburn highly recommended they give themselves more than one afternoon to decide where to have the wedding. After spending a few hours looking, Essy agreed. So they set the date for March 29th.

"Plenty of time," Essy said.

For being plenty of time, it melted away awfully quickly. Drew said to Essy, "I hardly see you anymore. Is there an end to your sewing on all these bridesmaids' dresses?"

"You'll see lots of me afterwards," Essy laughed.

"I would say you're working too hard, but it seems to agree with you," he said.

"It does," Essy said. "But it doesn't seem to agree with you. I always knew you would make the perfect melancholy hero, but now you really look the part."

"It's..."

"Well?"

"Oh, nothing," said Drew, but he looked troubled.

Essy shrugged and thought to herself, "It's probably just the sour milk Hannah used in those biscuits for dinner that's messing him up. I wonder what she was dreaming of that she didn't manage to smell it. I noticed right away and *I'm* the one in love here..."

About a week before the wedding Drew spoiled a third perfectly good piece of paper by trying to write to Essy and decided he'd have to say what he wanted to say in person or not at all.

When he came over he found her sitting on the living room table and whistling, one hand holding a notebook and the other drawing lines on it for the adjustments she intended to sew onto Hannah's bridesmaid dress that afternoon. There was nowhere else in the room to sit, for Fred had school books on one couch and himself on the other.

Essy pointedly didn't look up, but as she instead smiled broadly the pretense of oblivion was on the whole a failure.

"I wanted to talk to you," he said.

"Good afternoon Drew. Do you mind?"—handing him the dress to hold. "I need to measure the flounce down here."

"Okay," said Drew.

"Well?" said Essy, after a pause, and taking the dress back. "You're awfully silent for wanting to talk to me."

Drew brought a chair from the dining room over and sat in front of her. "Essy," he said, "it's just that..."

Essy's better angel got a hold of her. She put her pen down and gave him her full attention.

"I know you well enough," he said in a low tone, preferring not to be heard by Fred, "to know that you'd never have said you'd marry me if you didn't—like me pretty well—love me, in a way anyhow. But I know—I'm sure that—Essy, somewhere deep down you have a heart—"

"How kind of you to say so!" Essy thought, laughing inwardly, but Drew didn't give her a chance to say it.

"—and you could love someone with all of it. Essy"—he suddenly looked her firmly in the eyes—"if that someone—isn't—me—then don't marry me."

"Jolly!" thought Essy, in a sudden panic at the sight of Drew's set face. "He's going to make me say I love him. Man! He really will!"

Drew stood up and said, "You can think about it. If—" he turned a shade paler "—I'll break the engagement, if—please don't worry about how it will look to your family."

"Drew stop it!" Essy said, jumping to her feet and laughing a little hysterically. "All right!" she gasped desperately. "I'll say it then, but—" For a moment she glared at him with laughing eyes, then she suddenly said—"I love you, Andrew Leland—I love you with all my whole entire heart!"

By the time he recovered his wits she was already gone.

Gone, by the way, not to sob out her emotion on her pillow or any such thing, but gone to the mud room to buckle on her rollerblades and fly around the subdivision, trying to see what the cold wind could do toward getting a hold of that stupid smile that wouldn't stop smiling itself and wiping it off her face.

Chapter 38—Little Brother

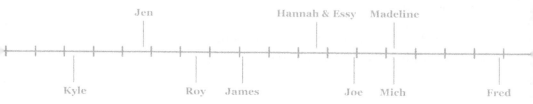

One hot day in August—quite a while after Essy and Drew's wedding—it happened that Fred was the only Ashburn child at home. Hannah was at a friend's house, James and Joe had both moved out for good, and the twins were babysitting for Paula, who was at the dentist.

This particular day in August happened to be Hannah and Essy's birthday—which was why Hannah was with a friend—and Mr. and Mrs. Ashburn had invited the children, grandchildren, and children-in-law for dinner and cake that evening. Mrs. Ashburn, who had not baked a cake in more than fifteen years, was determined to do her best.

She got to the second or third step of the process before she ran into a problem, and immediately suspected Fred. So she left her kitchen and went out back to Fred's reptile shed, where he kept three or four kinds of snakes and more lizards than any of his siblings had cared to count.

"Fred," Mrs. Ashburn called from a safe distance, "where is the baking soda?"

Fred showed up at the door, looking guilty. "I think the last of it got mixed up with vinegar and then ran away into the atmosphere after changing into carbon dioxide," he said.

Mrs. Ashburn did not look very surprised. "I need some for the cake," she said. "You'll have to run and get me some. While you're at it, I also need—just a second, I'll bring the list." Mrs. Ashburn wrote things down as she needed them on yellow sticky notes and always had one or two lists ready to hand to whoever was going shopping.

"Don't you need the baking soda real quick, mom?" Fred shouted after her.

"Oh, I'm not in that much of a hurry. I can work on dinner while you're gone," she said.

"The only car left here right now is the truck," she said when she came back. "Here are the keys, and the list for Walmart. Another one for Aldi's if you have time. Have fun!"

"All right," said Fred, looking more cheerful. He loved to drive the old truck, full of dents and scratches. Once he explained to Joe, "I know deep down all the teenagers driving snazzy new cars are jelly of me. I can scratch this up as much as I like without worrying about dad noticing."

Somehow it has become a stereotype that women are great shoppers—that is, that they enjoy it greatly. This may be true in some families, but in the Ashburn household it certainly was not. Mrs. Ashburn hated shopping, and the girls took after her, always treating shopping runs as if they were races against time—powering in, powering out. On the other hand several of the Ashburn boys enjoyed shopping very much—Joe in particular.

Once Joe explained to Fred, "It's just that there is a lot of scope for imagination in a supermarket. You know that skinny cashier who always has a pink bow in her hair? She's the suspect in a murder case. But the cashier in front of her—the one with the nerdy glasses—is the real culprit, and she has threatened to kill Pink Bow too if she doesn't keep her mouth shut. The pink bow is a sign of compliance. The beauty is, I don't have to worry about ever meeting these people and finding out that the reason they don't smile is just acid reflux."

"I see," said Fred admiringly, and looked around for an opportunity to use his own imagination. He found it in the intercom messages, and wove romances and tragedies for every name that got called. The least of these involved a determined mother-in-law tracking down her son's wife to inspect the groceries she planned on feeding her family with.

This shopping trip, he found himself in the bread aisle when he heard a license plate number called out.

"Who knows their license plate number, anyways?" Fred wondered, and immediately began to suppose that someone who had defaulted on his payments had just been caught by the bank, and his car was being repossessed and towed off.

"Calling again for the owner of a red 1991 pickup truck, license plate L7AP9T," the voice said.

Fred dropped the loaf of bread in his hand and stared in alarm. He'd driven a red 1991 pickup to the store. "But it's paid off," he thought. "Oh, maybe someone ran into the mirror."

He sauntered over to the information desk, looking casual.

"Red pickup?" he asked. "Not the one parked in the row right in front of the exit door, ten or eleven spots back?"

"I think that is about where it is," said the girl who was working the information desk, looking at him in a funny way.

Fred smiled. "What about it?"

"It's a—well, in fact, it's on fire."

Fred stared, and gasped, and pinched himself.

"Better go see if it's yours," she suggested.

So Fred did. It was his—and it was decidedly on fire, with orange flames rolling out the windows and thick black smoke billowing overhead.

A fire truck was pulling into the parking lot and Fred flew toward the scene, trying to see everything and getting in everyone's way.

"Oh dear!" he said finally, when the fire was out and the car was a smoldering shell of metal.

"Was that your truck, son?" a fireman asked.

"No, it was my dad's," Fred said.

"Oh! Well. Might wanna—find another ride home," he suggested.

"Did that really just happen?" Fred exclaimed.

"Come here," the fireman said, laughing. Then he went all around the car and talked Fred into reality by giving him a lesson on batteries and gas leaks.

Shortly after that Kyle's phone rang. "Hello?"

"Hey, Ky. It's Fred."

"Well hello little brother. I'm at work, you know."

"Yeah, I know—I mean I figured," said Fred, "but I couldn't get a hold of dad and mom's home without a car anyways. The truck got on fire while I was at the grocery store and now I'm stuck."

"The—what?" said Kyle.

"The truck, you know, the old red pickup—it caught on fire, and—"

"Fire? Like, flames and smoke and destruction?"

"Yeah, that kind of fire."

"Yow," said Kyle. "Well, I can probably get off for a family emergency like that. Where are you?"

"I'm at the Plainville Walmart," Fred said.

"All right little bro, be there in a minute. Sit tight and don't blow anything else up."

"All right, see you." Fred turned to the fireman. "My brother'll be here in a bit."

"I guess the insurance papers and so forth in the glove compartment burnt up," the fireman said thoughtfully. "Wait, where are you going?"

"I'm gonna go finish my shopping while I'm waiting for Kyle."

The fireman opened his eyes wide.

"I've already lost the truck," Fred explained. "I'd better come home with the baking soda."

Kyle squealed into the parking lot eleven minutes later and swung out of his car. "Here's a blessing in an impenetrable disguise if ever I saw one," he said, looking at the mangled remains of the pickup over the top of his sunglasses. "Where's my little brother?"

"Went inside to finish his shopping," someone explained.

Kyle raised his eyebrows. "Well, that's dedication. What do we need here anyway, ID and stuff? Towing service?"

By the time Fred was done shopping Kyle had gotten everything settled and was leaning against his car, spinning his keys on one finger and looking cool, except when he dropped his keys and had to bend over to scoop them up.

"Oh, Kyle!" Fred said. "Boy, you don't know what you missed. It was super exciting. They called the license plate over the store speaker system!"

"Hmm!" said Kyle.

"And the flames, boy they were really flaming out of the windows. You should have seen how dark the smoke was."

"Well, all I know is I'm pretty glad you weren't in that car," Kyle said, smacking Fred on the shoulder as if to see if he were still flesh and blood.

Fred looked suddenly thoughtful, and forgot to resent the smack.

"All right, let's go!" said Kyle cheerfully.

When they got home Kyle explained to Mrs. Ashburn what had happened while Fred took the groceries in.

"Oh dear," Mrs. Ashburn said, "I don't think I'll ever let Fred take the truck again."

"Don't think you have to worry about that," Kyle grinned.

Chapter 39—The End of an Era

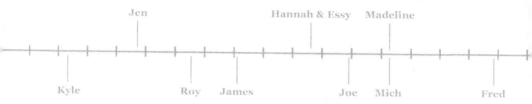

On the thirty-first of March, right after turning twenty-one, Madeline got married. Hannah got married the same day—it was a double wedding, in fact—but everyone called it "Mad's wedding," to the exclusion of her fiancé, Hannah, and Hannah's fiancé.

Essy, James, and Mich all spent the day and night before the wedding at home, since all three were taking an active part in the preparations—Essy and James as chefs, and Mich as their man-of-all-work. Mich had gotten a job in graphic design and moved into the city, but he took three days of vacation for his twin sister's wedding. He was very excited, and frequently mixed Essy and James' orders together.

"That hot sauce is not! —for the cake," Essy exclaimed, swooping down on Mich and rescuing the bottle which had been about to lose its lifeblood.

"Sorry," said Mich, "I know I'm awfully..."

"How's it going?" Mad asked, bouncing into the room. "Oh that cake looks beautiful. Oh it looks beautiful. Oh Mich I'm getting married tomorrow!" she exclaimed, shaking him vigorously by the shoulders.

"I know!" said Mich. "It's crazy!" He gave vent to his emotion by jumping up and high-fiving the roof.

"Just imagine—" Mad began, but Essy interrupted.

"You two need to either make yourself useful or get out of the kitchen," she said uncompromisingly.

"Have you seen my dress yet, Mich?" Mad asked.

"Oh yeah, let's go look at it!" Mich said, as if he hadn't already seen it a hundred times.

Essy sighed and shook her head as they left the room.

"I wonder if Peter knows he's marrying a lunatic," James said.

"He could hardly help knowing it," Essy retorted drily. "Boy I hope I was never that bad."

"As a general thing, I believe your composure on your wedding day was the talk of the family."

"Do you know," said Essy in a sudden burst of confidence, "I put my shoes on the wrong feet that day and didn't feel it until right after we said our vows. —Don't you dare tell anybody," she added quickly.

James chuckled. "I always knew you were really on cloud nine, and the down-to-earth stuff was just a facade."

"It was not! —mostly," Essy laughed.

Hannah came into the kitchen and asked, "Is there anything I can help with?"

"Yes," said James. "You can put a little of your calm sweetness into a bowl and force-feed Mad with it. Mich too, while you're at it."

"Also if you could make your eyes look a little less round and shining," Essy added, "it would be easier on the beholder."

Hannah laughed. "Mad is really a handful today, isn't she?" she asked sympathetically.

"Today? She's been a madhouse all week!" Essy retorted.

"We predict that Peter will have an exciting life," James grinned.

There was a sudden crash overhead.

"Better hurry with that dose of calm sweetness!" James exclaimed, as Hannah rushed to see what had happened.

The next morning Essy woke up with the sensation of being in a massage chair. "Wha—" she mumbled.

"Wake up! Wake up!" Mad said excitedly, shaking her. "It's my wedding day!"

"What time's it?" Essy asked, sitting up suddenly. "What is it, past nine or something?"

"Oh, no, it's only six," Mad said.

"You villain," said Essy, and buried herself under her covers again.

"But how can you sleep?" Mad exclaimed. "It's my wedding day!"

"Mad," said Essy, suddenly showing her face, "if you don't get out of this room and go somewhere where I can't see you or hear you, I'll—I'll sit on your cake."

Mad disappeared as quickly as she could, still thinking to herself, "How can she sleep? How can anybody sleep?"

She found Hannah in the music room, softly picking out Wagner's bridal chorus on the piano with one finger. "You look lovely," Mad said, admiring the strand of white flowers in Hannah's hair.

"Thanks," said Hannah, eyeing Mad doubtfully.

"I was too excited to get dressed," said Mad, who was still in her pajamas. "There's plenty of time. Oh! That should have been a sharp. Let me try."

Hannah ceded the piano to Mad, who instantly took off with a vigorous arrangement of Here Comes the Bride, her hands flying up and down the keyboard.

"You'll wake everyone up!" Hannah said.

"This is no day for sleep!" Mad replied—but she thought about Essy's threat, and did play more softly.

Essy said later that Mad's wedding was the craziest day of her own life, what with Mad always appearing in the places where she was least expected and least wanted. Mr. Ashburn, who had been nearly whisked off his feet while walking down the aisle, was tempted to agree with her.

Afterwards there were several car loads of wedding ruins— James' words—to load up and take back to the house. Then gradually Kyle and Paula, Drew and Essy, James, Joe, Jen and Caleb, and last of all Mich melted away and Mr. Ashburn said, "Well, Fred, now it's just you."

"Too bad I won't be here to enjoy it much longer," Fred said, stretching himself out lazily on the couch.

"You sure you want to go study biology?" Mrs. Ashburn asked. "It won't be as easy as taking care of your pet snakes, you know."

Fred said in an offended tone, "I can work, if I put my mind to it."

Mr. Ashburn stroked his chin. "It's the putting of the mind to it that we question—mostly," he said.

"You're such a social butterfly," Mrs. Ashburn added.

"Say chameleon," Mr. Ashburn suggested, "it's more up his alley."

Fred laughed. "Don't worry. I'll study hard—in my spare time, and get a good job at some zoo before you know it."

"A zoo!" Mrs. Ashburn exclaimed.

"Yeah," said Fred mischievously, "I'll bottle feed young monkeys and give panda bears baths."

"It's three o'clock," said Mr. Ashburn, "so I guess you're not really responsible for what you're saying."

"Is it really three o'clock?" Mrs. Ashburn exclaimed. "I'm going to bed."

Several months later Mr. and Mrs. Ashburn were once again together in the living room late at night—but without Fred. The reason they were up so late again, was because they had found so many little things to do to get Fred comfortably settled at his college campus, that they'd started their five hour drive home at eight o'clock.

"Well Jennifer," said Mr. Ashburn, saying well as if it had an H in it.

"Well, Jerry!" said Mrs. Ashburn—also pronouncing it whell.

"We did it!" said Mr. Ashburn, laughing.

"So strange to think of Fred at college," Mrs. Ashburn mused.

"Kyle married, Jen married," said Mr. Ashburn, counting the children on Mrs. Ashburn's fingers. "Roy—in India. James owning his own restaurant, Hannah and Essy married, Joe a plumber (you know, I used to think he'd be a poet), Mich off and working too, Mad married, and Fred at college."

"I remember when they were all babies," Mrs. Ashburn sighed.

Mr. Ashburn opened his eyes wide, trying to imagine all ten of his children being two-year-olds at the same time. After a pause he said with a sudden burst of seriousness, "I wonder if you can tell me, Jennifer, why they all turned out so good?" ("So well," Mrs. Ashburn murmured.) "What did we do to deserve it?"

"Nothing—"

"It's enough to make anyone humble, to think that God gave us so much," he said.

Mrs. Ashburn nodded thoughtfully.

"Well," Gerald finally said with a yawn, "shall we go to bed?"

"Yes, let's," Jennifer said.

But after Mr. Ashburn left the room she opened a notebook of her own and read over what she had written a few months before. "Jennifer Ashburn was a mother in Israel, and she changed more than 30,000 diapers, washed clothes more than 7,000 times, and made more than 17,000 meals. Moreover she believed the covenant promises of the Lord who answered her prayer that all her children would walk in truth."

Then Mrs. Ashburn got a pen and added, "And she rejoiced in God's salvation all her days."

Chapter 40—All Grown Up Now

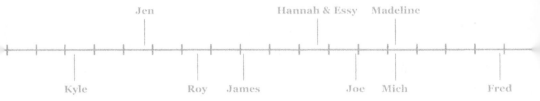

The Ashburns are all grown up now. Even Fred has a wife and two kids—though by the way, Mich does not.

They are not all successful, as the world counts success—not all rich, as the world counts riches—not even all happy, as the world counts happiness. Mr. and Mrs. Ashburn find as many reasons to pray for their children now that they're older, as they did when they were younger. But if happiness is more about trusting God, and loving him, and enjoying each other, than it is about making a fine show in a picture perfect house, then the Ashburns are all happy.

Kyle and Paula have three children now—three lovable, wild, fun, exhausting children—and Kyle sometimes has trouble making ends meet. But he can't tell Paula to cut back on her clothing style while he drives a forty thousand dollar car, so he straightens his tie and works overtime. And Paula sighs, and wishes he spent more time at home, and never thinks about the loads of once-used dresses she's taken to Goodwill.

To quote Mrs. Calhoun, "Caleb and I have seven kiddos so far," and so they certainly do. Jen is proud as a peacock of each one, and sighs over her nephews and nieces—and her children are all proud of her, and pity their cousins. Even the baby does—he pats Fred junior sympathetically on the shoulder whenever they meet. Of course Caleb thinks there never were such miracles as the Calhoun children. People who have seen those seven rambunctious children, dancing war dances around a room, suddenly fly to their seats and freeze when Jen snaps her fingers, sometimes agree.

Jen keeps up with her photography skills by practicing on her children, but she dropped her other work when her first girl came along. Caleb said, "Someday we should go into the photography thing together—I'll do the business side, you just take the pictures. After the baby grows up, maybe." Later he had to modify it to, "after all the babies grow up."

But for now Caleb works as a public relations specialist for a small local business, and somehow—Kyle can't figure out how—between his hard work and Jen's careful spending, they do quite well in their three-bedroom house.

Roy came back from India about a year ago for a long furlough—to recuperate his health and show off his wife. They're staying with Mr. and Mrs. Ashburn, and quiet Mrs. Roy Ashburn is slowly winning the approval of her critical siblings-in-law.

"I wish I dared to ask how they met," Hannah said one day to Essy. "It was probably very romantic."

Essy wrinkled her forehead. "Romantic baloney. They met in a hospital somewhere."

"Oh!" Hannah said, "was she his nurse?"

"Nurse! She mopped the floors and he drove a pickup truck as an ambulance."

"Oh," said Hannah. "Well that's romantic, don't you think, kind of?"

James owns a restaurant, and is getting to be a celebrated cook in a small way. But his wife does not like his cooking, which Mich thinks makes perfect sense. "It's why James married her," he said. "He was tired of his cooking too."

Hannah has two children, and Essy has three, and when they get together it's hard to tell whose children are whose. Essy has had to bite her tongue and remember her own younger days several times after driving home with the wrong cousin in the back seat. The surprising thing is, it's Hannah's daughter who gets Essy's to change places.

Hannah's husband owns a printing business and Hannah does the paperwork, besides homeschooling her two girls, hosting a small sewing club, writing once a week for her own blog, and beading in her spare time. "Aunt Hannah never sleeps," Kenny—Kyle's oldest—told his grandmother. Mrs. Ashburn secretly agreed, and looked worried; but Hannah never seems busy and always has time for guests, or a phone call, or an outing to the park—and how she gets everything done remains a mystery.

Drew is chief at the fire department now, and Essy pretends, even to herself, that she never worries about him.

Before his marriage, Joe wrote his wife three pieces of poetry—but apart from that, he has stuck to plumbing. He has one boy, Will, who is the most cheerful of babies, despite having been born with a bone deformation among other challenges. Joe's wife Kayla spends hours trying to help Will learn to walk.

Mich still works in graphic design and enjoys it thoroughly. Besides, he has dinner with one or another of his siblings almost every night. "Uncle Mich" is wildly popular among the cousins, partly because of the piggy back rides he gives even to ten-year-old Kenny, and partly because he always has candy in every pocket.

Two years after their marriage Madeline and Peter had a little girl who only lived a week. These days Peter works long hours and Mad gives piano lessons.

Halfway through college Fred got a job at a pet store, married, and started taking the college thing less seriously. So he still has a few classes left, but meanwhile he's worked his way to store manager and insists that the experience will look good on his resume when he applies for that zoo job he still pretends to hope for.

For their thirty-eighth wedding anniversary Mr. and Mrs. Ashburn allowed themselves to be persuaded to take an all-expenses paid trip to the lake of the Ozarks. Jen thought they should go to Europe, but Mr. Ashburn objected to spending that much time on a plane. Kyle thought they should go to the Grand Canyon, but Mrs. Ashburn objected to spending any time on a plane.

The day before they were expected back the ten Ashburn children got themselves—and where applicable their families—up bright and early and met at their old house. Mich was the last one there, but he protested that he'd stayed up working until two.

They planned to clean the house and get everything ready for a surprise dinner when Mr. and Mrs. Ashburn arrived the next day, but it had been five or six days since they'd last seen each other and everyone had lots to say.

The phone rang around eleven o'clock and Roy answered it. He came back into the living room looking serious.

"Guys, I need everyone's attention please," he said.

"'Sup?" Kyle asked.

"Change of plans. Heavy rainfall predicted for tomorrow. Mom and dad are driving home today."

"Oh my," Mad said.

"So far all we've done is make this place messier," said Essy, looking at the toys Kyle's children had scattered everywhere.

"All right," Kyle said, jumping from his seat. "No more time to waste! Jen, you'll be in charge of all the kids—"

"That's a lot of..." Jen began.

"Paula will help you with our three," said Kyle.

"Oh okay, that'll work. I can handle the rest."

"What are you implying?" Kyle asked.

"Hey, we're in a hurry here," James said.

Kyle frowned humorously and went on, "Roy, the dining room is all yours. Need it laid out for an elegant dinner. James, better get cooking. Hannah and Essy, forget the upstairs, it can't be that messy. Do the living room and school room. Joe and Kayla, I was thinking you could clean mom and dad's car, inside and out. Mind sweeping out the garage, Drew? Peter and Mad, congratulations, you get the bathrooms. Mich, get Caleb to help you go over the yard, there are a lot of sticks lying around. Fred, cast an eye over the hallway and the mud room. I'll install the new fridge and clean the kitchen. If there's anyone I haven't assigned a place, help James, he'll need some onion choppers. We ready to go?"

"Ready," Mich said.

"Wait a second, what time are they getting here?" Fred's wife asked Roy.

"They said they'd leave after lunch, so I guess they'll be here around four thirty or five," Roy said.

"Let's go!" said Jen, and led all the children outside.

When Mich and Caleb finished with the yard they went and asked James if there was anything they could do.

"What'd you say?" James asked. "Sorry, it's hard to hear."

"I asked if you needed any help," Mich said. "Boy those kids make a lot of noise."

"But you can still hear Jen over it all," Caleb said smugly.

James laughed and rolled his eyes at Caleb. "Anyway, we're out of cream cheese," he said to Mich, "and you're parked in the back so run and get me some, will you?"

"On it," Mich said.

"Not you, Caleb," James added. "I want you to chop these hot peppers."

Drew helped Kyle install the new fridge and the two of them got dreadfully in the cooks' way. So James and Fred's wives went to the dining room table to grate cheese and got in Roy's way. Roy took the chairs to the living room to drape them with white streamers and got in Hannah and Essy's way.

Hannah had brought a bunch of frozen pizzas with her and cooked them for lunch, and everyone except James—who said he got enough to eat taste-testing his own dishes—snatched a few minutes to go outside and eat them.

"We need to start getting these cars out of the driveway," Joe said. "It's a quarter past two already."

"Are we going to try to surprise them completely?" Jen asked.

"Of course!" said Kyle.

Jen looked over at Kenny, who was hanging upside-down from the branch of a tree and whooping. "Okay," she said doubtfully.

At five o'clock James was still putting the finishing touches on his meal, but the rest of the house was ready to go. Fred had volunteered to hide in the bushes at the corner of the street and give the house phone a call when he saw the rental car.

He called twice on a false alarm and Joe said over the phone, "It's a red car, Fred. Red. Shouldn't be so confusing."

"Okay, right. I knew it was a Lincoln, just didn't remember what color it was."

"It's red, like your hair," said Joe. "Call us back when you—"

"Oh here's a red car!" Fred exclaimed. "It's a Subaru though."

"Talk to you later, Fred," Joe said, hanging up.

The phone rang again almost immediately and Essy grabbed it. "I saw them!" Fred exclaimed.

"They're coming!" Essy said.

"Hurray hurray!" Kenny shouted.

"All right everyone, out of sight of the windows!" Kyle said. "Shout 'surprise' on three. Keep as quiet as you can!"

James dropped a plate and his wife banged the dustpan and broom together trying to clean it up.

Jen snapped her fingers and her children stopped playing drum rolls on the table and rushed to sit quietly on the couch.

Paula grabbed her youngest, who was crying under a chair, and offered her a sucker.

"Oh my oh my oh my," said Mad. "Which one of the children was it my job to keep quiet?"

"Oh—just keep yourself quiet," Peter said, hiding behind the door.

Fred, breathless, came flying in the back and slammed the door. "Oh! Sorry," he exclaimed. "They'll be here any minute."

"Surprise on three!" Kyle whispered.

"Don't you think counting to three will give it away?" Roy asked.

"Good point," Kyle said. "Oh! I heard the car door."

"Shh!" three or four adults said at the same time, and it sounded like a gust of wind blew through the house.

Kyle heard footsteps on the porch and held up one finger, then two fingers. At his third finger Peter whisked the door open and everyone shouted, "Surprise!"

"Oh wow, all this for me?" said Mich, grinning. "Sorry I'm late with the cream cheese. I got distracted talking to a cashier I knew. Mom and dad are right behind me—oh there they are, turning into the driveway."

"Way to ruin the surprise, Mich," Kyle said, as Mich turned and waved.

Mr. and Mrs. Ashburn were taken by surprise anyways and said several times that they had not expected anything like this. Essy said to Hannah, "How could they not have expected it? I would totally have expected it. Why do they suppose we paid for their vacation if not to have the fun of cleaning the house for them?"

"I suppose that's one perspective," Hannah said.

Kyle presented his parents with a frame full of family pictures and tried to give a short speech. He started by drinking an unnecessary amount of water.

"Well, I... just wanted to see if I could say a little something for all of us—and how much we appreciate all you've done for us... I doubt ten children are most people's definition of happily ever after... Ten children takes—okay, I'll say it—even my three children take a lot of patience, a lot of sacrifice, a lot of unselfish love. We've seen that day to day in the little things you've done for us, mom and dad—and we appreciate it, and you know we appreciate it—but I wanted you to know that we also appreciate the big picture. — There's so much incentive to follow your own career, be the star of your own story. But you never did that. You never sacrificed your family to the world's idols. You never measured success by fame or power or riches, or even by selfish dreams of happiness. So I guess what I want to say boils down to—thank you—thank you for showing us that there are some things that are better than happily ever after."

So ends the story of the Ashburn children. They have grown up, and left childishness behind. But they will always be childlike—always be humble—always be trusting, tenderhearted, and kind. And when they fail they will go to God, and ask his pardon, and take it, and go forth again boldly to meet the duties and dangers of life.

For those are the things, after all, that make an Ashburn an Ashburn.

Want to keep reading?

Short Stories
Geneva Durand

from hurricanes in Viking settlements
to mysteries in the Egyptian desert
to assasins in medieval Venice...

Find these and more on
amazon.com/author/genevadurand

Made in the USA
Middletown, DE
01 July 2023

34023058R00170